An Iron Rose

Peter Temple

W F HOWES LTD

This large print edition published in 2008 by
W F Howes Ltd
Unit 4, Rearsby Business Park, Gaddesby Lane,
Rearsby, Leicester LE7 4YH

1 3 5 7 9 10 8 6 4 2

First published in the United Kingdom in 2007
by Quercus

A CIP catalogue record for this book is available
from the British Library

ISBN 978 1 40741 381 5

Typeset by Palimpsest Book Production Limited,
Grangemouth, Stirlingshire
Printed and bound in Great Britain
by Antony Rowe Ltd, Chippenham, Wilts.

FSC
Mixed Sources
Product group from well-managed
forests and other controlled sources
Cert no. SGS-COC-2953
www.fsc.org
© 1996 Forest Stewardship Council

*For Josephine Margaret Temple and
Alexander Royden Harold Wakefield Temple:
first and best influences*

'Mac,' the voice said. 'Ned's dead.'

I couldn't take it in. I screwed up my eyes and tried to focus, head full of sleep and beer dreams.

'What?' I said.

He said it again.

'Jesus, no. When?'

'Don't know.' There was a pause. 'He's hangin in the shed, Mac. Can you come?'

Dead? Ned? What time was it? Two forty-five am. Sunday morning. I pulled some faces, fighting the fog and the numb incomprehension. Then I said, 'Okay. Right. Right. Listen, you sure he's dead?'

There was a long silence. Lew sniffed. 'Mac. Come.'

I was starting to think. 'Ambulance. You call the ambulance?'

'Yeah.'

'Cops?'

'No.'

'Call them. I'll be there in ten,' I said.

In the passage, Drizabone off the hook, straight

1

out the door. Didn't need to dress. I'd fallen asleep in a cracked leather armchair, fully clothed, half-eaten pie on the arm, television on.

I didn't see the dog but I heard him land on the tray. Little thump. Short route through Quinn's Marsh, saved a few minutes by bumping open the gate with the roobars and putting the old Land Rover across the sheep paddock behind Ned Lowey's house. You could see the house from a long way off: all the lights were on.

I slewed around the corner and Lew was in my headlights: arms at sides, hair wild, stretched tracksuit top hanging over pyjama pants, barefoot.

I got out at a run. 'Stay there,' I shouted over my shoulder to the dog. 'Where?'

Lew led me down the path between the garage and the chook run to the big machine shed. The double doors were open and a slab of white light lay on the concrete apron. He stopped and pointed. He didn't want to go in.

'Wait for the ambulance in front,' I said.

For a moment the light blinded me or I didn't want to see. Then I focused on Ned, in striped pyjamas, arms neatly at his sides, hanging against the passenger side of the truck. His head was turned away from me. When I got close I saw why Lew had not answered my question about whether he was sure Ned was dead.

I looked up. The rope was tied to a rolled steel joist about two metres above the truck cab. Ned had climbed up onto the cab roof, tied the rope to the joist, slid it along, tied a slipknot around his neck. And stepped off the cab roof.

'Mate, mate,' I said helplessly. I wanted to cry and be sick and run away. I wanted to be asleep again and the telephone not to ring.

Lew was sitting on the verandah step, shoulders slumped, head forward. I found the makings I kept in the Land Rover for when I needed a smoke, rolled a cigarette, walked the fifty metres to the gate. The night was black, absolutely silent. Then, far away, a speeding vehicle crossed the threshold of hearing.

I walked back, went into the house, down the long passage to Ned's bedroom. It was neat, like a soldier's quarters, the bed made drum tight.

Why was Ned in pyjamas?

On the way out, I paused in the sitting room, looking around the familiar space for no good reason. It was warm, the wood heater down low and glowing.

My eyes went to the photograph on the mantelpiece: Ned and my father, two big men in overalls, laughing, each with a king brown in hand. Between them the camera froze a thin boy in school uniform. He had a worried look. It was me.

I went outside and sat down beside Lew, looked at his profile. He was a mixture of Ned and his mother: long face, high cheek-bones, strong jaw. 'How'd you find him?' I said.

He shivered. 'I came back about eleven. He's always

asleep by then. Went to bed. Woke up, I don't know, half an hour ago, went to have a leak. Then when I got back into bed, I thought: he didn't say anythin.'

'Say anything?'

'You can't walk past his door without him saying somethin. Doesn't matter the time. Middle of the night. He hears everythin. And he didn't say anythin either when I went to the bathroom before I went to bed. But I didn't think about it then. So I got up and he wasn't in bed.' He paused. 'Then I went to look for the car and it was there, so I went to look for the truck. And . . .'

He put his head in his hands. I put my arm around his shoulders, gave him a squeeze, helpless to comfort him, to comfort myself. We sat like that until the ambulance arrived. The police car was about a minute behind it. Two cops. By the time Lew and I had given statements, it was after 5 am and there were two police cars and four cops standing in the warm sitting room, smoking cigarettes and waiting for someone from forensic to arrive.

I brought Lew home with me. He couldn't stay there, in that familiar house made strange and horrible. We drove in silence in the silver early dawn, mist lying in the hollows, hanging in the trees, dams gleaming coldly. The first smoke of the day was issuing from farmhouse chimneys along the way.

I felt that I should speak to him, but I couldn't. He's just a kid, I said to myself. Two weeks from now he'll be over it. But I wouldn't be over it. Ever. Edward Lowey had been part of my life since I was ten. He was the link with my father. There were lots of questions I wanted to ask Lew, but this wasn't the time.

At home, I made scrambled eggs, but neither of us could eat. We sat there like people in an institution, not saying anything, looking at the table, not seeing anything. Finally, I shook myself and said, 'Let's get some wood in. They say it's going to get colder.'

I fed the dog the scrambled eggs and we went out into the raw morning, low cloud, spits of rain. While Lew walked around, hands in pockets,

5

kicking things, I found another axe and put an edge on it on the grindstone. Then we chopped wood solidly, an hour, one on each side of the woodpile, not speaking, pausing only to take off garments. Chopping wood doesn't take your mind off things but it burns off the adrenalin and it sends you into a trancelike state.

Lew had just turned sixteen, but he was lean and muscled in the upper body and he matched me log for log and he didn't stop until I did. He was fetching a drink and I was standing there, leaning on my axe, sweat cooling, when an old red Dodge truck came up the driveway.

A tall woman, around thirty, dropped down from the cab: slim, long nose a little skew on her face, some weight in her shoulders, crew-cut dirty-blonde hair, overalls, pea jacket, no make-up.

'G'day,' she said. 'Allie Morris.'

I'd forgotten about our arrangement for today. I walked over and shook hands. 'Mac Faraday.'

Lew came out the house carrying two glasses.

'We've had a bit of a shock,' I said. 'His grand-father . . .'

I didn't want to say it. 'He found his grandfather dead this morning.'

'I'm sorry,' she said. 'That's terrible.' She shrugged. 'Well, the other thing. I don't suppose this is the day for it . . .'

I said, 'It's the day. Never a better day.'

I introduced Lew and we left him to stack the wood and went into the smithy. I'd cleaned out the forge on Saturday morning and laid the fire: paper and kindling over the tue hole, coke around that and green coal banked around the coke. I lit the paper and started the fan blower. Allie Morris came over with the watering can and dampened the green coal. She'd taken off her coat. Under her overalls, she was wearing a shirt with heavy canvas sleeves.

'Useful shirt,' I said.

'Blacksmith's wife in England makes them. Got tired of looking at all that burnt skin.'

'It's not a good look.'

'Sure you know what you're doing here?' she said. 'Never heard of anyone doing it.'

'People did it for hundreds of years.'

'Well, maybe they didn't have any choice. You could get a new one. Stick this thing in a museum.'

'Making things on this when Queen Victoria was a baby,' I said.

'Yes,' she said. 'And it's outlived its usefulness. Might as well hang on to your old underpants.'

I thought about this for a moment. 'Wish someone else would hang on to my old underpants,' I said. 'While I'm wearing them.'

Allie was pushing coal towards the glowing coke. She looked up, bland. 'Surprised to hear that position's vacant,' she said. 'Give it a blast. We'll be here all day.'

I gave the fire a blast. Allie Morris was a qualified farrier and blacksmith, trained in England. For a long time I'd been looking for someone

7

to do the horse work and help in the smithy. Then I saw her advertisement in the Situations Wanted.

'I'd be in that if the terms were right,' she'd said on the phone. 'But I've got to tell you, I'm not keen on the business side.'

'You mean extracting the money?'

'In particular.'

'You want to come around on Sunday? Eight-thirty? Or any time. Give me a hand with something. We'll talk about it.'

I'd explained what I wanted to do.

It took a good while to get the fire right: raking and wetting until we had a good mass of burning coke that could be compacted.

'What I had in mind,' I said, 'you do the horse work, I take the bookings, keep up the stores, send out the bills, and get the buggers to pay.'

'Last item there,' said Allie. 'That's the important function. That's where I fall down.' She shook her head. 'Horse people.'

'Tight as Speedos,' I said.

'I had to tell this one bloke, I'm coming around with two big men and we're going to fit him with racing shoes, run him over the jumps. And he still took another week to pay up.'

'I'll need your help with some general work too,' I said. 'Sometimes I can't cope. And I'm not all that flash on the finer stuff.'

'Sounds good to me,' said Allie, banking coal around the coke. 'Got to get even heat for a job

8

like this. Get the heat to bounce off the coal, eat the oxygen. Reducing fire, know the term?'

'Use it all the time,' I said.

Lew and the dog came in to watch. The dog went straight to his spot on a pile of old potato sacks in a corner, well away from sparks and flying bits of clinker.

Finally, Allie said, 'All right, let's do it.' She was flushed from the heat. It was an attractive sight.

I had a sliding block and tackle rigged from the steel beam in the roof and a chain around the battered anvil's waist. Lew and I pulled it up, an unwieldy 285 pounds of metal. You could tell the weight from the numbers stamped on the waist: two-two-five, standing for two hundredweights, or 224 pounds; two quarters of a hundredweight, fifty-six pounds; and five pounds. To get it under the smoke hood and onto the coke bed, Allie slid it slowly down a sheet of steel plate.

When it was in place, I unshackled the chain.

'Got any tea?' Allie said. 'This'll take a while.'

'I'll make it,' said Lew. He looked glad of something to do.

It took about an hour in the intense heat to get the face of the anvil to the right colour. We put on gloves and I got the chain around its waist, pulled it to the lip of the forge and Lew and Allie hoisted it. The day was dark outside and we had no lights on in the smithy. But when the anvil came out and hung in the air, turning gently, the room filled with its glowing orange light and we stood in awe for a moment, three priests with golden faces.

Carefully, we set the dangerous object down on the block of triple-reinforced concrete I used for big heavy jobs.

'Well,' said Allie, 'the thing will probably break in half. Put your helmet on.'

I handed her a six-pound flatter and a two-pound hammer and we went to work, hammering, dressing the face and edges of the anvil, trying to get the working surface back to something like its original flatness.

'Lew's grandfather found this anvil,' I said. 'In the old stables at Kinross Hall. Bought it off them for twenty dollars. Gave it to my old man.'

Allie Morris had just left when they arrived, two men in plainclothes in a silver Holden. I heard the car outside and met them at the smithy door. The dog came out with me. His upper lip twitched.

'Lie down,' I said. He turned his head and looked at me, lay down. But his eyes were on the men.

'MacArthur John Faraday?' the cop in front said.

I nodded.

'Police,' he said. They both did a casual flash of ID.

I put out my hand. 'Look at those.'

They glanced at each other, eyes talking, handed over the wallets. The man who'd spoken was Detective Sergeant Michael Bernard Shea. His offsider was Detective Constable Allan Vernon Cotter. Shea was in his forties, large and going to flab, ginger hair, faded freckles, big ears. He had the bleak look men get on assembly lines. Cotter was dark, under thirty, neck muscled like a bull terrier's, eyes too close, hair cropped to a five-o'clock shadow. Chewing gum.

I gave them the wallets back.

'Lewis Lowey here?' Shea said.

'Yes.'

'Like a word with you first, then him. Somewhere we can sir down?'

'What kind of word? We've given statements.'

Shea held up a big hand. 'Informal. Get some background.'

I put my head back in the door. 'Police,' I said. 'Don't go anywhere, Lew.'

I took them over to the shed that served as the business's office. It held a table, three kitchen chairs, and a filing cabinet bought at a clearing sale. I sat down behind the table. Cotter spun a chair around and sat down like a cowboy.

Shea perched on the filing cabinet behind Cotter. He looked around the room, distaste on his face, sniffing the musty air like someone who suspects a gas leak. 'So you been here, what, five years?' he said.

'Something like that,' I said.

'And you know this bloke?'

'A long time.'

'First on the scene.'

'Second.'

'You and the kid. First and second.'

I didn't say anything. Silence for a while. Shea coughed, a dry little cough.

'You, ah, friendly with the kid?' This from the offsider, Cotter. He was staring at me, black eyes gleaming like sucked grapes. His ears were pierced, but he wasn't wearing an earring. He smiled and winked.

12

I said to Shea, 'Detective Constable Cotter just winked at me. What does that mean?'

'I'll do this, Detective Cotter,' Shea said. 'So Lewis rang you at . . . ?'

'Two forty-five. It's in the statement.'

'Yeah. He says you got there about two fifty-five. Looking at his watch all the time.'

'About right.'

'Clarify this for me,' Shea said. 'It's twenty kilometres from here. You get dressed and drive it in ten minutes. Give or take a minute.'

'It's fifteen the short way,' I said. 'I didn't get dressed. I was dressed. I fell asleep dressed. And I didn't obey the speed limit.'

Shea rubbed the corner of his right eye with a finger like a hairy ginger banana. 'Old bloke worth a bit?'

'Look like it?'

'Can't tell sometimes. Keep it under the mattress. That his property?'

I nodded.

'Who stands to benefit then?'

'There's just Lew, his grandson.'

'Then there's you.'

'I'm not family.'

'How come you inherit?'

I said, 'I'm not with you.'

'We found his will,' Shea said. 'You get a share.'

I shrugged. This was news to me. 'I don't know about that.'

Cotter said, 'Got any gumboots?' Pause. 'Mr Faraday.'

I looked at him. 'Dogs got bums? Try the back porch.'

Cotter got up and left.

'We'll have to take them away,' Shea said.

I got up and went to the window. Cotter had the Land Rover passenger door open and was poking through the mess inside.

'Your man got a warrant?' I said.

'Coming to that,' Shea said. He took a folded piece of paper out of his jacket pocket. 'Here's your copy.'

'Got something in mind?' I said.

It was Shea's turn to say nothing, just look at me, not very interested.

I heard the sound of a vehicle, then another car nosed around the corner of the house. Two men and a woman.

'The gang's all here,' I said. 'Go for your life.'

Shea coughed. 'I'm going to ask you to come into town for an interview. When we're finished here. The young fella too. Don't want you to talk to him before. Okay? So you can't travel with him. He can come with me or you can make some other arrangement, get a friend. You're entitled to be represented. Kid's gotta have someone with him. You don't want to come of your own accord, well, we do it the other way. Believe me.'

There wasn't a way around this. 'Let me explain this to Lew,' I said.

Shea nodded. We went over to the smithy. Lew was where I'd left him, puzzled and frightened. I sat down next to him.

'Lew,' I said, 'listen, mate. They're going to search the place. Then they want us to go into town so they can ask us some more questions. They'll record everything. You'll have a lawyer with you, just so everything's done right. All right?'

'We told them,' Lew said.

'I know. It's just the way they do it. I'll tell you about it later. I'm going to arrange for your lawyer now. We can't talk to each other again before the interviews. I'll be there when you finish.'

He looked at me, looked away, just a child again in a world suddenly turned from stone to water. He was on the edge of tears. I gave him a little punch in the arm. 'Mate, this'll be over in next to no time. Then we can have a feed, get some sleep. Hold on. Right?'

He moved his head, more tremble than a nod. He was exhausted.

I rang the lawyer who'd handled my father's estate. 'You're better off with someone who specialises in crime,' he said. 'What's your number?'

I waited by the phone. A tall cop came in, opened the Ned Kelly stove and poked around in the ashes. When he'd finished, he started on the chest of drawers, working from bottom to top like a burglar.

The phone rang.

'Mr Faraday?'

I said yes.

'I'm Laura Randall.' Deep voice. 'Mike Sherman said you had a matter.'

15

I told her what was happening.

She said nothing until I'd finished. Then she said, 'Ring me just before you leave. I'll meet you there.'

The search took nearly two hours: house, smithy, all the out-buildings. When they'd finished, the five of them had a conference outside. Shea came into the office and said, no expression, 'Firearm on the premises.'

I nodded.

'.38 Colt Python.'

I nodded again.

'Licence?'

'No.'

'Unlicensed firearm?'

I savoured the moment. 'Special permit.'

'Special permit. That's for what reason?'

I said, 'See if they'll tell you, Detective Sergeant.'

He didn't like this. 'I will. I will.'

When they'd bagged the gun we set off for town, Shea and Cotter in front with Lewis, then me in the Land Rover, then the other car. It began to rain as we crested the last hump of the Great Dividing Range, all sixty metres of it.

I parked behind Shea and Cotter in front of the police station, an old two-storey redbrick building with an ugly new annexe. The other cops drove through an entrance marked OFFICIAL PARKING ONLY.

As I got out, the door of a BMW on the other side of the narrow street opened and a tall woman

16

with dark hair pulled back in a loose ponytail got out. She took a leather briefcase out of the back seat and came over.

'Mr Faraday?' she said. 'Laura Randall.' Her breath was steam in the cold afternoon. She was in her thirties, thin, plain, pale skin, faintly amused twist to her mouth. The clothes were expensive: brown leather bomber jacket, dark tartan trousers over gleaming boots.

We shook hands. Shea, Cotter and Lew were out of the car, standing on the pavement. Cotter had his hands in his pockets and a cigarette in his mouth. He looked like a bouncer on his break.

I moved around so that I had my back to them. 'That's your client,' I said. 'The young fella. He told them the story this morning. He doesn't know anything. The fat one over there, Shea, he's hinting he thinks the kid and I might be in it, killed Ned for the inheritance. Maybe more than just friends, too.'

She looked me hard in the eyes. 'Sexually involved?' she said. 'Are you?'

'Only with the opposite sex,' I said. 'And that infrequently.'

She didn't smile.

I said, 'There's nothing like that. Lew's a good kid, been messed around by his mother. His grandfather was my father's best friend.' I paused. 'He was my best friend too.'

Laura Randall said, 'You need to understand, if he makes an admission in this interview, they'll

17

call me as a witness. I won't be able to represent him.'

I shook my head. 'Can't happen. Nothing to admit. I just want someone with him, make him feel he's not alone with these blokes.'

'You'll need someone with you too,' she said.

'No,' I said. 'Not with this lot. I've been on fishing trips with pros.'

She gave me an interested look. 'Talk to you later,' she said. 'Mr Faraday.'

'Ms Randall.' To the dog, I said, 'Stay.'

It was dark before we got home and we were both staring-eyed with fatigue. After I switched off the engine, we sat in silence for a while. Finally, I shook myself into action. 'Okay. Lew, that's over. There's two big pies in the top rack of the freezer. Bang them in the microwave, twenty minutes on defrost. I'll get the fire going.'

We ate lamb pies, made for me by the lady down the road, in front of the fire, watching football in Perth on television. Lew drank half a glass of beer. I drank half a bottle of red. He had barely stopped chewing when his head fell onto his shoulder. I made the bed in the spare room, put a pair of pyjamas on the pillow, woke him and pushed him off to bed. Then I started work on the second half of the bottle.

In the night, far from dawn, I sat up, fully awake, swept the blankets from my legs. Deep in sleep, some noise had alarmed me. Not the wind nagging at the guttering and the loose tiles, shaking the windows, making the trees groan like old men being massaged. Not the occasional slash of rain hitting the panes like pebbles. Not the house timbers creaking and ticking and uttering tiny screeches, not the plumbing gargling and knocking, not the creatures moving in the roof.

Something else.

When I'd first come from Melbourne, to my father's house at the crossroads, the old life's burden of fear and vigilance heavy on my back, I'd sat in the dark in every room in turn, eyes closed, listening, pigeonholing sounds. And I had slept fitfully for weeks until I knew every night noise of the place. Only then was I sure that I would hear the sounds that I was always listening for: a vehicle stopping on the road or in the lane, a squeak of the new gravel I'd put around the house, the thin complaint of a window being forced.

Now I heard the sound again: the flat, hard smack of a door slamming.

It was the smithy door. Once or twice a year I'd forget to slide the bolt. The wind would gradually prise the door open, then slam it triumphantly and start prising again.

I got up and went into the black, wet night. The dog came from nowhere to join me, silently.

Francis Keany was waiting for us in front of the dilapidated mansion called Harkness Park, sitting in his warm Discovery, smoking a panatella and listening to *La Traviata* on eight speakers. When the window slid down, the warmth and the aromatic Cuban smoke and the music floated out to us where we stood in the cold and the rain and the mud.

'Boys,' he said. 'You know I don't like to wait around when you're on my time.'

Stan Harrop cleared his nose and spat, a sound like a blow dart being fired. The missile hit the right front hubcap. 'We're not on your fucking time, Frankie,' he said. 'We're here to look at a job. Don't like it, off we fuck.'

Francis's eyes narrowed. Then self-interest clicked in and he cocked his head and smiled, the smile that had won many a society matron's heart. And the rest, so the word went. 'You're absolutely right, Stan,' he said. 'I'm getting ahead of myself. Let me show you the magnitude of the task.'

He got out of the vehicle, put a Barbour hat on his sleek head to complete his Barbour outfit, and led us down the driveway and into the wilderness. We couldn't get far: this was a garden gone feral. Francis started down what was once a path and was now a dripping tunnel that narrowed rapidly. He wrestled with branches for a few metres, gradually losing confidence. Finally, faced with an impassable thicket, he gave up. We reversed out, Lew in front, then me, then Flannery, then Stan, then Francis.

Francis pushed his way past us and tried another matted and sodden avenue. A few metres in, he missed an overgrown step, fell forward and disappeared into a dank mass of vegetation. His shriek hung in the cold air, wild enough to send hundreds of birds thrumming skywards.

We all stopped. Stan began to roll a cigarette one-handed as we waited for Francis to emerge. 'Hurt yourself?' he said, no trace of sympathy in his voice, as the wet figure struggled upright, cursing.

'Course I fucking hurt myself,' Francis said, each word a small, distinct explosion. 'Look at this shit on my trousers.'

'On?' Stan said. 'We know there's a shit *in* your trousers. What are we looking for here, Frankie? Don't have to hack my way with a bloody machete to see it's a jungle.'

Francis was examining the slime on his palms, mouth pursed in disgust. 'My clients want it restored,' he said. 'I was trying to show you the enormity of the task.'

'Enormity? That's not the word you want, Frankie,' Stan said. He was a pedant about language.

'Try enormousness. And if they want it bloody restored, what do they want it bloody restored *to*?'

'I don't know,' Francis snarled. 'Don't fucking care. Its former fucking glory. That's your department.'

'Francis Keany doesn't know and doesn't fucking care. You should put that on your business cards.'

Stan took pleasure in giving Francis this kind of needle. The only reason Francis tolerated it was because without Stan he wouldn't be able to take on jobs like this. Francis had started out as a florist and conned his way into the garden design trade. He apparently wasn't too bad at doing little squares of box with lollipops in the middle and iceberg roses lashed to dark-green trellis. But then one of his satisfied society matrons commissioned him to do a four-acre garden from scratch near Mount Macedon. Francis panicked: you couldn't fill four acres with little squares of *Buxus sempervirens*. You couldn't copy another big garden. People would notice. And then, somehow, he heard about Stan Harrop.

Stan had started work at twelve as a garden boy at Sefton Hall in the south of England. Four years later, he lied about his age and went off to war. When he came back, five years on, he was all of twenty-one, sergeant's stripes on his arm, the ribbon of the Military Cross on his chest, and a long bayonet scar on his right forearm. It was twenty years before he left Sefton Hall again, this time to catch the P&O liner to Sydney to be head gardener on an estate outside Mittagong. Over the next twenty years, he ran four other big gardens.

Then he bought fifty acres with a round hill on it down the road from Ned Lowey and started a nursery. That was where Francis Keany found him. It was the luckiest day of Francis's life. And for Ned and Flannery, and later for me, it meant fairly regular work at a decent rate of pay.

'There's a little clear bit over there,' Lew said. We followed him through a grove of plane trees into a clearing. For some reason, rocky soil perhaps, nothing had grown here. You could at least see some way into the jungle. Overgrown shrubs were everywhere. Mature deciduous trees – oaks, ashes, elms, planes, maples, birches – stood in deep drifts of rotting leaves. To the left, what might once have been a tapestry hedge of yew and privet and holly was a great impenetrable green barricade. Rampant, strangling holly had spread everywhere, gleaming like wet plastic. All trace of the garden's form, of its design, had been obliterated by years of unchecked growth.

'These clients of yours,' Stan said, 'they understand the *magnitude* of what they're getting into here? Financially speaking.'

'Leon Karsh,' Francis said. 'Food. Hotels. Travel. Leon and Anne Karsh.'

Stan looked at me. 'Food. Hotels. Travel. How do you suggest we approach this thing, Mac?'

I said, 'Food. Hotels. Travel. From the air. We approach it from the air. Aerial photography.'

'My feelings exactly,' Stan said. 'Francis . . . ?'

'Aerial photographs?' Francis said. 'Are you

23

mad? Can you imagine the expense? Why don't you just poke around and . . .'

'Aerial photographs,' said Stan. 'Aerial photographs and other research. Paid by the hour. Or we fuck off.'

You could see Francis's fists clench in the Barbour's roomy pockets. 'Of course,' he said through his capped teeth. 'Whatever it takes.' Pause. 'Stan.'

Before we left, we went down the road and looked at the derelict three-storey bluestone flour mill on the creek at the bottom of the Karsh property. Flannery went off to look at the millrace pond. He was obsessed by machinery, the older the better. When he came back, he had a look of wonder on his face, the face of a naughty thirty-five-year-old boy. 'Sluicegate'll still work,' he said. 'Someone's been greasing it.'

The wind had come up and, while we looked at the building, a slate tile came off the roof and sailed down into the poplar thicket along the creek.

'Dangerous place to be, down the creek,' Flannery said.

We drove back via the country cemetery where we'd buried Ned. It was a windblown acre of lopsided headstones and rain-eroded paths on a hillside above a weatherboard Presbyterian church. Sheep grazed in the paddock next door, freezing at the sight of the dog.

'I'll just pop this on,' Stan said. He'd made a wreath out of ivy and holly for Ned's grave. He hadn't come to the funeral. 'I can't, Mac,' he'd said on the phone. 'I can't go to funerals. Don't know what it is. Something from the war. Ned knew. He'll understand. Explain to the boy, will you?'

We all got out, into the clean, biting wind. This was my third visit to the place. My father's grave was here too. You could see for miles, settled country, cleared, big round hills with necklaces of sheep, roads marked by avenues of bare poplars. Ned's grave was a bit of new ploughing in the cemetery. Two magpies flew up angrily at our approach, disturbed at the rewarding task of picking over the rich new soil for worms.

Stan put the wreath on the mound. 'Sleep well, old son,' he said. 'We're all better for knowing you.'

I walked around to my father's grave. It needed weeding and the silver paint in the incised inscription was peeling. *Colin MacArthur Faraday,* 1928–1992, it said. Under the date, a single line, Ned's choice: *A free and generous spirit come to rest.*

Ned had made all his own arrangements for his burial: plot, coffin, picked and paid for. It was typical. He was organised in everything, probably why he got on so well with my father, who made life-changing decisions in an instant at crossroads and regarded each day as the first day of creation.

'You ask yourself why,' Stan said as we neared his gate.

'You ask yourself who,' I said.

Allie Morris had just arrived when we parked next to the smithy. She was wearing her bluey and a beanie and yellow leather stockman's gloves. Although she hadn't known Ned, she'd come to the funeral.

'I saw your legs at the funeral,' I said. 'First time.' She'd worn a dark-blue pinstripe jacket and skirt and a black shirt and black stockings. Ned would have approved. All the other men at the funeral did, many of them sober.

She scratched her forehead under the beanie with a thumb-nail. 'Legs?' she said. 'You only had to ask. What's happening today?'

We went over to the office to look at the bookings and check the answering machine.

'You've got two over at Miner's Rest, then the Shetland lady wants you. After that, there's a new one at Strathmore. In the badlands.'

'Badlands,' she said. 'Take the badlands before the Shetlands. Last time one of the things tried to bite my bum.'

'The Shetland,' I said. 'A discerning creature. Knows a biteworthy bum when it sees one.'

26

'I'm not sure how to take that.'

'The right way. Leave you free on Thursday? Bit of hot work here.'

After she'd gone, I got the forge going, got to work on some knifemaking.

We had the reading of the will the day after Ned's funeral. He'd made it soon after I reopened the smithy opposite the pub in the potato country, an hour and a half from Melbourne. It was the year Lew came to live with him following his mother's drowning off Hayman Island. Monica Lowey tried a lot of strange things in her time but scuba diving on speed was the least well-advised. The property was Ned's main asset. He wanted it sold and the proceeds divided 60:40 between Lew and me, Lew to get his share when he was twenty-five. I got the tools and the backhoe. Lew got everything else. And then there was a little personal matter: he asked me to use some of my share to look after Lew.

I was working with the file when I heard the vehicle. I went to the door. Silver Holden. Shea and Cotter. Shea got out, carrying a plastic bag.

'They say you can have this back,' he said.

I took the bag. I'd forgotten how heavy the Python was.

Shea looked around as if contemplating another search. 'Buy any rope recently?'

'Fuck off,' I said.

He gave me the look. 'Not helpful, the Feds,' he said. 'Fucking up themselves.'

27

'That right?'

Shea put both his hands in his pockets, hunched his shoulders, shuddered. 'Jesus, how d'ya live out here? Santa's dick. Fella down the road here, he can't sleep. Knows your noise. Puts a time on you goin past. Good bit after the kid called the ambulance.'

'Amazing what best practice detective work will reveal,' I said. 'What's forensic say? There's no way Ned would top himself.'

He sighed, moved his bottom jaw from side to side. 'Listen, I asked before. In his background. Anything we should know? Old enemies, new ones, anything?'

I shook my head. 'I never heard anything like that.'

'Well,' Shea said. He took his hands out of his pockets, rough, ruddy instruments, and rubbed them together. 'It's not clear he done himself or there's help. Anyway, doesn't look like he had health worries. Ring me you think of anything.' He took out his wallet and gave me a card. As he was getting into the car, he said, 'So there's life after, hey?'

'After what?' I knew what he meant.

'After being such a big man in the Feds they let you keep your gun.'

'You've got to have life before to have life after,' I said.

He pursed his lips, nodded, got in.

I went back to work on the knife, thinking about Ned. Suicide? The word burned in me.

It took me three days to clean out Ned's house. I started outside, working my way through his collection of sheds, carting stuff back to my place. On the morning of day three, I steeled myself and went into the house. There had been no fire for more than a week now and the damp cold had come up from under the floorboards and taken hold.

I did Ned's room first: there was no other way. I packed all the clothes into boxes, put the few personal things in Ned's old leather suitcase. Then I started to pack up the rest of the house. It wasn't a big job. Ned's neatness and his spartan living habits made it easy. I left the sitting room for last. It was a big room, made by knocking two rooms into one. There were two windows in the north wall, between them an old table where Ned had done his paperwork. There were signs that the cops had taken a look. Both drawers were slightly open.

I took the deep drawers out. One held stationery, a fountain pen, ink bottle, stapler, hole punch, thick wads of bills and invoices held together with rubber bands, a large yellow envelope, Ned's work diary, a ledger. The other one held a telephone book, a folder with all the papers relating to the purchase of the property and the regular outgoings, three copies of the *Dispatch*, string, a magnifying glass, a few marbles, and a wooden ruler given away by a shop in Wagga Wagga. The yellow envelope was unsealed. I looked into it: staples, rubber bands, string, assorted things. I stuffed the newspapers into a garbage bag and packed everything else into a box.

At the end of the day, I had all the things to go to the Salvation Army in one shed, the things to keep in another, and the contents of Lew's room and Ned's personal things on the back of the Land Rover. I also had two large bags of stuff to be thrown away.

I drove home via the shire tip and dumped the bags. Then it was all speed to the Heart of Oak, the pub a few hundred metres from the smithy. I was parked outside, taking out the key, taste of beer in my mouth, when the question came to me.

Why would Ned keep three copies of a newspaper in his drawer? All the other papers were in the shed, tied in neat bundles for the recyclers.

Forgot to throw them out.

No. Everything else in that drawer had a purpose.

I turned the key. Back to the tip. The man was closing the gate as I arrived.

'Don't tell me,' he said. 'You want it back.'

The bags were where I'd left them, and the papers were on top of the one I opened.

I took them into the Heart of Oak with me. It was just me and Vinnie the publican and a retired potato farmer called George Beale. Vinnie and George were playing draughts, a 364-day-a-year event contested in a highly vocal manner.

'Now that's what I call a dickhead move,' George was saying as I came in. 'Told you once, told you a thousand times.'

'Funny how I keep winnin,' Vinnie said.

'Sometimes,' said George, 'the Lord loves a dickhead.'

They said Gidday and Vinnie drew a beer without being asked.

The papers were about six weeks old, the issues of a Monday and Tuesday in April and a Thursday in June. The front-page lead in Monday's paper was headlined: BODY IN OLD MINE. I vaguely remembered reading this, people talking about it in the pub. The story read:

Police are investigating the discovery of a skeleton at the bottom of an old mine shaft at Cousin Jack Lead in the State forest near Rippon.

The macabre find was made by Dean Meerdink of Carlisle, whose dog uncovered the shaft entrance and fell about ten metres, landing on a ledge.

'We were out with the metal detector,' Mr Meerdink said. 'Deke was off looking for rabbits and he just vanished. I was calling his

31

name and I heard a faint bark. Then I saw this hole and I thought: he's a goner. I didn't want to get too close in case there was a cave-in, so I went back and rang the shire.'

Three CFA firemen with a ladder went to the scene and shone a spotlight down the shaft.

'The shaft goes almost straight down and then branches off parallel to the surface,' said CFA fireman Derek Scholte. 'The dog was fine and I was about to go down when I saw the skull. We called in the police.'

A police spokesman said the remains were human and had been taken to Melbourne for forensic examination.

I turned to Tuesday's paper. The follow-up story was also on the front page, under the headline: MINE BODY IS YOUNG WOMAN.

It began:

The remains of a body found in an old mine shaft near Rippon yesterday have been identified as those of a young woman.

Melbourne forensic scientist James LaPalma said yesterday the skeleton was that of a woman, probably under twenty. It was at least ten years old. The cause of death had not been positively ascertained but an initial examination suggested that her neck had been broken.

A spokesman for the Victoria Police said the discovery was being treated as a murder. An inquiry was underway.

The third paper, published on a Thursday in June, didn't have a front-page story on the skeleton in the mine. The story was on page three, under a photograph of a chain with a broken catch. On the chain was a small silver star.

MAN'S CHAIN FIND NEAR DEATH MINE
A man fossicking for gold with a metal detector near the mine shaft where the remains of a young woman's body were discovered last month yesterday found a silver ankle chain police say may belong to the woman.

The man, who does not wish to be identified, found the broken chain about one hundred metres from the entrance to the mine shaft and two hundred metres from the track through the State forest near Rippon.

The story went on to repeat the information in the two previous ones. The police asked anyone who recognised the chain to come forward. I read all three stories again, finished my beer and went home.

I rang the newspaper and asked for Kate Fegan, the name on the stories about the skeleton.

'Kate, my name's Milton, Geoff Milton. *Canberra Times*. I wonder if you can get me up to date on a story you handled about six weeks ago?'

Lying comes easily when you've lived my kind of life.

'Well, sure. If I can.' She was young, probably just out of her cadetship.

'The body in the mine shaft. Has that been identified?'

'No. The teeth are really all they've got to go on and they're no help. She had all her teeth, no fillings. She probably never saw a dentist, so there wouldn't be any dental records. They're pretty sure it isn't someone local. That's about all.'

'Why's that?'

'There's no-one missing from around that time. No-one that age.'

'They've put a time on it?'

'Within a year, they reckon. Around 1985.'

'How'd they do that?'

'The shire put a track in there in late 1984.

Before that you had to walk about five kilometres through dense bush to reach the mine. Then there's the decomposition. There's a scientist in Sydney who specialises in that. Reckons no later than 1985 to '86. Firm on that.'

'And her age?'

'Around sixteen. They can tell from the wrist bones.'

I said, 'So there's nothing with the remains? Clothes, stuff like that?'

'Nothing. No trace of clothes or shoes, no jewellery. She was probably naked when she was thrown down.'

'And the cause of death?'

'Difficult to say. Her neck was broken. But that might have happened after death. That was in another story I wrote. Are you doing a story?'

'Just a general piece on missing girls,' I said. 'So they don't hold out much hope of identifying her?'

'It would be pure luck, they say. I could fax you the clippings.'

'Thanks, but I think I've got everything I need. You've been a big help.'

As I put the phone down, Lew came in, tracksuit and runners, hair wet with rain, sallow skin shining.

'You play in this?' I said.

'Just the short game. He made me hit about a million.'

'He's a hard man. Hope it's worthwhile. Listen, I want to talk to you about school.'

Lew had dropped out of school at the beginning

of the year. I knew Ned had tried everything to prevent it happening but the boy became withdrawn and Ned gave up. I think his fear was that Lew would end up running away, as his mother had.

'School.' Lew took on a wary look. 'I've got to shower.'

'Hold on, mate,' I said. 'Ned asked me to look after you. That doesn't give me any rights. But I want you to know what I think, okay?'

He didn't look at me. 'Okay.'

'Leaving school at sixteen is for people who for some reason don't have any choice. That's not you. I want you to think about going back.'

He screwed up his face. 'Mick says I could be a pro.'

'Millions of kids want to do that, Lew. Maybe it'll happen. But give yourself some other options.'

He looked at me for a moment, in his dark eyes something I couldn't read. 'Got to shower,' he said and left the room.

I'd done my duty. Ned would have wanted me to try, but pushing it wouldn't work. I wasn't much and I wasn't family but I was all Lew had now and he was at the age when the testosterone and the self-doubt turn some boys into unpredictable explosive devices. I couldn't be a parent to him. The best I could hope for was that he would value my friendship, trust me. I had always been comfortable with him, liked the dry sense of humour he'd got from his grandfather's genes and example. From the moment he came into my house to stay on that grim early morning, he'd fitted into the routines of the place. He helped out without being asked, washed clothes, vacuumed, made fires, cooked. By Ned's account, Lew's life with his mother had been anything but easy. You could read some of that in his self-contained manner, but he was still just a boy in most ways.

I started work on supper: beef and vegetable stew. Open freezer door, take out two portions of beef and vegetable stew, made two weeks before. Place in microwave to defrost. Open bottle of beer. All the while I was trying to recall myself at Lew's age. But I couldn't remember where I'd been then, the places came and went so quickly.

I took the beer to the sitting room, lit the fire and switched on the early television news. A man with a face immobilised by cosmetic surgery said: *Heading tonight's bulletin: Victoria goes to the polls in five weeks. The Premier, Mr Nash, today called a snap election fourteen months before the end of the government's term.*

James Nash appeared on the screen seated next to his deputy, the Attorney General, Anthony Crewe, who was the MP for these parts. Nash was short and balding, with a worried expression. His suits had an inherited look. Crewe, on the other hand, looked like the advocate you want to plead your case to an all-female heterosexual jury: sharp features, smooth hair, dimpled chin. He had a wry, knowing smile and his suits lay on him like a benediction.

'The Nash government hasn't been afraid to take the hard decisions,' the Premier said. 'We're

37

confident that the people of Victoria value that and want us back for a third term of office.' He didn't look at all confident.

'Premier,' said a male voice, 'how do you react to allegations within your own party that this election is designed to stave off a leadership challenge from Mr Crewe, the Attorney General?'

Crewe smiled his wry smile and said, 'I'll answer that if I may, Premier. Mr Nash has my complete support and loyalty. There is no leadership challenge, election or no election. I'm happy to repeat that as many times as you want me to.'

The rest of the news was the usual line-up of accidents, strikes, bomb threats and businessmen in court, concluding with the heartwarmer: a man had rescued a guinea pig from a burning house.

Lew was silent during our meal but I couldn't feel any tension in him, so I didn't make an effort to talk. When we'd finished, he said, 'Good stew. Gotta show me how to do it. I'll wash.'

I left him washing up and went out to the office, picking up the dog on the way. The night was still and clear. I heard a car door slam down at the pub and a woman's laugh. I thought about the naked girl falling down the mine shaft, into the absolute blackness of the earth. Was she still alive when she was stuffed into the opening in the ground?

I'd put the boxes with Ned's papers and personal things in a corner. The one holding the work diary was on top. I took the old ledger over to the table and leafed through the pages recording about twenty years of Ned's working life. In his neat, slanting hand, he had noted every job he did: date, client, type, number of hours worked, amount charged, expenses. The last entry read: *July 10. Butler's Bridge Nursery. Rip subsoil approx acre. Four hours. $120.00. Fuel 36 km.*

I turned back to 1985. The first half of the year had been lean, sometimes no more than three or four small jobs a week, entries like: *Mrs Readshaw. Fixed garage door. Half hour. $5.00. 14 km.*

In July, things began to pick up. He had three weeks fencing a property at Trentham, then he did a big paving job, demolished a house, spent five weeks putting in a drive-way, gates and fences on a horse property. In October, he built a wall at Kinross Hall, the first of a series of jobs there that took up most of his time until late November. That was where he had found the old anvil. December and January were quiet, but from mid-February, for most of 1986, Ned worked on an old school being turned into a conference centre.

I read on, through 1987 and 1988, 1989, 1990. I went back and read 1982 to 1984. Then I sat back and thought. About fifteen employers' names occurred regularly across the years, people who gave Ned jobs big and small. I looked at 1982 again. Two employers appeared for the first time: J. Harris of Alder Lodge, the horse property, and Kinross Hall. I read forward. Alder Lodge became a regular source of work, most recently in May when Ned repaired a kicked-about stable. Kinross

Hall employed him three times in 1982, for two long periods in 1983, for almost three months in 1984, and in 1985 he did five separate jobs there, the last a three-week engagement ending on 22 November. That was the end of Kinross Hall. Ned never worked there again.

I told Lew where I was going and the dog and I walked over to the pub. Half a dozen or so regulars were in place, including, down at the end of the bar talking to Vinnie, Mick Doolan. He was a small man, chubby, florid, head of tight grey curls and eyes as bright and innocent as a baby's. Everything about Mick was Australian except his Irish accent. I sat down next to him.

'Well, Moc,' he said, 'just sayin to Vinnie, can't get over Ned goin out like that. No sense in it. Not Neddy.'

'No,' I said.

He drank some stout. 'Had these police fellas around today. Murderers roamin the countryside and they're out makin life difficult for small businessmen such as misself.'

Mick was a dealer in what he called Old Wares, mostly junk, and the police took a keen interest in the provenance of his stock.

I said, 'Small businessman? The police think you're a small receiver of stolen property.'

He sighed. 'Well and that's exactly what I'm sayin, Moc. They form theories based on nothin but ignorance and then they devote the taxpayers' time to provin them. And naturally they can't.

40

Vinnie, give us a coupla jars and a bag of the salt and vinegar. Two bags.'

'One, Vinnie,' I said. 'Mick, what's Kinross Hall?'

'Kinross Hall? It's what they used to call a place of safety. For naughty girls. They won't let you in, Moc.'

'Did Ned ever talk about working there? Late '85?'

He scratched his curls. 'Well, you know Ned. Not one to gossip.'

Vinnie arrived with the drinks and the chips. I paid.

I persisted. 'Did he ever say anything about the place?'

Mick munched on chips, washed them down with a big swallow, wiped his mouth. 'From what I could gather,' he said, 'he thought the place should be closed down. He said he wouldn't work there again.'

'Why?'

'He heard some story. Went to see the police about it and they told him basically piss off, mind yer own business. That's how I remember it.'

'What kind of story?'

'I couldn't tell you. He never said. You know Ned. Y'had to read his mind.' He offered me the chip packet. 'Now you're a cert for Satdee? And you'd be settin an example to the young fellas by attendin Wednesday trainin. I've bin workin on a new strategy, could be revolutionary, turnin point in the history of the game.'

I said, 'New strategy? What, we kick a goal? That'll shock 'em rigid.'

A girl with a broken neck, a naked girl, thrown down a mine shaft and the entrance covered. I couldn't get it out of my mind.

I thought about these things all through the morning as Allie Morris and I worked at the forge on an order for four dozen garden-hose hooks. It was pleasant enough work once we had forty-eight lengths: heat the flat steel to glowing red, use jaws in the anvil hardie hole to put a bend in one end, bend sixty centimetres down to make a flap, squeeze the top half in the vice to make a doubled length. Then curve the rest into a three-quarter circle over the anvil horn. The job was finished by putting a stake point on the end that went into the ground. Two people working with red-hot metal can be awkward, but we found a rhythm quickly, taking turns at heating, bending and hammering, Allie's deftness compensating for my occasional clumsiness.

We finished just before one pm: four dozen hose hooks, neatly stacked on Allie's truck to be dropped off for priming and painting.

'That's a day's work,' Allie said. 'Does the pub do a sandwich?'

We took turns to clean up in the bathroom I'd built on to the office so that I didn't have to traipse into the house in a filthy condition, and walked down the road in silence. The dog appeared ahead of us: taken a short cut through the neighbour's paddock. The sky was clearing, the cloud cover broken, harried fragments streaming east in full retreat.

Suddenly the world was high and light and full of promise. I hadn't talked much to Allie since she started. She had a reserved way about her, not rude but not forthcoming. And I didn't have any experience of working relationships like this. Man and a woman working with hot metal.

At the pub, it was just us and Vinnie and two hard-looking women in tracksuits playing pool. The fat one had a lipstick smear at the edge of her mouth. It looked like a bruise when she bent her head. Allie put the beers down and said, 'Know someone called Alan Snelling?'

'Know who he is.'

'What's he do?'

'Runs a few horses. Nice house. Nice cars. Gets married every now and again.'

'He asked me out.'

'Available to be asked out?' I instantly regretted the question.

She smiled, drank some beer, wiped away a thin tidemark of foam on her upper lip with a fingertip. 'I'm between engagements. He was at Glentroon

43

Lodge yesterday, looking at a horse. Asked my opinion.'

'Who wouldn't,' I said. 'An older man. They can be attracted to capable young women.'

She put her head on one side. 'Older man? He's about your age.'

'That's what I mean.'

She laughed. Vinnie arrived with the toasted sandwiches.

'That was quick,' I said.

'Cook's day off,' said Vinnie. 'Everything's quicker on his day off. Including the time. Passes too fast.'

We talked business while we ate. On our way back, I said, 'About Alan Snelling.'

Yes?'

'You want to think.'

'Meaning?'

'Alan's lucky,' I said. 'His old mum popped off. Nobody thought she had much, just the house, falling-over weatherboard. Not so. She had lots of things. Jewellery, coin collections, stamp collections, and a box with about $100,000 in cash in it. All up, worth about $400,000.'

'Well, I suppose there's an explanation,' said Allie.

I said, 'Also, Alan had a business partner, ran their little video hire business in Melbourne. Top little business, big as a phone booth, cash flow like Target. Then the partner was working out in his home gym and the machine collapsed on him. Fatal.'

'That's not lucky,' Allie said.

'They had key executive insurance,' I said. 'Half a million.'

We were going down the lane, when Allie said, 'What's that about his mother mean? I don't get it.'

'People could think Alan was parking invisible earnings with his mother.'

'Invisible? You mean illegal? Like drugs?'

I shrugged. 'Among the possibilities.'

'Jesus,' Allie said. 'How do you know this stuff?'

'I forget where I heard it,' I said.

Allie went off to a job. I should have worked on the knives but instead I rang the library at Burnley Horticultural College and asked them if they had any information on Harkness Park. The woman took my number. She rang back inside half an hour.

'I've tracked down a dozen or so references to it,' she said. 'There'll probably be more.'

'Any pictures or drawings?'

'No. It was designed by a man called Robert Barton Graham, an Englishman. It's not clear but he seems to have been brought out by a Colonel Stephen Peverell in 1896 to design the garden. He designed other gardens in Victoria while he was here, but they're all gone as far as we know.'

'Anywhere else I could try?'

She sighed. 'Our collection's pretty good. The State Library doesn't have anything we don't have. Not that you can get to, anyway. I'll keep looking.' As an afterthought, she said, 'Sometimes the local history associations can help. They might know who has information.'

45

I drove over to Brixton, the town nearest Harkness Park. I knew where the local history museum was, a brick and weatherboard building near the railway station. It had once been a factory with its own rail siding. Two elderly women sitting behind a glass display counter in the front room of the museum looked surprised to see a visitor.

'G'day,' said the smaller of the pair. She was wearing a knitted hat that resembled a chimney pot. Wisps of bright orange hair escaped at the temples. 'You're just in time. We're just having a cup of tea before we close.'

A hand-lettered sign said: Adults $2, Children $1, Pensioners Free. I put down a coin.

The second woman took the money. 'On your own, are you?' she said. She looked like someone who'd worked hard outdoors: ruddy skin, hands too big for her wrists.

'I'm interested in gardens,' I said. 'Old gardens.'

The women looked at each other. 'This is a local history museum,' the smaller one said apologetically.

'I thought you might be the ones to ask about old gardens around here,' I said.

They exchanged glances again. 'Well, there's a good few that open to the public,' the taller one said. 'The best'd be Mrs Sheridan's, wouldn't it, Elsie? Some very nice beds.'

'You don't know of a place called Harkness Park?' I said.

'Oh, Harkness Park,' she said. 'Mrs Rosier's house.

46

I don't think that's ever been open. She had nothing to do with the town. Didn't even come to church. People say it was a grand garden once, but you can't see anything from the road except the trees. It's like a forest.'

'Old Col Harris used to work there,' the other woman said. 'Him and that Meekin and another man – I can't remember his name, lived out on Cribbin Road. Dead now. They're all dead.'

'There wouldn't be photographs, would there?' I said.

The taller woman sighed exaggeratedly. 'Don't talk about photos. There's a whole room of unsorted photos. Mr Collits was in charge of photographs. Wouldn't give anyone else a look-in, would he, Elsie?'

'He's not around anymore?'

She shook her head. 'Blessing, really. Had a terrible time.'

'I told the committee we needed to appoint someone to sort the photos,' Elsie said. 'But will they do anything practical?'

'These men who worked at Harkness Park,' I said, 'do they have family still here?'

'Why don't you just go out there and knock on the door?' Elsie said. 'It's still in the family. Some cousin or something got it.'

'They sold it. I'm interested in knowing what it was like twenty or thirty years ago.'

'Col Harris's boy's here,' the taller one said. 'Dennis. Saw him a few weeks ago. Wife went off with the kids. Shouldn't say that. He works for

Deering's. They're building the big retirement village, y'know.'

I said thanks and had a look around the museum. It was like a meticulously arranged garage sale: nothing was of much value or of any great age, but assembling the collection had clearly given the organisers a lot of pleasure.

Finding the new retirement village wasn't a problem. It was at an early stage, a paddock of wet, ravaged earth, concrete slabs and a few matchstick timber frames going up.

A man at the site hut pointed out Dennis Harris on one of the slabs, a big man in his forties with long hair, cutting studs to length with a dropsaw. At my approach, he switched it off and slid back his ear protectors. Dennis's eyes said he didn't think I was the man from Tattslotto.

'Sorry to bother you,' I said. 'Ladies at the museum thought you could help me.'

'Museum?' Deep suspicion, stiff shoulders.

'They said your father worked at Harkness Park. I'm trying to find old photos of the place.'

Dennis's shoulders relaxed. He nodded. 'There's pictures in his old album. Lots. He used to work in the vegie garden when he was a young fella. Before the war. Huge. Wall around it. There was five gardeners there.'

We arranged to meet at the pub after knock-off. Dennis brought the album. 'Take it and copy what you want,' he said.

'I could give you some kind of security for it,' I said.

'Nah. What kind of bloke pinches old photos? Just bring it back.'

I bought him a beer and we talked about building. Then I drove home and rang Stan.

'Research,' I said. 'Paid for by the hour. I've got photographs from the 1930s.'

'No you haven't, lad,' he said. 'Not yet. Not enough hours.'

Ten minutes into the last quarter, it began to rain, freezing rain, driven into our faces by a wind that had passed over pack ice in its time. We only needed a kick to win but nobody could hold the ball, let alone get a boot to it. We were sliding around, falling over, trying to recognise our own side under the mudpacks. Mick Doolan was shouting instructions from the sideline but no-one paid any attention. We were completely knackered. Finally, close to time, we had some luck: a big bloke came out of the mist and broke Scotty Ewan's nose with a vicious swing of the elbow. Even in the rain, you could hear the cartilage crunch. Scotty was helped off, streaming blood, and we got a penalty.

'Take the kick, Mac,' said Billy Garrett, the captain. He would normally take the kick in situations like this, but since the chance of putting it through was nil, he thought it best that I lose the game for Brockley.

'Privilege,' I said, spitting out some mud. 'Count on my vote for skipper next year. Skipper.'

I was right in front of goal but the wind was lifting my upper lip. I looked around the field.

There were about twenty spectators left, some of them dogs sitting in old utes.

'Slab says you can't do it,' said the player closest to me. He was just another anonymous mudman but I knew the voice.

'Very supportive, Flannery,' I said. 'You're on, you little prick.'

Squinting against the rain, I took my run-up into the gale, scared that I was going to slip before I could even make the kick.

But I didn't. I managed to give the ball a reasonable punt before my left leg went out under me. I hit the ground with my left shoulder and slid towards goal.

And as I lay in the cold black mud, the wind paused for a second or two and the ball went straight between the uprights.

The final whistle went. Victory. Victory in round eight of the second division of the Brockley and District League. I got up. My shoulder felt dislocated. 'That'll be a slab of Boag, Flannery,' I said. 'You fucking traitor.'

'Brought out yer best,' Flannery said. 'Psychology. Read about it.'

I said, 'Read about it? *Psychology in Pictures*. I didn't know they'd done that.'

We staggered off in the direction of the corrugated-iron changing room. On the way, Billy Garrett joined us. 'Pisseasy kick,' he said.

'That's why you didn't want it, Billy,' I said. 'Not enough challenge.'

After we'd wiped off the worst of the mud and changed, we drove the hundred metres to the Heart of Oak. Mick Doolan had about twenty beers lined up.

'Magnificent, me boyos,' he said. 'Out of the textbook. And good to see you followin instructions, Flannery. Hasn't always bin the case.'

'Instructions?' Flannery said. 'I didn't hear any instructions.'

The outside door opened and the big bloke who'd broken Scotty Ewan's nose came in. Behind him were four or five of the other larger members of the Millthorpe side, just in case. He came over to Mick.

'Bloke of yours all right?' he said. 'Didn't intend him no harm. Sort of run into me arm.' He looked down at his right forearm as if inquiring something of it.

'Perfectly all right,' Mick said. 'Hazard of the game. Nothin modern medical science can't handle. Won't be out for more than three or four. Shout you fellas a beer?'

'Thanks, no,' the man said. 'Be gettin back. Just didn't want to go short of sayin me regrets.'

'You're a gentleman, Chilla,' Mick said. 'There's not many would take the trouble.'

After they'd left, Flannery said, 'There's not many would have the fuckin front to come around here afterwards. Might as well've hit Scotty with an axe handle.'

'Think positively,' Mick said. 'Some good in the worst tragedy. Got the penalty. And we won.'

52

'Bloody won a lot easier if you'd play Lew,' Billy Garrett said. 'Be the only bloke under thirty in the side.'

I said, 'Also the only bloke who can run more than five metres without stopping for a cough and a puke.'

Mick took a deep drink, wiped the foam from his lips, shook his head. 'Don't understand, do ya lads? Young fella's pure gold. Do ya put your young classical piano player in a wood-choppin competition? Do ya risk your young golf talent on a frozen paddick with grown men, violent spud-grubbers and the like? Bloody no, that's the answer. Boy's goin to be a champion.'

'Speakin of champions,' said Flannery. 'Reckon I'm givin away this runnin around in the mud on Satdee arvos, big fellas tryin to bump into me. All me joints achin.' He scratched his impossibly dense curly dog hair. 'Could be me last season.'

Mick's eyes narrowed. He rubbed his small nose. 'Last season? That so? Well, Flanners me boyo, get to the Grand Final, I'll point out a coupla fellas ya can take into retirement with ya.'

I took the next shout. Then Vinnie came in from fighting with the cook and sent the beers around. Flannery's younger brother came in with the lovely and twice-widowed Yvonne and shouted the room. Things were good in trucking. Other rounds followed. In due course, Mick broke into 'The Rose of Tralee' and Flannery's voice, shockingly deep from the compact frame, joined him.

53

The air warmed, thickened, became a brew of beer fumes, breath, tobacco smoke, cooking smells from the kitchen. The windows cried tears of condensation and my shoulder was healed of all pain. It was after ten, whole body in neutral, when I decided against another drink. I was saying my farewells when Mick put his head close to me and said, 'Moc, other day. That Ned thing we were discussin. Met the fella today, works on the gate at Kinross Hall. Says Ned was there a coupla days before. Before he – y'know.'

I wandered out into the drizzle, cold night, black as Guinness, smell of deep and wet potato fields. The dog appeared and we found our way across the road. I stopped for a leak beside the sign that said *Blacksmith, All Metalwork and Shoeing.* Flannery had done it for me in pokerwork and it wasn't going to get him a place in the Skills Olympics. Down the muddy lane the two of us went home, both happy to have a home. Homes are not easy to come by.

The sign saying *Kinross Hall, Juvenile Training Centre* directed you down a country road. Five kilometres further, another sign pointed at a long avenue of poplars. At the end of it, huge spear-pointed cast-iron gates were set in a bluestone wall fully three metres high. Above them, an ornate wrought-iron arch held the words *Kinross Hall*, the two words separated by a beautiful wrought-iron rose. Through them you could see a gravel driveway flanked by bare elms. An arrow on the gate took the eye to a button on the right-hand pillar. A sign said: RING.

I got out of the vehicle, admired the craftsmanship of the iron rose on the arch, and pushed the button. After a few minutes, I rang again. Then a man in standard blue security guard uniform came walking down the drive – moon face, fat man's walk, not in any hurry.

'Yes,' he said.

'I'm trying to find about someone who was here about two weeks ago,' I said.

He didn't say anything, just looked at the Land Rover and looked back at me blankly.

'Bloke called Ned Lowey,' I said.

He nodded. 'I heard about him. He was here. Hold on, tell you when.' He went off to my right, out of sight. When he came back, he had a black and red ledger, open. He riffled through it, then said, 'Tuesday 9 July, nine twenty am.'

I said, 'What was it about?'

Still expressionless, he said, 'Wouldn't know, mate. Had an appointment with the director at nine-thirty am.'

'How do you get to see the director?'

'Ask. Want me to?'

I nodded.

'Name and purpose of visit.'

I gave him my name and said, 'Inquiry about Ned Lowey's visit.'

He wrote it in the book and went off again. He was away no more than two minutes. 'Better put the dog in the cab,' he said. 'Park in front of the main building. Turn right as you go in the front door. Down the passage. There's a sign says Director's Office.'

I opened the passenger window and whistled. The dog jumped onto the cab roof. His back legs appeared, scrambled their way over the windowsill, and then the whole animal dropped into the cab. The guard shook his head and opened the gate.

No inmates were to be seen, only a man on a ride-on mower in the distance. The main building was stone, someone's house once, a mixture of

56

castle and Gothic cathedral with a hint of French chateau, set in immaculate parkland. It could have been an expensive country hotel but it had the feeling of all places of involuntary residence: the silence, the smell of disinfectant, the disciplined look of everything, the little extra chill in the air.

The secretary was a pale, thin woman in her thirties with very little make-up. Her bare and unwelcoming office was cold and she had her jacket on.

'Please take a seat,' she said. She tugged an earlobe. Blunt nails. 'Dr Carrier will see you shortly.'

It was a ten-minute wait in an upright chair, probably an instructional technique. The secretary pecked at the computer. There wasn't anything to read, nothing on the walls to look at. I thought about Ned. Had the director kept him sitting here, too? On this very chair? Finally, the secretary received some kind of a signal.

'Please go through,' she said.

The director's office was everything the secretary's wasn't, a comfortable sitting room rather than a place of business. A fire burned in a cast-iron grate under a wooden mantelpiece, there were paintings and photographs on the walls and chintz armchairs on either side of a deep window.

A woman sat behind an elegant writing table. She was in her mid-forties, tall, and groomed for Olympic dressage: black suit with white silk cravat, dark hair pulled back severely, discreet make-up.

'Mr Faraday,' she said. She came around the table and put out her right hand. 'Marcia Carrier. Let's sit somewhere comfortable.' There was an air of confidence about her. You could imagine her talking to prime ministers as an equal.

We shook hands and sat down in the armchairs. She had long, slim legs.

'I understand it's to do with Mr Lowey,' she said. 'What a shock. A terrible thing. Are you family?'

'Just a friend,' I said. 'I wonder if you can tell me why he came to see you?'

She smiled, put her head on one side in a puzzled way. 'Why he came to see me? Is this somehow connected with what happened?'

'I don't know.'

'It was about work,' she said.

I waited.

'He'd done some work for us before. A long time ago. I confess I didn't remember him. He was inquiring about the prospect of future work.'

'You hire the casual workers yourself?'

'Oh no.' She shook her head. 'Our maintenance person does that. But Mr Lowey asked to see me.' She smiled, an engaging smile. 'I try to see anyone who wants to see me.'

'So he was looking for work?'

'Basically.'

'He did quite a lot of work here in 1985. Can you tell me why you didn't use him again?'

She shrugged, puzzled frown. 'I really can't say.

Lots of people work here. The maintenance person may have had some reason. Then again, we didn't use many outside contractors from '86 to '91. Budget cuts every year.'

I looked out of the window. You could see bare trees, gunmetal clouds boiling in the west. 'Did you know that he went to the police about something to do with this place?' I said.

Her eyes widened. 'No.' She appeared genuinely surprised. 'You mean in 1985 or now?'

'In 1985.'

'Do you know what about?'

I shook my head.

'Well,' she said, 'he certainly didn't mention anything a few weeks ago. I can't imagine what it could have been.'

'You had no inquiries from the police in 1985?'

'The local police? I'd have to check the records. I can't recall having anything to do with them.'

'There wasn't anyone missing?'

'Missing?'

I said, 'I presume some of your charges do a runner occasionally.'

She laughed. It brought her face alive. She was very attractive. 'They do from time to time, and we notify the Department of Community Services and they handle the business of looking for them. They generally find them in a few days, back in their old haunts.'

'And you didn't have one like that in late '85?'

She clasped her hands. 'Mr Faraday, I'm happy

to answer your questions but I'm not sure what this is about.'

I wasn't sure either but I said, 'I had the vague thought that Ned's death might be connected with something that happened here in 1985.'

She was looking at me in a way that said she had grave doubts about my grip on reality. 'I'll find out,' she said. 'It'll take a few minutes. Can I offer you coffee? Tea?'

I declined and she left me. I walked around the room looking at the pictures. The paintings were all oils, small, signed by the same hand – B.I. or B.L. From a distance they looked like bush camp-fire scenes. Close up, they had the power to disturb. Something unpleasant seemed to be happening in them, primitive sacrifice or torture, people in poses of prayer and supplication and indistinct flesh-toned objects in the flames. There were six of them, not markedly different, not hung in any order I could detect.

Marcia Carrier was in most of the photographs, family scenes with another dark-haired girl and a couple who might have been their grandparents. The man was stern-looking, handsome, hair intact, cleft chin. The woman was overweight, dowdy. I went back to looking at the paintings.

'Painted by my father,' Marcia Carrier said. 'Just a weekend painter.'

'Very dramatic weekend painter,' I said.

She laughed again. 'I must say I don't quite understand them. Now. There was no-one absent

60

without permission from here in late 1985. In fact, no-one strayed in 1985. Two girls took unofficial leave in 1986, both returned to us within a fortnight. Is that helpful?'

I said, 'Thanks. I won't waste any more of your time.' 'Coffee's on its way,' she said. 'I insist.'

I sat down. The secretary came in with a tray holding a silver coffee jug, big French coffee cups, warm milk, shortbread. Marcia Carrier poured.

'What sort of work do you do, Mr Faraday?'

'I'm a blacksmith, metalworker.'

'Really? I've never met a blacksmith. How do you become one?'

'Years of training under a master craftsman. Intensive study of the properties of metals. Also, you have to be able to hit hot things with a really heavy hammer. How do you get to run a place like this?'

Her serious look did not leave her. 'Well, you have to be a public-spirited person, utterly selfless, with an abiding faith in the essential goodness of human beings. You also need a deep understanding of psychology. Then you have to be a superb administrator who thinks nothing of working long and unpredictable hours.'

'So,' I said, 'basically anyone can apply.'

She had an engaging laugh. 'Your inmates . . .' I said.

'Clients.'

'Clients. How do they get here?'

She was serious now. 'The courts send us all

61

sorts of girls – rich kids, poor kids, kids you can help, kids you can't. They've all got one thing in common. No-one wants them except for the worst reasons. They've usually landed up on the street and someone, sometimes a number of people, is pushing them towards drugs and prostitution. If no-one intervenes, most of them won't see twenty. If the department can convince a court that a girl's in significant danger, she might get sent here.'

'Then what happens?'

'We try our best to help them. You have to under-stand, some of these girls have had no childhood. Shunted around, never felt wanted, sex at an early age, often raped. They're fifteen going on forty. Our aim is to convince them that their lives have worth and that they can live worthwhile lives.'

I had the feeling she'd said all this before. Many times. 'Doesn't sound easy,' I said.

'No.' She looked out of the window. 'Mostly we're too late. And for some girls I sometimes think it's always too late.'

I didn't say anything.

She turned her eyes on me. 'Do you believe in evil, Mr Faraday?'

I thought about this for a while. It wasn't the kind of question people often asked me. Finally I said, 'I don't doubt that some people are evil. I'm not sure there's an evil that's independent of evil people.'

Marcia Carrier nodded. 'Have you noticed,' she said, 'that evil people have a kind of force about them? A kind of independence? It's a very powerful thing to have. It's a stillness, an absence of doubt, an indifference to the world. It draws people to them. The moral vacuum sucks people in. The weak go to the strong. We see girls like that here. Some of them come on like victims, like wounded creatures. But sooner or later the other side shows through. The side that's the predator, the side that inflicts wounds. The evil side.'

She shook her head, quick self-chastising movement. 'But that's all too serious,' she said. 'We do what we can for the girls. They can study if they want to. Some do. For others, it's too late. For now anyway. For them, we have a range of programmes. Self-esteem. Life skills. Job skills. That sort of thing.'

That was the end of talking about Kinross Hall. She moved the conversation over to the possibility of spring ever coming. We talked about coffee-making, her ignorance of football, the effects of sun deprivation. It was an easy exchange. When I got up to go, she said, 'This is going to nag at me. I'll have another look at the records, see if there's anything I didn't spot that might have worried Mr Lowey. What's your phone number?'

At the door, we shook hands. She had a nice, dry grip and she held it for a second.

'I'm pleased to have met a blacksmith, Mr Faraday,' she said.

'Mac.'

'Marcia.'

The security man had the gate open when I rounded the corner. He gave me a little wave.

I went home, lit the Ned Kelly in the forge and got back to work on the knives. I had made my first knife for George Tan, a chef friend of Vinnie the publican. He'd lost the index finger on his chopping hand to a boat winch. When he got back to work after two months off, he found his knives unbalanced in his hand. George showed me the problem in the pub one Monday night, and I drew a knife shape that might compensate for the missing finger. It took four or five versions to get the distribution of weight right. George was ecstatic. He rang me to say he wanted a full set. Another chef in his kitchen, a tenfingered one, tried the knives and ordered three. He showed them to a chef in Sydney, who ordered a full set. I now had orders for about thirty knives.

Filing and fitting, stove gradually warming the room, I thought about my visit to Kinross Hall.

I couldn't believe Ned had gone to see Marcia Carrier about work. Ned never asked anyone for work. And leaving aside Ned's nature, he had no need to drum up work. His diary showed an almost full workload of bookings for two or three months.

Marcia Carrier had not told me the real reason for Ned's visit to Kinross Hall the day before he died. Why? I kept turning my meeting with her over in my mind. Then I went to the office and rang Detective Sergeant Michael Shea. He was out. They would pass on a message. I left my number. I was sorting out Allie's appointments when the phone rang.

'Shea.'

I said, 'There's something. Ned Lowey complained to the cops about Kinross Hall in late 1985. November. Can you check that?'

Silence. He cleared his throat. 'November '85? Why the fuck would I want to check that?'

'You might find out something.'

There was a long silence. I could hear traffic noises. Then he said, 'I'm the policeman.'

'Trying to help,' I said. 'Don't want that, fine.'

Silence again. Someone said something in the background. Probably skinhead Cotter. 'Get back to you,' Shea said.

In the half-awake dawn, rain hissing in the downpipes, I lay on my back and, for the first time in years, thought about the old life. When I'd come to my father's house and the smithy to stay, I had schooled myself to shy away from thinking about my recent past until the people in it seemed unreal and unimportant, as if I'd created them or seen them in a film. In my mind, I called that the old life. I wanted a new life, a life among ordinary people, people like Ned and Stan Harrop and Flannery. Now Ned's death had shaken everything loose and I didn't try to fight the thoughts.

The old life. It had been my life for thirteen years. The old life. The Job. The endless, seamless job that had no clear beginning and was never finished. 'Your job!' Susan had screamed one night. 'Don't call it your fucking job! It's not a job. It's your fucking life! It's your fucking personality! It's *you*. It's what you are. You don't exist without it. There isn't anything fucking else in your world, don't you understand that?'

I did understand that. And then again I didn't. Not that it made any difference. She left me anyway. I came home one day and she was on the pavement putting suitcases into her car. It was a sunny day in early spring and, from a full block away, I saw the gold of her hair catch the light. A flash, like sun on a helmet.

Another departure. My whole life seemed to be about departures. My father and I changing towns every year or two, the two of us packing everything into the truck, sometimes no-one to say goodbye to, driving away from some forlorn fibro house in the grey dawn. I used to put myself to sleep thinking about the towns, trying to picture the few friends I'd made. Wal in Cunnamulla who gave me a Joseph Rodgers pocketknife. Sleepy-eyed Gibbo in St George whose mother always wanted to feed me. Russell in Baradine whose dog had spotty pups. For many years, I had the feeling that it was vitally important to keep the memories of these and other people and places alive. To let them fade away would somehow be an act of betrayal, of disloyalty. Perhaps this was because I had no recollection of my mother, and I felt that this was somehow my fault, as if I had not cared enough about her, as if I had cast her off, thrown away her memory. Your mother. Other people's mothers ask you about your mother. The fathers ask: 'So what's yer father do?'

Why did we keep moving? I never really understood. I asked my father once, one night in my first university vacation, watching him work in the smithy. He didn't stop what he was doing. After a while, he said, 'Never wanted to stop anywhere long after I lost your mum.' There was a long silence, then he said, 'Nothin's forever, John. Enjoy what you can and don't be scared to move along.'

Before I was in my teens, I could tell when we were going to move. My father became morose, pacing around at night, not fishing, not reading, saying things like: 'Jesus, imagine endin up in a dump like this.' Once that started, it was over. Mentally, he was already somewhere else. It only remained for me to tell the teacher and get my sealed envelope. And prepare myself for the fight.

That's the thing I remember most clearly about the string of tiny towns that looked as if they'd been dumped on the site from the air. The fight in the first week. They trailed you after school like mongrels following a bitch on heat. Big boys, small boys, fat boys, thin boys, all aroused by the prospect of violence, strutting, jostling. You walked on, whole body tense, heart like a piston in your chest, feeling them getting closer, half hearing the taunts through the blood noise in your head. Then someone would try to trip you, usually a small one, over-excited, wide-eyed, flushed. Or a few would run past you, turn and block your path or dawdle along, finally stopping. That was the moment.

By the time I was twelve, I'd learned to short-circuit the process, stop, turn, issue the challenge, draw out some pale-eyed, mouth-breathing boy, spitty lips, hands too big for his wrists. You couldn't win these fights. Some bigger boy always dragged you off if you got the upper hand. But what my father taught me was that you had to show the whole baying mob that you were a dangerous person, a person prepared to kick, bite, pull hair, tear ears, gouge eyes, squeeze testicles, anything. 'Don't worry about fair,' he said. 'Dangerous is what you want to be. Go mad. Nobody wants to fight a mad person. Nobody wants fingers stuck up his nose.'

He was right. He also taught me the barfighters' tricks: the quick chest shoves to get the opponent off balance, the heel scraping down the shin and stamping on the instep, the Adam's apple punch, the thumbs pressing under the ears, the chop under the nose, the many painful uses of the elbow, the double ear slap, the protruding knuckle in the chestbone. I learned these things and I survived.

Ned Lowey. In all this movement, this rootlessness, this life in shabby houses and scuffed caravan parks and shearers' quarters that smelled of sweat and ashes, Ned Lowey was the still point. We were on our way to another town, another fight, another departure, when I met him for the first time. It must have been some time after my ninth birthday, but I had been hearing about Ned as far back as I could remember, things like 'We need bloody Ned Lowey for work like this', or 'Here's a little trick Ned Lowey showed me', or, at picnic races, 'Back Ned Lowey ridin sidesaddle against this lot'.

We drove into Ned's backyard and he came out and shook hands with my father. They stood there smiling and slapping each other's arms.

'This is the young fella,' my father said. 'John. We named him for the wife's father.' I remember my surprise at two things. One was that Ned was Aboriginal. My father had never mentioned it. The other was that Ned Lowey was not a giant. I remember that he took me by the shoulders, picked me up and held me to his chest. Then we went into the house to meet his wife. She was sitting in a patch of sun in the kitchen, not doing anything, a gaunt woman with faded blonde hair. I knew without being told that there was something wrong with her.

Ned Lowey. I shook the thoughts away and got up. By seven am, I was in the smithy getting ready to start work on Frank Cullen's latest contraption. Frank inherited the huge property that had been in his wife's family, the Pettifers, for generations. That was the end of farming. Now he spent all his time designing strange and usually counterproductive devices. Every six months or so, he came in with a set of plans for another machine that was going to change the face of rural life. The first one I made for him was designed to help elderly farmers mount horses. It featured a hydraulic piston and was said to have enabled the test jockey to mount a tree. The latest one was a sort of tray on wheels that fitted on the back of a ute. By fitting tracks, the tray could be run off the back and loaded. A winch operated by the driver then pulled it back up.

'Came to me in a flash, Mac,' Frank said. 'Can't think why no-one's ever thought of it.'

'Takes a special kind of mind,' I said.

It was almost noon and I had just finished welding the heavy-gauge steel mesh into the angle-iron base when Frank and Jim Caswell arrived. Jim was rumoured to be old man Pettifer's illegitimate son. Frank was somewhere in his seventies with a big, bony head, patches of hair, exploding eyebrows and ears like baseball mitts. Jim was about fifteen years younger, full head of grey hair cut short, small-featured, neat. He looked like a clerk in some old-fashioned shop. Usually they both wore the squatter's uniform: tweed jacket, moleskins, blue shirt and tie. Today Jim was in a dark suit, white shirt and navy tie.

They sat down on the bench against the wall and watched me marking the position of the axle mountings. These visits were a feature of the construction period.

'Nice job so far, Mac,' Frank said. 'Paying attention to the plans? Worked out in every detail.'

'Like I was building a Saturn VI,' I said.

'Good man.' He turned to Jim. 'So who was there?'

'Langs, Rourkes, Carvers, Veenes, Chamberlain, Charlie Thomson, Ormerods, Caseys, Mrs Radley, Frasers. Just about everyone. Old Scott.'

71

'Old Scott?' Frank said. 'Danny Wallace hated the miserable old bastard. What did he want?'

'Same as everyone else, I s'pose. Came to pay his respects.'

'Anybody ask after me?'

'No.'

Frank scratched a moulting patch of hair. 'Not a word? What about old Byrne? He must've noticed I wasn't there.'

'Didn't say anything.'

'Well,' said Frank. 'That's that bloody mob for you. I knew Danny Wallace since '47, day I king-hit him in the Golden Fleece. Used to put him to bed. That drunk he'd get on a horse backwards.' He patted his jacket. 'What happened to my smokes?'

'I though he was cryin a bit at the end,' Jim said. 'By the grave.'

'Who?'

'Old Kellaway.'

Frank found his cigarettes and lit one with a big gold lighter. He coughed for a while, then he said. 'Old Kellaway? Bloody crocodile tears. Sanctimonious old bastard. Spent his whole life crawlin up the cracks of the rich. You know where the bastard was in the war? Y'know?'

'I know,' Jim said.

'Chaplain in the Navy, bloody Australian Navy, two pisspots and a tin bath. Hearin the bunnyboys' confessions.' He put on a high voice. ' "Forgive me, father, I cracked a fat at Mass." ' Then a deep voice:

' "My son, the Lord forbids us to lust after petty officers' bums. Say fifty Hail Marys and report to my cabin after lights out." '

'He's all right,' Jim said. 'Hasn't been much of a life for him.'

'All right?' said Frank. 'All right? He's far from bloody all right. If he was all right he'd never have landed up here so he wouldn't have much of a life. He'd a been a bloody cardinal, wouldn't he?'

Frank took a small leather-bound flask out of his inside pocket. 'Just thinkin about bloody Kellaway gives me a need for drink,' he said. He took off the cap and had a good swig.

Jim muttered something.

'What's that?' Frank said, wiping his lips. 'You say somethin?'

'Nothin.'

'Don't bloody nothin me. Somethin to say, spit it out.'

'Bit early for the piss, innit?'

Frank nodded knowingly. 'Sonny,' he said, 'don't come the fuckin little prig with me. I've had disapproval from a whole family of disapproval experts. I feel like it, I'll give myself a whisky enema for breakfast.'

I was looking at the plan. 'What's this twisty thing you've drawn here, Frank?'

He eased himself up and came over. 'It's a spring, Mac. A shock absorber.'

'Right,' I said. 'That horse mounter needed a shock absorber.'

73

'I need a bloody shock absorber,' Frank said. 'Shares goin down like the *Titanic* and the bastards call an election. This country's buggered, y'know that, Mac. Get butchered for bloody king and country twice, then it's for the Yanks. Now everythin's for sale. Power stations. Telephone. Bloody airports. Negative gear this bloody Parliament buildin chock-a-block with liars, thousands of bloody bent police thrown in. Buy the whole country.'

'What about Crewe?' I said. 'Going to get back, is he?' I went over to the cabinet to look for some suitable springs for the shock absorber.

'Anthony Crewe,' Frank said. 'Lord only knows how they made that bastard attorney-general. Bloody miscarriage of justice if ever there was one. Done that shonky will for old Morrissey.'

'That's enough, Frank,' Jim said.

Frank turned his big head slowly. 'What?' he said. 'What did you say?'

Jim looked away. 'You know what Mr Petty always said about repeatin gossip.'

A look somewhere between pleasure and pain came over Frank's face. 'Little man,' he said, 'don't quote The Great Squatter to me. I've told you that before. I had those sayins straight from the horse's arse for thirty-five years. Now a miniature ghost of the old shit follows me around repeatin them. Is that what they mean by everlastin life? You're dead but your miserable opinions linger on to haunt the livin?'

74

He turned back to me. 'Now, as I was sayin, the bastard Crewe shoulda been in jail over that will.'

'What will?' I was looking in the box for springs.

'Will he produced after old Morrissey turned up his toes. Half the bloody estate to the physio-thingamajig. Who happens to be Mr Shonky Crewe's current rootee. Lorraine was her name, I recall. Latest in a long line. Once he got his cut, he was into that Kinross Hall warder. Dr Marcia somethin or other. All legs and hair.'

I looked up. 'Crewe had an affair with Marcia Carrier?'

'That's what they say,' Frank said. 'He's the boss cockie out there, y'know. Chairman of the council, whatever. They should take a bloody good look at that place. God knows what goes on there. I see the quack switched off his lights the other day. Hanged himself down there in Footscray. Least he picked a place with a decent footy team.'

'Frank,' Jim said. He had a habit of sitting with his hands clamped between his knees, palms together.

'Shut up,' Frank said. 'Dr Barbie. Good name, eh? I'd take the wife rowin, though. That Irene.'

'What's he got to do with it?' I said.

Frank lit another cigarette. It started a coughing fit. When it ended, he wiped moist eyes and said, 'Where was I?'

'Dr Barbie. Where's he fit in?'

'Kinross quack. Inherited the job from old

75

Crewe. Looks just like old Crewe, too. Now Dr Barbie's mum, she was the receptionist for umpteen bloody years.'

'You never bloody stop, do you?' Jim said.

'Take that girl Sim Walsh picked up,' Frank said. 'Now where did she come from? Naked as your Eve. On Colson's Road. Out there in the middle of the night. Covered in blood. Been whipped like a horse.'

'That's serious,' I said.

'Bloody oath. Told me about it one night he'd pushed the boat out to bloody Tasmania.'

'Drunk talk,' said Jim. 'Sim Walsh was drunk for forty years. Most likely made the whole thing up.'

I said, 'When was this?'

'Good way back,' Frank said. 'Around '82, could be '83. Thereabouts.'

'What happened?'

'Nothin. Said he took her home, cleaned her up. Girl wouldn't go to hospital, wouldn't go to the police. Scared out of her wits. Put her to bed. Next day, gone.'

'She tell him what happened?'

'No. Kept talkin about a bloke called Ken. You got springs, then?'

'I want the right springs,' I said. 'Not any old springs. Who was the girl?'

Frank stumped over to the door and flicked his cigarette end into the yard. 'Juvenile harlot from Kinross Hall,' he said.

'She told him that?'

Frank thought about this. 'Well,' he said, 'near enough. Sim said she was ravin. Drugs, he reckoned. Mind you, he was ravin a bit himself that night.'

'Never reported it?' I said.

'Don't know,' Frank said. 'Come round the next day, eyes narrer as bloody stamps side-on. Said, do me a favour, what I said about that girl, forget it. Load of rubbish I made up.'

'And here you are doin it,' said Jim. 'He told you it was a load of rubbish. What more d'ya want?'

'I want you to keep your mouth shut,' Frank said. 'Sim didn't make it up. He could bloody bignote himself – me and Douglas Bader and Sailor Malan saved the world from the bloody Nazis – but he wouldn't make anythin up. Not out of nothin. Not in his nature. Oh no, it happened. Believe you me. He never came near me after that. Saw me comin, he'd cross the street. Another bugger I wouldn't go to his bloody funeral.'

Alex Rickard was ten minutes late but that was a misdemeanour by his standards. 'Mac, Mac,' he said, sliding onto the plastic barstool seat. 'Back from the fucking dead. Where you been, mate?'

'Here and there,' I said. 'What is it with you and these grunge pits?'

Alex looked around at the pub: yellow smoke-stained walls, plastic furniture, scratched and cigarette-burnt formica-topped bar, three customers who looked like stroke victims. It was on Sydney Road and John Laws was braying at full volume to overcome Melbourne's worst traffic noise. The house smell was a mixture of burnt diesel, stale beer, and carbolic. 'I dunno,' he said, shrugging his boxer's shoulders in the expensive sports coat. 'It's the kind of bloke I am. True to my roots.'

'That's the thing they all value most about you,' I said.

'You drinking?' said the barman. He'd modelled his appearance on the barmen in early Clint Eastwood westerns.

'Beer,' said Alex. I ordered a gin and tonic. I

wasn't going to drink anything that came up from this pub's cellar.

'No tonic,' said the barman. 'No call for it.'

'What do they drink gin with?' I said.

'Coke,' said the barman. 'You drink Coke with gin.'

'Whisky and water,' I said. 'You got any call for water?'

He muttered something and left.

Alex rubbed the tip of his long nose between finger and thumb. 'Y'know a Painter and Docker got it right where you're sitting?' he said. 'Bloke walked in the door, up behind him, took this big fucking .38 out the front of his anorak. Three shots. Bang. Bang. Bang. Back of the head, two in the spine. Walks out the door. Gone.'

'They get him?' I said.

'No witnesses,' Alex said. 'Sixteen people in the pub, no-one saw a fucking thing.'

'Funny that,' I said. 'You get so wrapped up talking footy, they shoot someone next to you, covers you with blood, you don't notice a thing.'

The drinks arrived. Alex paid, keeping his wallet well below the counter. 'So they say you looked the other way on Lefroy,' he said, not looking at me.

'Who's they?'

'I done a few jobs for Scully.'

'Scully tell you?'

'Nah. The offsider.'

'Hill? Bianchi?'

'Hill. Bianchi's dead. Went to Queensland and drowned.'

'Wonderful news,' I said. 'Saves me killing him. Listen, your boy any good on the Human Services Department?'

He flicked his eyes at me, away, back. 'Human Services? What the fuck you want with Human Services? They dealing now?'

'It's a private thing. I need the records of a place called Kinross Hall for 1985. It's a kind of girls' home. Who went in, who came out. All that.'

Alex drank some beer, took out a packet of Camel. 'Smoke?'

I shook my head.

He lit up, blew plumes out of his nostrils. 'Could be easy. Could be fucking hard. It's in the database, my boy's probably in there like a honeymoon prick. Not – well, there's ways. But it'll cost.'

'How long to find out?'

Alex took out a grubby little notebook and a pen. 'How d'ya spell this place?'

I told him.

'Eighty-five. What's the mobile?'

I gave him my number.

'He can probably get in and look at the database inside an hour. Not there, I'll have to think. I've got this sheila in the archives, knockers absent but Jesus, the arse on her. She can get all kinds of stuff. Thinks it's sexy. Like I'm a spy.'

'In your special way, Alex,' I said, 'you are. Want to talk about money?'

He gave me a long look, drawing on the cigarette. There was something of the fox about him.

'Not now,' he said. 'Maybe if we have to go the next step.'

I was looking at the military history shelf in Hill of Content bookshop when the phone rang. I went outside into Bourke Street. It was lunchtime, street full of smart people in black.

'That thing we were talking about,' Alex said.

'Yes.'

'Don't have to go the next step. Where are you?'

'Bourke Street. I'm parked in Hardware Lane.'

'The one on the corner?'

'Right.'

'I'm closer than you are. See you outside the side door.'

I spotted him from a long way away, across the lane, back to the car park, brown packet under his arm. When I got close enough, I saw him watching me in the shop window. I gave a spy-type wave, close to the hip. He turned and came over.

'Here,' he said. 'Fucking phone book of stuff. Boy downloaded all the '85 material in the file.'

I took the packet. 'How'd he get in?'

Alex smiled his foxish smile. 'They've got a link with Social Security. He reckons their data protection's good as a knitted condom.'

'What's the bill?'

'I'll put it in the bank,' Alex said. 'Day will come.'

We shook hands. He looked at me for a while, deciding something. 'Look after yourself,' he said. He walked off, hand in pockets, chin up, at ease with himself.

It was just before dark as I entered the home straight, the long avenue of bare poplars, the light turning steely blue-grey, the wet road shining like a blade. I was thinking about the girl in the mine shaft. Could she have been brought from far away? Whoever pushed her into the hole in the ground had to know that it was there: you wouldn't travel a long distance with a dead body unless you had some burial spot in mind. Perhaps a local person, someone who knew the area, had murdered the girl in Melbourne. Had the police eliminated all the girls missing in Melbourne around that time? Surely not.

But why would Ned be interested in the finding of her body? Why did he go to Kinross Hall?

Allie was still working in the smithy. Face shining, she was making curtain poles, bending and twisting the red-hot iron into shepherd's crook shapes with smooth, economic movements. I stood in the doorway watching her. She reminded me of my father at work. I was never going to be that good.

'Looking smart,' she said, putting the last pole

in the rack. 'Debonair, even. That's the first time I've seen you wearing a tie.'

'You only had to ask,' I said, taking it off and putting it in a jacket pocket. 'Everything all right here?'

'Booming,' she said. 'Woman over at Kyneton wants two sets of gates. She saw the ones you made for Alan Frith.'

'That's nice,' I said. 'Frith doesn't pay for his inside a week, I'll take them round to her.'

'And a man called Flannery was here. He put a case of beer in the office.'

'That's nice too,' I said. 'How many did he drink?'

'Just one.'

'Must be Lent,' I said. 'You in a hurry?'

She looked at me speculatively. 'No.'

'Mind helping me read something?' I told her about Ned working at Kinross Hall in 1985, Mick Doolan's story about the complaint to the police, Ned's visit four days before his death, and my meeting with Marcia Carrier.

'Pretty weird,' she said. 'What's the reading matter?'

'Kinross Hall records.'

'How'd you get them?'

'Some bloke gave them to me. I forget who.'

She scratched her short hair, face impassive. 'Maybe it was the same bloke who told you about Alan Snelling and you've developed a block about remembering him.'

I tore the continuous print-out Alex had given me into pages while Allie showered. She came back in jeans, a grey polo-necked sweater and her half-length Drizabone, and we walked down the road. Her skew nose and wet and shiny crew cut gave her the look of a boxer. A rather sexy female boxer. She caught me looking at her.

'What?' she said.

'Nothing.'

The pub was empty except for Vinnie and George Beale playing draughts and a farmer reading the *Weekly Times* at the bar. We got two beers and went into the small lounge where a fire was dying in the grate. I fed it some kindling and a log from the bin.

'I'm hoping there's something that'll jump out at you,' I said, giving her half of the print-out pages.

'Like what?'

'Christ knows. Something happening to a girl. Trouble of some kind. Anything out of the ordinary.'

We settled down in the sagging armchairs and started reading. I'd taken the first half of 1985 and it quickly became clear that the department liked paperwork. Kinross Hall filed monthly accounts, fortnightly pay sheets, weekly lists of admissions and discharges, and reports by Dr Ian Barbie on medical visits. Every three months, it produced a budget operating statement and a report card on each inmate. The department filed full personal dossiers on all new admissions. Once a month, Kinross Hall was visited by two senior department staff and they filed a report.

It took us more than an hour to skim through the

print-outs. Midway, I fetched more beer. Finally, Allie said, 'Well, nothing sticks out to me. I mean, here's a major event. The inspectors had four written complaints about the food in October. Dr Carrier says the reason was the cook was off sick and the second in charge was having domestic troubles and basically couldn't give a bugger about the food.'

'No-one jump the wire in November?' I said.

'No. There were five admissions and three discharges in November. The three had all turned seventeen. They don't seem to be able to hold them after that.'

'Nothing else?'

'The hot water system broke down.'

'You hungry?'

'Why?'

'I've got a farm chook, raised on insects and berries in the wild.'

'Now you tell me. I'm going out.'

'Well,' I said, 'hot date with Alan Snelling could be better than a hot chook.'

'It's not Alan Snelling. You took the shine off Alan Snelling. A vet.'

'Pure animal, some vets,' I said.

She smiled at me. 'This one comes on like he's got a Rottweiler stuffed down the front of his jeans.'

'Probably a Jack Russell thinks it's a Rottweiler.'

'It's not the size of the bite that counts.'

'What counts?'

'How long they gnaw at you.'

★   ★   ★

At home, Mick Doolan and Lew were watching a golf video. As I came in the door, Mick was saying, 'It's all that wantin to hit the ball to kingdom come, lad. Bin the ruination of many a great talent. What I'm tryin to do is to get you to play the game backwards.'

'But drivin's where the game starts,' Lew said.

'And ends fer a lotta the fellas. We'll get to the drivin. We've got the puttin down flat. Now we've got to get the approach right. Not twice outta ten, not three times. Ten outta ten. Lookit this fella on the screen here. Ya can't putt like that. See. Bloody country mile.'

'Can't you watch porn videos like everyone else?' I said.

Mick looked around. 'When I'm done coachin this lad,' he said, 'they'll be askin us to *star* in the porno videos.'

'Golf porn,' I said. 'There could be a market for that.'

I went to work on the chicken. My father's recipe, made a hundred times: rub the skin with butter, stuff with a mixture of breadcrumbs, finely chopped onion, Worcester sauce, grated lemon rind, chopped raisins, half a cup of brandy. Stick in oven until brown.

I opened a bottle of the Maglieri. Mick came in to say goodnight and had a glass. He studied the label. 'Lay this drop on,' he said, 'they'd be fightin to get in for communion.'

After supper, Lew and I played Scrabble. He

was good with small words, quick to see possibilities.

'"Zugzwang"?' I said. 'Two zs. What kind of a word is "zugzwang"?'

'You challengin it?'

'Zugzwang? I am most certainly challenging zugzwang.'

'We playin double score penalty for failed challenges?'

'We are. And we are playing minus-score penalty to a player who doesn't take the opportunity to withdraw when challenged. Are you withdrawing zugzwang?'

'Surprised at you, Mac. Everybody knows zugzwang.'

'Withdrawing, Lewis? Last chance.' I put my hand on the *Concise Oxford Dictionary*.

'Open it,' he said. 'At "z".'

I did. 'Zugbloodyzwang,' I said. 'You little . . .'

There was no recovering from zugzwang. We were packing up, when I said, 'Think about what I said about school?'

He didn't look at me. 'Thinkin about it,' he said. 'Thinkin about it a lot.'

When Lew went off to bed, I put another log on the fire, fetched a glass of the red, got out a book Stan had lent me called *The Plant Hunter: A Life of Colonel A. E. Hillary*. I was on page four when Lew came in wearing pyjamas.

'Forgot to tell you,' he said. 'I was lookin in Ned's Kingswood for my stopwatch. He used to take me out on the road and drop me for my run and I left the watch in the car one day.' He held out a piece of paper. 'This was on the floor.'

I took it. It was a ticket from a parking machine, a Footscray Council parking machine in the Footscray Library parking area. It was valid until 3.30 pm on 11 July. That was two days before Ned's death.

'Make sense to you?' I said.

Lew shook his head. 'Ned had to go to Melbourne, he started complainin a month before.'

'Must be some explanation,' I said. 'Sleep well.'

When he'd gone, I got out the Melways street directory and found the Footscray Library parking lot. Then I got the Melbourne White Pages and looked up Dr Ian Barbie.

I put the Melways and the phone book away, refilled my glass in the kitchen, slumped in the armchair staring at the fire.

Ned had parked within two hundred metres of Dr Barbie's consulting rooms. Two days later, Ned was dead. Hanged. Two days after that, Dr Barbie was dead. Hanged.

The wind was coming up, moaning in the chimney, sound like a faraway wolf. The dog and I went out to the office in search of a telephone number I hadn't used in years.

I saw Brendan Burrows from a long way away. He had a distinctive walk, his left shoulder dropping as his left heel hit the ground. Even from fifty metres, I could tell that he'd aged about twenty years since I'd last seen him. You could count the straw hairs he had left, deep lines ran down from the thin, sharp nose. It's hard to be a policeman and an informer on your colleagues. The days are cold, the nights are worse.

'Fuck,' he said, sitting down next to me. 'Used to be able to do this stuff on the phone. How ya goin? Fair while.' We shook hands. The country train platform at Spencer Street Station in Melbourne held us and a fat woman, exhausted, and two small children bouncing off each other like atoms in some elemental physical process that produced tears.

He put his hand into his leather jacket and took out a sheet torn from a notebook. 'Ian Ralph Barbie, forty-six, medical practitioner, 18 Ralston Street, Flemington, hanging by the neck in disused premises at 28 Varley Street, Footscray. Your man?'

I nodded.

'Got this on the phone in a hurry. Body found approx eleven am, 16 July. Estimated time of death between nine pm and midnight, 15 July. Cause of death, a lot of technical shit, but it's strangulation by hanging. Significant quantity of pethidine. Lots of tracks. No injuries. Last meal approx eight hours before death.'

'On him?'

'Wallet. Cards. No cash. Car clean like a rental. Jumped off the top. Drove inside the building, got on the roof, chucked the rope over a beam.'

'Don't you need some special knot for a noose?'

'Something that'll slip. Must've looked it up. There's nothing isn't in books.'

'Note?'

'No.'

'Any interest?'

Brendan's head turned slightly. A shaven-headed man in an anorak carrying a bulging sports bag was coming down the platform. His eyes flicked at us as he passed. You could hear Brendan's jaws unlock.

'They look at you,' he said, 'they're not on.' But he watched the man go down the concrete peninsula. 'Need a break. You get para. You bastards owe me. No, no interest. Another medico on the peth, can't take the lows anymore, goes out on a high. Happens with the quacks a lot. Guilt. Feel a lot of guilt. Pillars of fucking society sticking stuff up the arm. Don't call peth the doctor's drug for nothing. Still, dangling's a worry. Unusual. Needle, that's the way they go. You got it, you use it.'

'That's it, then?'

'Well, watch's gone, clear mark of watch on left wrist. Probably nicked by the deros.'

'Deros?'

'They found him.'

'Right. Brendan, listen. Scully – what's happened to him?'

'Been livin in Queensland? Outer space? Good things only for the man. Next deputy commissioner. To be anointed soon.'

'I've been away. How'd he do that?'

'Plugged a bloke into Springvale, suburb of smack. Smackvale. Three years in the making. Had to import this cop from Vietnam. Any day now they'll announce he's delivered half the Vietcong and a fucking mountain of smack. Scully's going to be the hero of the day. Course, most of the stuff'll be back on the street by dark. Catch the upward move in price.'

'He's a lucky man.'

'Blessed.' Brendan looked around, scratched his scalp. 'You heard the shit's flying sideways about surveillance records? About ten years' worth gone missing in Ridley Street.'

'They're on disk, right?'

He made a snorting sound, like a horse. 'They scanned everything onto a hard drive, three sets of backup floppies. But the bloke taking the floppies over to Curzon Street for safekeeping, he got hit from behind by a truck. And while they're sorting it out, his briefcase gets nicked. Can you believe that? Oh well, there's always the paper. But no, all the paper has vanished. Fucking truckload. Well, this is bad, but thank Christ there's the hard disk.'

Brendan paused, looking as happy as I'd seen him.

'Guess,' he said.

I'd guessed. 'Don't know.'

'Hard drive's like the Pope's conscience. Not a fucking thing on it. Hacked into, they reckon. Supposed to be impossible.'

'So?'

'Lots of people happy.'

'You reckon what?'

'Dunno. People don't get together to make something like that happen. More like one very big person got together with some friends. Couldn't just take out the bit the person wanted, they took the lot.'

I said, 'And you take the view one friend could be Scully. How come the Commissioner doesn't think that too?'

Brendan gave me a long, unblinking stare. 'Yeah, well, the view's different from the thirtieth fucking floor. Ground level's where you smell the garbage. They're all overdue, that mob.'

'I hear Bianchi drowned.'

'A fucking tragedy. Cop resigns, buys waterside mansion in Noosa with modest pension and savings. Found floating in river. New wife says he went out for a look at the new boat, she falls asleep.

Exhausted from a marathon dicking probably. Next morning the neighbour sees poor Darren bobbing around like a turd.'

'What about Hill?'

'Bobby's making lots of money in the baboon hire business. Calls himself a security consultant. Need muscle for your rock concert, nightclub, anything, Hill Associates got baboons on tap, any number. Also provides special security services for rich people. Drives this grey Merc.'

'I knew the boy would amount to something.' We shook hands. 'Thanks,' I said. 'Appreciate it.'

'I only do it because you can get me killed,' he said, unsmiling. 'You go first. I'll just have a smoke, watch the trains a bit.'

I was a few paces away when he said, 'Mac.'

I turned.

'The Lefroy thing,' he said. 'I heard Bianchi was in that pub in Deer Park one day around then.'

'Yes?'

'Mance was there too. That's all I heard.' He looked away.

'**M**uch maligned creatures, chooks,' said Dot Walsh, frisbeeing out another precise arc of grain to the variegated flock of fowls. 'Quite intelligent, some of them. Unlike sheep, which are uniformly stupid.'

She pointed to a large black-and-white bird. 'That's Helen, my favourite. After Helen of Troy.'

By her voice, Mrs Walsh was English, in her seventies, deeply lined but unbowed and un-dimmed, with hair cut short and sharp. I'd told her my business at the front door. She'd shown no interest in why I wanted to know more about the story her husband had told Frank Cullen.

'I'm surprised Frank remembers it,' she'd said. 'I used to make a special trip to the tip with bottles after one of their sessions. Anyway, I don't suppose it matters now that Simon's gone. Come through. It's chook feeding time.'

When she'd exhausted the grain, we went on a tour of the garden. Even in the bleak heart of winter, it was beautiful: huge bare oaks and elms, black against the asbestos sky, views of farmland at the end of long hedged paths, a pond with ducks, a rose walk that narrowed to a slim gate just wide enough for a wheelbarrow.

'How big?' I said.

'Two acres,' she said. 'All that's left of nearly a thousand. From a thousand acres to two in a generation. That was my Simon's accomplishment. Simon and Johnny Walker Black Label. The old firm, he used to say. Still, he was a lovely man, lovely. Just unfirm of purpose.'

She moved her head like her hens as she talked, quick sideways jerks, little tilts, chin up, chin down, eyes darting.

I got on to the subject. 'You never saw the girl that night?'

'No,' she said. 'I was in Queensland with Fiona, our daughter. She was having domestic trouble. Temperament like Simon, I'm afraid. Forty-six and still thinks that responsibility is something for grown-ups.'

'Could you put a date on that trip?'

'Oh yes. October 1985. My granddaughter had her tenth birthday while I was there.'

'May I ask you what your husband told you happened?'

'Simon ran out of cigarettes at about ten o'clock. It often happened. It was a Thursday night I think, my first night away. He drove down to the Milstead pub. He used to take the back roads. He was coming back down Colson's Road, do you know it?'

I nodded.

'Well, he came around a bend and there was this

95

girl by the side of the road. Not a stitch on. Naked. She'd been beaten. He got her into the car and brought her back here.'

'He didn't think of going to the police?'

'The police? No. He thought she needed medical attention.'

'She was badly hurt?'

'He thought so at first. Lots of blood. But most of it had come from her nose. That was swollen. Simon thought it might be broken. There were red puffy welts all over her body as if she had been whipped, he said. And she had scratches every-where and dust and what looked like cement stuck to her. But he didn't think she was seriously hurt.'

'Why didn't he take her to casualty?'

She gave me her sharp little look. 'Simon was a drunk, Mr Faraday,' she said, no irritation in her voice, 'but he wasn't a fool. It was half past ten at night. He would have had at least half a bottle of whisky under his belt by then. He'd already had his licence suspended once. The safest thing for both of them was to bring her here and get someone else to take her to hospital.'

'Did he find out how she got her injuries?'

She didn't answer for a while. We were walking between low walls of volcanic stone towards the back of the old redbrick farmhouse. The sky had cleared in the west and the last of the sun was warming an aged golden Labrador where it sat watching us, fat bottom flat on the verandah boards.

'In the beginning, in the car, Simon said she

was crying and babbling and saying the name "Ken" over and over again. He couldn't get any sense out of her. He thought she was on drugs. When they got here, he gave her a gown to put on and he went to the telephone to ring Brian. That's his nephew, he farms about ten minutes from here. He wanted Brian to take her to casualty. That's when the girl attacked him.'

'Attacked him?'

'Tried to get the phone away from him and punched him.'

'He'd told her what he was doing? Phoning someone to take her to hospital?'

'I suppose so. He said she shouted, "Don't tell anyone. I'll say you raped me". Her nose was bleeding again and her blood got all over him. I saw his jumper when I got back.'

'So he didn't phone?'

'No. It wasn't the sort of thing he was used to, Mr Faraday. Went into shock, I imagine.'

We'd reached the verandah. The dog came upright by sliding its forelegs forward until they went over the edge and dropped to the first step.

'This bloke's in worse shape than I am,' Mrs Walsh said. 'Needs two new hips. Can I offer you a beer? I have a Cooper's Sparkling this time every day.'

We sat on the side verandah in the weak sun and drank beer. I had a pewter mug with a glass bottom and an inscription. I held the mug away from me to read it: *To Sim, a mad Australian, from his comrades, 610 Squadron, Biggin Hill, 1944.*

'He was in the RAF,' Mrs Walsh said. 'He was in England doing an agriculture course when the war broke out, so he joined up. He was billeted with my aunt for a while. That's where I met him.'

I said, 'Biggin Hill was a fighter station, wasn't it?'

'Yes,' she said, looking up at the sky as if expecting to see a Spitfire come out of the sun. 'He never got over the war. None of them did, really. All that expecting to die. Every day. For so long. And they were so young.'

A silence fell between us, not uneasy, until she said, 'The girl calmed down after that, said she was sorry. Simon found some of Fiona's pyjamas and a pair of her riding jeans and an old shirt. She showered and went to bed in the spare room. The bed's always made. Simon said he brought her a mug of Milo but she was asleep. The next day, she asked if he could take her to a station and lend her the fare to Melbourne. Simon said she looked terrible, swollen nose, black eyes. He took her to Ballan, bought her ticket and gave her fifty dollars. And that was that.'

'Did he find out her name?'

'No.'

'And he never reported it to anyone?'

'No. He should have. It was too late by the time I got back.'

'Did he think she was from Kinross Hall?'

'Well, she wasn't a local. You get to know the locals.'

'But there wasn't any other reason to think that?'

'No.'

'Do you ever think about how she might have found herself in Colson's Road?'

She shrugged, took a sip of beer. 'Simon thought she might have been pushed out of a car.'

I finished my beer, got up, said my thanks. At the front gate, Mrs Walsh said, 'Things left undone. Sins of omission. Most of us err more on that side, don't you think, Mr Faraday?'

Howard Lefroy's apartment, the blood up the tiled walls, came into my mind.

'Amen,' I said.

A naked girl, neck broken, thrown down a mine shaft, some time after 1984. A naked girl, beaten, by a lonely roadside in October 1985.

Ned worked at Kinross Hall in November 1985.

And never set foot there again. Until a few days before his murder.

I took the long way home, down Colson's Road to Milstead in the closing day. There was a pine forest on the one side, scrubby salt-affected wetlands on the other. Dead redgums marked the line of a creek running northwest. The last of the light went no more than four or five metres into the pines. Beyond that, it was already cold, dark, sterile night. Nothing cheered the heart on this stretch of Colson's Road.

Neither did anything in the bar at the Milstead pub. An L-shaped room with a lounge area to the right, it had fallen in the formica wars of the seventies. The barman was a thin, sallow man with greased-back curly hair and a big nose broken at least twice. A small letter J was crudely tattooed in the hollow of his throat. As an educated guess, I would have said four or five priors, at least one involving serious assault, and a degree or two from the stone college. He hadn't studied beer pulling either.

'Helpin out,' he said, putting down the dripping glass. 'Owner's on the beach in fucking Bali, regular bloke got done this arvo, wouldn't take the breathie, the bastards lock him up.'

'Thought you had some rights,' I said. 'You local?'

He gave me a long look and made a judgment. 'Wife,' he said. 'Well, ex, pretty much. Bitch. Fuckin family swarm around here. Get the motor goin, I'm off to WA. Bin there? Fuckin paradise.'

He took my five-dollar note and short-changed me without going near the till.

'Who owns the pine forest down the road here?' I said.

He was pouring himself a vodka. Three vodkas, in fact.

'Wooden have a fuckin clue, mate.' He raised his voice. 'Ya breathin there, Denise? Who owns the pine forest?'

'Silvateq Corporation,' a husky voice said from around the corner. 'S-i-l-v-a-t-e-q.'

I took my glass and made the trip. A woman somewhere out beyond seventy, face a carefully applied pink mask matching her tracksuit, was sitting at a round table playing patience. She was drinking a dark liquid out of a shot glass.

'G'day,' I said. 'John Faraday. What's Silvateq Corporation?'

She looked me over and went back to the cards. 'A company,' she said.

'Right,' I said. 'Is it local?'

'Collins Street,' she said. 'They sent me a letter tellin me not to use their road. *Their* road. It's bin a public track since God was in nappies. Wrote back, told 'em to bugger off. Not another word.'

'They backed off?'

'No. Put a bloody great barbed-wire fence across the road and dug a trench behind it. Looks like the bloody Somme.'

She took a sip of the black liquid and ran her tongue over her teeth. 'Course the shire's bought off. Only takes about ten quid.'

'This was when?'

She flipped a card. 'More than ten years. When did that Hawke get in?'

'In '82.'

'Round about then. Bought it from old Veene. He planted the trees along the road. Twenty rows, I remember. This other bunch planted the rest. Know what they call bloody pine plantations? Green graveyard. Nothin lives in 'em.'

Green graveyard. I thought about that on the trip home. The mine shaft the girl was thrown down was in a pine forest near Rippon. How far was that from Colson's Road?

101

On the way home, gloomy, I stopped at Flannery's place, a small village of dangerously old sheds surrounding a weatherboard house. He lived with a cheerful nurse called Amy who wouldn't marry him. 'Marry a flogged-out back-yard mechanic whose first wife walked off with a water diviner?' she once said. 'I'd need time to think about that. A lifetime.'

'Just as easy been the fence bloke,' Flannery had said, 'but then I'da had a new fence. This bugger's got a bit of wire, coathanger wire, picks three spots, bloody wire's vibrating like a pit bull's chain. Down we go, drillin halfway to the hot place, fifty bucks a metre. Two holes bone dry, third one a little piddle comes out, takes half an hour to fill the dog bowl. Still cry when I think about it.'

Flannery was in one of the sheds working under the hood of a Holden ute by the light of a portable hand lamp. The vehicle was covered in stickers saying things like *Toot to Root* and *Emergency Sex Vehicle* and *Bulk Sperm Carrier*.

'My cousin's boy's,' he said. 'Virgin vehicle. Never had a girl in it.'

'I can see he's waiting for someone special,' I said. 'Listen, you know of Ned ever going around asking for jobs?'

Flannery was wiping his large hands on his jumper, a garment that qualified as a natural oil resource. 'Ned? Ask for a job? You smokin something?'

'Second question. He ever talk about a doctor called Ian Barbie?'

'What's this? Doctor? Ned wouldn't know a doctor from a brown dog.'

I looked into the engine. 'Dirty.'

'Clean inside that matters,' Flannery said. 'Let's get a beer. Got some in this little fridge over here, bought it off Mick.'

'I can see the dent.'

'What dent?'

'Dent it got falling off the truck.'

The perfect is the enemy of the good. Making knives would be easy if all you wanted was a good knife. But you don't. You want a perfect knife. And so, in the endless grinding and filing and fitting and buffing, the mind has plenty of time to dwell. Today, moist Irish day, sky the colour of sugar in suspension, I dwelt on Brendan Burrow's parting words. All I wanted from Brendan were the details of Ian Barbie's suicide. And then he said: *The Lefroy thing. Heard Bianchi was in that pub in Deer Park one day around then.* And I said: *Yes?* And he said: *Mance was there too.*

Mance was there too.

The feeling of missing a step, of walking into a glass door, of being shaken from deep sleep. With Bianchi? At the same time as Bianchi? I knew the answer. Just before noon, I finished polishing a small paring knife and the dog and I went over to the office.

The file was at the back of the cabinet, not looked at for years. I sat down at the table and took out the record of interview. I didn't want to read it again. I read it.

RECORD OF INTERVIEW

DATE: 5 June 1994.

TIME COMMENCED: 3.10 pm.

TIME TERMINATED: 3.25 pm.

NAME: MacArthur John Faraday, Detective Senior Sergeant, Australian Federal Police.

OFFICERS PRESENT: Colin Arthur Payne, Inspector, Australian Federal Police. Wayne Ronald Rapsey, Detective Inspector, Internal Affairs Division, Australian Federal Police. Joseph Musca, Detective Inspector, Victoria Police.

SUBJECT: Matters relating to the surveillance of Howard James Lefroy.

D-I RAPSEY: For the record, this is a resumption of the interview with Detective Faraday terminated at five forty-five pm yesterday. Detective, do you have anything to add to your statements yesterday?

DSS FARADAY: No. Sir.

D-I RAPSEY: I want to go over a few things. The decision to wait for Howard Lefroy to dispose of the heroin. You made it.

DSS FARADAY: Yes.

D-I RAPSEY: Did you inform your superiors that Lefroy was in possession of the heroin?

DSS FARADAY: No.

D-I RAPSEY: Why was that?

DSS FARADAY: I was afraid it would jeopardise the operation.

D-I RAPSEY: Reporting something to your superior officer would jeopardise an operation. Serious statement, detective.

DSS FARADAY: Yes, sir. As I said last time and the time before, it was not my superior officer I was worried about but other officers.

D-I RAPSEY: Equally serious. What was your reason for waiting?

DSS FARADAY: I believed Lefroy was dealing with a top-level distributor. We had no idea who. Just take Lefroy out, some other importer takes his place. Nail everyone at the pick-up, we at least have a chance of finding out who's buying. Small chance, but a chance.

D-I RAPSEY: You say you discussed this with Inspector Scully.

DSS FARADAY: I told him. Correct.

D-I RAPSEY: What was his view?

DSS FARADAY: I don't recall him offering a view.

D-I RAPSEY: Did he disagree?

DSS FARADAY: I don't recall that he offered an opinion.

D-I RAPSEY: What if Inspector Scully says that he made it clear to you that he

106

strongly opposed waiting for Lefroy to dispose of the heroin and wanted to . . . ?

DSS FARADAY: He did not.

D-I RAPSEY: So he'd be lying?

DSS FARADAY: Draw your own conclusions.

D-I RAPSEY: Moving on. Howard Lefroy's flat. Visual contact?

DSS FARADAY: Three windows. Only the dining room blinds were left open at night.

D-I RAPSEY: And audio?

DSS FARADAY: All rooms except the hall. Sitting room was weak. Had been for a couple of days.

D-I RAPSEY: Why didn't you fix it?

DSS FARADAY: Too risky. Too close.

D-I RAPSEY: Too close to what?

DSS FARADAY: The pick-up.

D-I RAPSEY: There was going to be a pick-up at Lefroy's place?

DSS FARADAY: According to my information.

D-I RAPSEY: Source?

DSS FARADAY: I had information.

INSP. PAYNE: Answer the question, Mac.

DSS FARADAY: Lefroy's woman, Carlie Mance.

D-I RAPSEY: She was a registered informant?

DSS FARADAY: No. I believed registering my informant would endanger her.

107

D-I RAPSEY: You going to stick with this line?

DSS FARADAY: Yes, sir.

D-I RAPSEY: We'll come back to it. Believe me, we'll come back to it. Moving on. So Lefroy had five kilos of heroin in the flat and you were waiting for someone to come along and collect it?

DSS FARADAY: That's correct.

D-I RAPSEY: How long were you going to wait?

DSS FARADAY: As I said before, I had reason to believe that we didn't have long to wait.

D-I RAPSEY: How long had you been waiting?

DSS FARADAY: It's on record.

D-I RAPSEY: Tell me.

DSS FARADAY: Two days.

D-I RAPSEY: According to Inspector Scully, you initially informed him that the pick-up would take place within four days of the heroin's arrival at Lefroy's flat. Is that correct?

DSS FARADAY: Yes.

D-I RAPSEY: How did you know?

DSS FARADAY: Informant.

D-I RAPSEY: Ms Mance? The unregistered informant?

DSS FARADAY: Correct.

D-I RAPSEY: We'll revisit this. Moving on. Let's talk about the night.

DSS FARADAY: This'll be the third time.

INSP.PAYNE: Don't be an arse, detective. You're in serious trouble here. This isn't about dry-cleaning on the house or free screws.

D-I RAPSEY: What time did Ms Mance arrive?

DSS FARADAY: Just before Howie went for his walk. Around noon.

D-I RAPSEY: What did they talk about?

DSS FARADAY: The usual. Nothing. Howie didn't talk business to her.

D-I RAPSEY: So how did she know his business?

DSS FARADAY: She didn't. All she knew was that the pick-up was going to be at Howie's.

D-I RAPSEY: So Howard's on his walk? What then?

DSS FARADAY: Dennis rang. Said he was coming around. Eight-thirty sharp.

D-I RAPSEY: You were listening?

DSS FARADAY: It sounded like Dennis. It still sounds like Dennis.

D-I RAPSEY: Dennis been to Howard's place before?

DSS FARADAY: Not while we were on him, no.

D-I RAPSEY: Didn't think it strange Dennis suddenly decides to visit Howard?

DSS FARADAY: They're brothers. Their mother needs to go into a home and she doesn't want to. Howie takes her side. Dennis is on the phone to Howie for weeks trying to talk him round and he's getting nowhere. No, I didn't think it was strange he wanted to see Howie.

INSP.PAYNE: Your people made a positive ID of Dennis when he showed up?

DSS FARADAY: Good as they could. Mackie knew him. His car. Tinted glass. We took pictures. We've enhanced them. Looks like him.

INSP.PAYNE: But they didn't get a good look at him.

DSS FARADAY: They saw him for about thirty seconds. He drove up, the garage door opened, he drove in.

D-I RAPSEY: Opened?

DSS FARADAY: It's a high-security building. You need a remote control with your own code to open the garage door. Or someone in the building can press a button and open it.

D-I RAPSEY: So someone was watching for Dennis?

DSS FARADAY: They knew when to expect him.

D-I RAPSEY: Who was on duty?

DSS FARADAY: Mackie and Allinson.

D-I RAPSEY: You didn't think this was important enough for you to be there?

DSS FARADAY: No. Mackie knew Dennis. He knew Dennis better than I did. What would me being there help?

D-I RAPSEY: And with hindsight?

DSS FARADAY: With hindsight, I should have spent twenty-four hours a day on the job instead of just twenty.

D-I RAPSEY: Let's go on. Mackie rang you.

DSS FARADAY: Correct. I was asleep.

D-I RAPSEY: What did he say?

DSS FARADAY: He said Dennis'd turned up.

D-I RAPSEY: And you said?

DSS FARADAY: I said: So?

D-I RAPSEY: Mackie suggested a tail on Dennis when he left. What was your response?

DSS FARADAY: I said no.

D-I RAPSEY: Didn't even consider it? Five kilos of smack up there, brother shows up on short notice.

DSS FARADAY: Dennis is clean, no history, no connections. Rotary clean. In the time we covered him, he did nothing. He thinks Howie made his money on the stockmarket. He's not going to courier smack for Howie.

D-I RAPSEY: So Dennis drives off. When did Mackie call you again?

DSS FARADAY: Nine o'clock. Just after.

D-I RAPSEY: The reason?

DSS FARADAY: He was worried about a call Howie made as Dennis came out.

D-I RAPSEY: Listened to it?

DSS FARADAY: I've listened to it.

D-I RAPSEY: Howard's voice.

DSS FARADAY: Howie's voice.

D-I RAPSEY: Sound a bit stagey?

DSS FARADAY: Yes.

D-I RAPSEY: Know the person on the other end?

DSS FARADAY: As you know, the person doesn't say anything.

D-I RAPSEY: One-way conversation.

DSS FARADAY: Not unusual for Howie. They pick up the phone, he talks.

D-I RAPSEY: Never raised a doubt in your mind?

DSS FARADAY: Not when Mackie described it, no.

D-I RAPSEY: What did you tell Mackie?

DSS FARADAY: Told him I'd listen the next day.

D-I RAPSEY: Ten minutes later, he rings you again. What did he say this time?

DSS FARADAY: Someone rang Howie. Howie didn't make any sense, didn't answer questions, said goodbye in the middle of something the guy was saying.

D-I RAPSEY: That didn't alarm you? Didn't interest you?

DSS FARADAY: No. Sounded like vintage Howie.

D-I RAPSEY: And when you listened to the tape?

DSS FARADAY: I had the benefit of hindsight.

D-I RAPSEY: Would you have picked it if you'd been there?

DSS FARADAY: Yes.

D-I RAPSEY: And exactly when did you listen to the tape?

DSS FARADAY: The next day.

D-I RAPSEY: Mackie says he asked you to come back and listen. Is that right?

DSS FARADAY: He did.

D-I RAPSEY: And you didn't.

DSS FARADAY: I didn't see any reason to.

D-I RAPSEY: So let's get this straight. Lefroy is sitting in his flat with five kilos. You believe that a pick-up could take place at any time. He gets a visit from his brother. Something that hasn't happened before. Your man calls you to suggest a tail because he didn't get a good look at Dennis. You say no. Howard makes a phone call to someone who doesn't talk back. Your man calls you. Forget it, you say. Then someone calls Howard and it sounds weird to your

113

man. He calls you. You say, I'll listen tomorrow. Is that a fair account?

DSS FARADAY: You have to understand, Mackie was new on Howie. I've listened to hundreds of Howie's conversations. This stuff wasn't weird for him.

D-I RAPSEY: Nothing else happened that night?

DSS FARADAY: No. Loud music. Stopped about midnight. Often that way.

D-I RAPSEY: No more calls.

DSS FARADAY: No.

D-I RAPSEY: Let's go to the morning. What kind of routine did Lefroy have?

DSS FARADAY: Call to his broker. Six forty-five, Monday to Friday.

D-I RAPSEY: This Thursday he didn't.

DSS FARADAY: No.

D-I RAPSEY: What else did he always do?

DSS FARADAY: Open all the curtains. Make coffee. Walk around naked. Phone people.

D-I RAPSEY: Didn't happen either.

DSS FARADAY: No.

D-I RAPSEY: Who was on duty?

DSS FARADAY: O'Meara. Stand-in.

D-I RAPSEY: Briefed on Lefroy's habits? Knew what to expect? Shown the log?

DSS FARADAY: He was a stand-in. He was covering for two hours.

D-I RAPSEY: What time did you show up?

DSS FARADAY: Just after seven am.

D-I RAPSEY: Was that late?

DSS FARADAY: Depends. I had a flat. Happens.

D-I RAPSEY: What did you do when you finally arrived?

DSS FARADAY: Listened to the tape. Two minutes. We went straight in.

Howard Lefroy was in the wide hallway, near the sitting room door. He was wearing one of his big fluffy cotton bathrobes, the one with navy blue trim. The carpet was pale pink, the colour of a sexual blush. Except around Howie's head and upper body, where it was dark with his blood. He'd been killed where he lay, his head pulled back by the ponytail and his throat cut. More than cut. He was almost decapitated. The bathrobe was bunched around his waist, displaying his short hairy legs and big buttocks.

Carlie Mance was in the bathroom, naked. She had tape on her mouth and her wrists were taped to the chrome legs of the washbasin. The man had been behind her when he cut her throat, kneeling between her legs, a fistful of her dark, shiny hair in his right hand, dragging her head back.

Her blood went halfway up the mirror over the basin, a great jet that hit the glass and ran down in neat parallel lines.

I should have stayed to ID Dennis. Or I could have put Mackie in a car right outside the garage to ID him. Or we could have had Traffic Operations pull him over nearby and had a good look at him. Carlie would have been alive. Lefroy too, not that I cared about that: cheated, that's all I felt when I saw him.

But I didn't do any of those things . . . And I didn't put a tail on the car. Thirteen years on the job and I didn't do any of those things.

The portable phone had a device that looked like a dictation machine attached to it. Howard Lefroy was on the tape, the two phone calls that had made Mackie suspicious. They were composites.

D-I RAPSEY: Tell us about this lockup of yours.

DSS FARADAY: As I've said about twelve times, it's not my lockup. I hired it for my wife. I took some of her stuff there. Once. I gave her the key.

D-I RAPSEY: We're assuming here that it would be out of character for your wife to keep 100 grams of smack and $20,000 in cash in her lockup. Fair assumption?

DSS FARADAY: I'd go with it.

D-I RAPSEY: So it would belong to someone else. Right?

DSS FARADAY: Jesus, charge me, why don't you?

D-I RAPSEY: In good time. You've had dealings with Howard Lefroy, haven't you?

DSS FARADAY: Dealings? I don't know about dealings. I was on a job where we tried to get in touch with him. Seven, eight years ago.

D-I RAPSEY: You tried to roll a bloke. One of Lefroy's runners.

DSS FARADAY: We rolled him.

D-I RAPSEY: But it didn't work out.

DSS FARADAY: No. We put him in a safe house and somebody came around and took him away.

D-I RAPSEY: Dead, would you say?

DSS FARADAY: I would say.

D-I RAPSEY: You aware the talk was Lefroy was tipped off?

DSS FARADAY: That is what generally happens in Sydney. People get tipped off.

D-I RAPSEY: By you?

DSS FARADAY: I'll say yes? I'm supposed to say yes, am I? Trick question, is it?

D-I RAPSEY: So first Lefroy gets lucky with you around and then he gets unlucky.

DSS FARADAY: I'm sorry, is that a question?

D-I RAPSEY: It's the central question on my mind, Detective Faraday. It's the central question on many people's minds. And we'll answer it before we're finished. Interview terminated at three twenty-five pm.

That wasn't the last interview, not by a long way. But as I had sat there, looking at the men who weren't looking at me, I had known without doubt that I wasn't one of them anymore. It was the end of that life. Thirteen years. Thirteen years of belief and self-respect. Pride, even. Come to an end in a grubby little formica-lined office reeking of disbelief.

I could have lived with that. What I couldn't live with was that my negligence, my confident negligence, killed Carlie Mance.

I put the file away, made a phone call and set off for Melbourne to look for the scene of Dr Ian Barbie's end.

It took me the best part of two hours to get to Varley Street, Footscray. And when I got there, I didn't want to be there. It was a short narrow one-way street that ended in the high fence of some sort of container storage depot. Newspaper pages, plastic bags, even what looked like a yellow nylon slipper had worked their way into the mesh.

The right side of the street was lined with the high rusting corrugated-iron walls of two factories. The steel doors of the first building appeared to have been the target of an assault with a battering ram, but they were holding. At the end of the street, one of a pair of huge doors to the second building was missing, leaving an opening big enough for a truck.

The left side of Varley Street consisted of about a dozen detached weatherboard houses, small, sad structures listing on rotten stumps behind sagging or collapsed wire fences. Several of them had been boarded up and one was enclosed by a four-metre-high barbed-wire fence. About a tonne of old catalogues and other pieces of junk mail had been dumped on the porch of the house three from the corner.

My instinct was to reverse out of Varley Street and go home. There was nothing to be gained here. But I parked at the end of the street outside a house that showed a sign of being lived in: a healthy plant was growing in a black nursery pot beside the yellow front door. I got out, locked the door, put on the yellow plastic raincoat I kept in the car, and crossed the street.

The missing door had opened on to what had probably been a loading bay, a large concrete-floored space with a platform against the right-hand wall, which had two large sliding doors in it.

Opposite the entrance was another doorway with both doors open. Trucks had once driven through to the tarmac courtyard visible beyond.

I walked out into the courtyard. There was a blank corrugated wall to the left, a low brick building that looked like offices to the right and ahead a high cinder-block wall. The day of the weeds had come. Everywhere they were pushing contemptuously through the tarmac and their reflections lay in the cold puddles in every depression.

To my right, about twenty metres along, there was another doorway, big enough for a vehicle.

I walked over and stood on the threshold.

It was a big space, dimly lit from small windows high in the street wall. People had been using it recently: there were deep ashes in a corner, surrounded by empty cigarette packets, beer cans and the ripped cartons and wrung-out bladders of wine casks. In the air was the chemical smell that comes from burning painted wood.

I walked into the middle of the space and looked up. The beams were low.

A voice said, 'Not there, mate. Over to ya right, that's where.'

There was a man standing in the doorway, a dark shape against the light. He came towards me, his details emerging as he moved into the gloom: long, unkempt grey hair, grey stubble turning to beard, thin body in a black overcoat over a tracksuit, battered training shoes, one without laces.

'Ya come to see where the bloke strung hisself up, have ya?' he said, stopping about five metres away.

'That's right,' I said.

'Not a cop,' he said. It was a statement of fact.

'No.'

'Got a smoke on ya?'

I shook my head.

'Should be chargin admission. See that beam up there?'

He pointed at the roof to my left, to one of the trusses. The crossbeams were about four metres up. 'Rope went over there. Jumped off the car roof.'

'How d'you know that?'

'No other way, mate. He was hangin there right up against the car, bout three feet off the ground. Head looked like it was gonna pop.'

'Did you find him?'

'Na. Me mate Boris. But I was right behind.'

I took a short walk, looking up the beam, looking at the floor, looking at the campfire zone. I came back and stopped a short distance from the man. The skin under his eyes was flaking.

'The bloke's mum asked me to take a look,' I said.

He nodded. 'Be a bit upsettin, rich bloke an all.'

'What's your name?'

'Robbo, they call me. Robert's me proper name.'

'Robbo, how do you know he was a rich bloke?'

He thought for a moment. 'Had a tie on, y'know. Funny that.'

'Anything else catch your eye?'

'Na. Tell ya the truth, I'd had a few. Went down the milk bar to call the cops.'

'You and Boris know this place well?'

He looked around as if seeing it for the first time. 'I reckon,' he said. 'Make a bit of a fire, have a drink.'

'You do that often? Every night?'

'When it's warm we just stay in the park.'

'Must have been pretty cold that night. How come you weren't here?'

'When?'

'The night the bloke hanged himself.'

'Dunno. Can't remember.'

'So you came here the next day. In the morning?'

Robbo fingered the skin under his left eye. 'I reckon,' he said. 'Boris'd know. He's a youngster.'

'I might like to talk to Boris,' I said. 'Is he going to be around some time?'

Robbo looked off into the middle distance. 'Well,' he said, 'ya see him and ya don't.'

I took out my wallet and found a ten-dollar note. 'Where do you buy your grog?' I said.

'Down the pub. Geelong Road. Just near the park.' He waved vaguely.

'They know your names there?'

He thought about it. After a while, he said, 'Reckon.'

I gave him the ten dollars. 'I'll leave a message for you at the bottle shop. Be sure you tell Boris. I'll give you another twenty each when I see him.'

He gave me a long look, nodded and shuffled off.

I carried on with my look around. The wood for the fire came from cupboards and counters in the office building. Only bits of the carcasses remained. Ripping up of the floorboards had started. To the left of the office building was a laneway ending in a gate, its frame distorted and with large pieces of mesh cut out.

There wasn't anything else to look at, so I left. As I was driving away, I looked in the rear-view mirror and saw a boy of about twelve, one foot on a skateboard, watching me go. I hoped he didn't have to do all his growing up in Varley Street.

The Streeton pub. Solid redbrick building, twenty metres long, small lounge on the left, bar on the right, standing at a skew crossroads on a windy hill. I made a hole in a steamed-up pane of a bar window and watched a Volvo pull up outside: Irene Barbie, short red hair lighting up the sombre day like the flare of a match. What daylight was left was retreating across the endless dark-soiled potato fields. She was wearing a tweed jacket and jeans, didn't seem to notice the thin rain falling, took a small black suitcase from the front passenger seat and locked it in the boot. Vet's bag, full of tempting animal drugs. It wasn't an overly cautious thing to do: there were men drinking at the bar who looked capable of snorting Omo if it promised a reward.

I drained my glass and went through to the empty lounge to open the door for her. She was medium height, slim, nice lines on her face. It was hard to guess her age – somewhere in the forties. There was no grey in the springy red hair.

'Mac Faraday,' I said. 'Irene?'

We shook hands.

'I'll take a drink,' she said. 'Double scotch. Just had a horse die on me. Perfectly healthy yesterday, now utterly lifeless. Massive bloody things go out like butterflies. Thank God there's a fire.'

When I came back, she had her boots off and her feet, in red Explorer socks, warming in front of the grate.

'Thanks,' she said. 'Disgusting to take off your shoes in public, but I feel like I've got frostbite.'

'I'd join you,' I said, 'but I'm not sure my socks match.'

'I changed mine at lunchtime,' she said. 'I had a gumboot full of liquid cow shit.' She moved both sets of toes, waving at the fire.

We drank. I'd spoken to her on the phone. Allie knew her from working around the stables and that got me over the suspicion barrier.

'She's a real asset around here, Allie,' she said. 'District's full of self-taught farriers.' She had another large sip, put the glass on the floor beside the chair. 'Well,' she said, 'the pain is receding. I'll tell you straight away, I had very little to do with Ian in the last two years.'

'Something involving Ian puzzles me,' I said. 'A friend of mine, man called Ned Lowey, not a patient of Ian's, went to see him in Footscray. Now they're both dead. Both hanged. Ned, then Ian. Two days in between them.'

She was silent. Then she said, 'Well, that's hard to explain.'

'I'm not convinced Ned killed himself,' I said.

'Can I ask you whether you could see Ian killing himself?'

She considered the question, looking at me steadily, grey eyes calm under straight eyebrows. 'Yes,' she said. 'Yes, I could.'

'Why's that?'

Sip of whisky, audible expulsion of breath, wry face. 'It's not easy to talk about this.' She looked into my eyes. 'Are you married?'

'Not any more. Does that disqualify me?'

'People who haven't been married have trouble understanding how things can change over the years. I was married to Ian for nearly twenty years and I knew less about him at the end than I did at the beginning. Yes, he could kill himself.'

Now you wait.

'If you ask around about Ian, you won't hear anything but praise. Everywhere I went, people used to tell me how wonderful he was. It's worse now that he's dead. People stop me in the street, tell me how they could ring him in the middle of the night, never get a referral to a duty doctor, never get an answering machine. How he'd talk to them for twenty minutes, calm them down, cheer them up, make them feel better, traipse out at two am to comfort some child, reassure the parents, hold some old lady's hand. And it's all true. He did those things.'

'Sounds like the old-fashioned doctor everyone misses,' I said.

She smiled, without humour. 'Oh, he was. Like his partner, Geoff Crewe, seventy-nine not out. And

126

Ian wasn't just a good doctor. He was wonderful company. Mimic anyone, not cruelly, sharp wit. He noticed things, told funny stories, good listener.'

She looked around the room, looked into her glass.

'But,' I said.

'Yes. The But. That was Ian's public face. Well, it was his private face too. In the beginning. There was an unhappiness in Ian and it got worse over the years. After about five years, it was like living with an actor who played the part of a normal human being in the outside world and then became this morose, depressed person at home. He'd come home full of jokes, talkative, and an hour or two later he'd be slumped in a chair, staring at the ceiling. Or in his study, head on his arms at the desk, or pacing around. He cried out in his sleep at night. Almost every night. I'd wake up and hear him walking around the house in the small hours. He used to love skiing, one thing that was constant. Went to Europe or Canada every year for three weeks. Then he just dropped it. Stopped. If he'd been drinking, he'd try to hurt himself, hitting walls, doors. He put his fist through a mirror once. Forty stitches. You couldn't reason with him. All you could do was wait until the mood swung. It happened a few times a year when we were first married. I was in love. I sort of liked it. It made him a romantic figure. In the end, we didn't speak ten words a day to each other. I stuck it out until our daughter left home and then I left him.'

'Did he have treatment?'

'Not while I was with him. I'd try to talk to him about it but he wouldn't, he'd leave the house, drive off, God knows where. And I was always too scared to push it for fear he'd do something in front of Alice.'

'He wasn't like that when you met him?'

'You had to live with him to see that side. People who'd known him for donkey's years had no idea. I met him at Melbourne Uni. He was fun, very bright, near the top of his class. We went out a few times, but I didn't impress his friends and he dropped me. Then I met him again here when I started practice.'

'He was a local?'

'Oh yes. Part of a little group from here at uni. Tony Crewe, Andrew Stephens, Rick Veene.'

'Tony Crewe – is that the MP?'

'Yes. All rich kids. Except Ian. His father was a foundry worker. Left them when Ian was a baby. His mother was Tony's father's receptionist for about forty years. I think Geoff Crewe paid Ian's way through St Malcolm's and through uni. They ended up partners.'

'And the group? Did Ian stay friends with the others?'

Irene had a sip of whisky, ran a hand through her hair. 'It's not clear to me that they ever were friends. Not friends as I understand friends. Mind you, I'm just a Colac girl. Ian was sort of . . . sort of in their thrall, do you know what I mean?'

'Not exactly.'

'Andrew Stephens was a golden boy. Clever, rich, spoilt, got a sports car when he turned eighteen. Scary person, really. Completely reckless. His father was a Collins Street specialist, digestive complaints or something, friend of Geoff Crewe's from Melbourne Uni. They were very close once, I gather. Andrew was sent to St Malcolm's because Geoff's boy went there. The Stephenses had a holiday place outside Daylesford called Belvedere. Huge stone house, like a sort of Bavarian hunting lodge. Andrew lives there now. With the gorillas. Sorry. Shouldn't say that.'

'Why not?'

She emptied her glass. 'I'm going to risk another one. What about you?'

'I'll get them,' I said.

She shook her head and went to the serving hatch. I was admiring her backside when she turned and caught me at it. We smiled.

'The gorillas?' I said when she came back with the drinks.

'Doesn't do to talk about valued clients. I'm due out there to look at a horse tomorrow. Still. Andrew's got two large men with thick necks living on the property. We call them the gorillas.'

'What do they do?'

'Nothing as far as I can see. Well, except take turns to drive the girls around.'

'His children?'

She laughed. 'Right age. No. He doesn't have children. Two marriages didn't take. There's

129

always a new girl at Belvedere, two sometimes. Some of them look as if they should be at school. Primary school, my partner once said.'

'What's Andrew do for a living?'

'It's not entirely clear. Developer of some kind. They say he owns clubs in Melbourne. His father apparently left him a heap. He used to talk shares with Tony Crewe – shares and property and horses.'

'So you've been with them?'

'Oh yes. We'd go to dinner with Tony and current woman and Andrew and sometimes Rick Veene and his wife two or three times a year. I have to say I hated it. I think Ian did too. He turned into a kind of court jester when he was with Tony and Andrew and Rick. I once suggested we turn down a dinner invitation and Ian said, "You don't say no to Tony and Andrew". I said, "Why not?" and he said, "You wouldn't understand. They're not ordinary people". Anyway, Andrew and Tony had some kind of falling out and the dinners stopped.'

'Did Ian ever talk about Kinross Hall?'

'No. Geoff Crewe was the place's doctor for umpteen years and I think it sort of passed on to Ian. The director came with Tony Crewe to dinner a few times. Marcia Carrier. Very striking. Ian didn't get on with her so he gave up the Kinross work.' She swirled her drink around and finished it. 'Night falls,' she said. 'None of this helps in finding out why your friend went to see Ian, does it?'

'No,' I said. 'Why did Ian give up his practice and move to Footscray?'

Irene shrugged. 'No idea. Seems to have happened overnight. About a year ago, he phoned Alice, our daughter, and gave her a new phone number. She rang me.'

'Thanks for taking the time,' I said, getting up.

She gave me a steady look. 'If you want to talk again, give me a ring.'

We went out to her car in the deepening dark. There was a house across the road and I could see into the kitchen. A man in overalls was staring into a fridge as if he had opened a door on hell. As she was getting in, I said, 'Ian's pethidine habit. How long did he have that?'

Irene closed the door and wound down the window. The light from the pub lit half her face. 'What makes you think Ian had a pethidine habit?'

'Heard it somewhere,' I said.

She looked away, started the car. 'News to me,' she said. 'Give me a ring. We'll talk about it.'

I watched the cheerful Swedish tail-lights turn the corner where the ploughed paddock ran to the road and nothing interrupted the view. The line between night and day was the colour of shearers' underwear. Far away, you could hear the groan of a Double-B full of doomed sheep changing gear on Coppin's Hill. In the pub, a hand grenade of laughter went off.

The man across the road slammed the fridge door: hell contained. For the moment.

'Well, get on with it. What d'you want to know about Ian Barbie?'

'Why would he kill himself?'

Dr Geoffrey Crewe, age seventy-nine, gave me a sharp look from under eyebrows like grey fish lures. He was a big man, parts of whom had shrunk. Now the long face, long nose, long ears, long arms did not match the body. The body was dressed in corduroy trousers, what looked like an old cricket shirt, an older tweed jacket, and a greasy tweed hat. What had not shrunk was the value of his house. He lived across the road from the lake, redbrick double-storey facing south. I'd arrived as he was leaving on a walk. He set a brisk pace, even though his left leg buckled outward alarmingly when it met the ground. It occurred to me to ask him whether he fancied a game of football on Saturday. He could certainly outpace Flannery over a hundred metres.

'Don't know if there's a sensible answer to the question,' he said. 'What's it matter anyway? Made his choice. You make your choice. Serious choice, but just a choice.'

'His wife says he was often depressed.'

He gave me a look that said he'd met smarter people.

'Could be said about half the people in the line of work – more. Not shuffling bloody paper, y'know. Pain and suffering and bloody dying.'

A fat pink woman in a lime-green towelling tracksuit, large breasts swaying and bouncing out of control, lurched around a corner. 'Gidday, Dr Crewe,' she panted.

Dr Crewe touched a finger to the brim of his tweed hat. 'Don't know what they think they're doing,' he said. 'Do herself a lot more good jumping up and down naked on that miserable bloody shopkeeper she's married to.'

I rolled up my right sleeve. The day was clear, almost warm. I'd left my jacket in the car. 'Didn't surprise you?'

'Too late for surprises. Precious bloody little surprises me. What's that on your arm?'

I looked down. 'Burn.'

'Burn? What kind of work d'you do?'

'Blacksmith.'

He nodded. 'Reasonably honest trade.' Pause. 'This interest in Ian Barbie, say it again.'

I told him about Ned's visit to Footscray.

'Sure he went to see Ian?'

'The receptionist remembered him. He didn't have an appointment, said it was a private matter. She told Ian and he saw him after the next patient. He was with Ian for about ten minutes.'

Dr Crewe didn't say anything for a while. Out on the calm water, a man in a single scull was sitting motionless, head bowed, shoulders slumped, could be dead. Then he moved, first stroke slow and smooth, instantly in his rhythm, powerful insect skimming the silver surface. At the end of each stroke, there was a pause, missed in the blink of an eye.

'This Ned,' he said. 'Any drug problem there?'

'No.'

We walked in silence for perhaps fifty paces. 'Ian had a drug problem,' I said.

He didn't say anything, didn't look at me. We passed a scowling group of seagulls on a jetty, identical commuters waiting in anger for an overdue train home.

'I left the practice on my seventieth birthday,' said Dr Crewe. 'Nine years ago last month. Saddest day of my life. Second saddest. Nobody feels seventy, y'know. Not inside the heart. Always twenty-five inside.'

More silence. Two runners came from behind, short chunky men, hair cut to stubble, big hairy legs. Footballers. Then a tall blonde came into view, white singlet, tight black stretch shorts, hair pulled back. She was at full stride, moving fast, balanced, arms pumping. As the balls of her feet touched the ground, her long thigh muscles bunched above the knee. Her legs and torso were flushed pink, her head was back, mouth open, eyes slits.

We both turned to watch her go. Our eyes met.

134

'Always twenty-five inside,' he said. 'And some-times you feel you could be twenty-five outside too.'

'Eighteen,' I said. 'Eighteen.'

He gave a snort and picked up the pace. We were going up an incline between two huge oaks when he said, 'You don't want to accept your friend's suicide.' A statement.

'No.' It came out sharply.

'I won't talk psychological bullshit to you, but some questions you have to leave alone. They didn't do it to hurt you. They did it because some-thing hurt them and they wanted to put an end to that pain.'

'Dr Crewe,' I said, 'I don't know about Ian, but Ned wouldn't kill himself.'

He stopped. I was taken by surprise, went a pace further.

'They don't end up hanging by accident,' he said. 'So I don't know what you're saying.'

I said, 'I think Ned's suicide was staged. I think he was murdered.'

He put his head back and looked at me down the long nose. 'Police think what?'

'Investigating officer seems to think it's a possi-bility.'

'Probably humouring you. You reckon the same might hold for Ian?'

'If I'm right about Ned, it's possible.'

Dr Crewe sighed and started walking. After a while, he said, 'Loved the boy, y'know.'

I didn't say anything.

'Loved his mother, too, might as well tell you. People say he's mine, but he's not. Often wished he was. Instead I've got Tony – every inch a Carew, not a trace of Crewe in him. Mean-spirited, selfish, whole bloody clan's like that. Mean-spirited and selfish genes pass on to every generation, doesn't matter who they marry. Tony's mother was a prime example.'

A small, round man in a tracksuit overtook us, wobbling as he ran. 'Doc,' he gasped. It sounded like an appeal for help.

'G'day Laurie. Walk, you bloody fool.'

The man gave a feeble wave.

'Three Carews joined up the same day I did,' said Dr Crewe. 'Wife's brother, two of his cousins. You'd think one of 'em would see some action. Hah. Whole war in Canberra, fighting the paper, all three. More than luck involved, I can tell you. Tony's the same. If there's an easy way, he'll find it.'

'Ian was at Melbourne Uni with Tony,' I said. 'Little group of local boys, I gather.'

Dr Crewe looked at me, shook his head. 'Done anything to keep Ian away from Tony and Andrew Stephens and the Veene boy. Andrew's father was a good man, fine man, fought with the Greek partisans in the war. Good doctor too. Andrew. Young Andrew's just rubbish. Too much too soon. Like Rick Veene. Rick's got Carew in him somewhere down the line. His mother's Tony's mother's third cousin or something. Poisonous breed. Buy

136

their way through life. Bought off bloody Carew, that was easy enough.'

'Carew?'

'Carew College, University of Melbourne. Tony's mother's grandfather paid for it. Out of ill-gotten gains. Unjailed criminal. College. Place you stay in. Know about that?'

'Only just,' I said.

He gave me a look and an appraising nod. 'Blacksmith. Name again?'

'Mac.'

'Mac. I remember. Mac.'

There was a sound like sandpapering behind us and a group of male runners split to pass us, came together, all one physical type, a big pack of brothers sent out to run until supper time.

'So,' I said, 'Carew.'

'Carew?'

'Bought off. Carew.'

'Bought off?'

'The college.'

'Oh. That's right. Bought off. Andrew Stephens, Carews and the Veenes. Bloody Carew family trust gives the college some huge sum every year. Clive Carew and Bob Veene were on the council then. Bob Veene. Bloody rabbit. Pathetic. Rick's the only son. Four girls. Nice things, bit on the big side mark you, but nice, healthy girls, never heard a bad word about them. One's married to a carpenter. That'd make the bloody Veenes' fore-skins curl.'

'Why did they buy off the college?'

'Business with a girl. Didn't hear about it till years later. Tony's mother and the rest of them did the dirty work. Kept me in the dark 'cause they knew me. I'd have let the buggers take the consequences. Jail if necessary. Never been any consequences for Tony and Andrew. Never. Not in their lives. Now Tony's the bloody attorney-general. Unbelievable. Makes you think even less of politics. Never thought that'd be possible. Not an ounce of respect for anything. Went into politics because he saw it was easy money. All talk and some bloody public servant does the work. Or doesn't.'

He shook his head. 'Shocked me that old Andrew'd get involved in something like that. Doted on that bloody boy of his. We had a big blue, not the same after that. Friends for going on thirty years. Still, bribery's bloody bribery. Can't brush over it.'

'So Ian was involved in this Carew business?'

'Don't know. Suppose so. Time I found out, it was pretty pointless to ask.'

We had reached a marker that said two kilometres. Dr Crewe said, 'Turnaround time.'

'Kinross Hall,' I said. 'Why did Ian stop being Kinross Hall's doctor?'

His shoulders seemed to sag a little at the mention of the place.

'Don't know. Gave me the brushoff when I asked him. That Carrier woman, probably. Picked her for a cast-iron bitch moment I laid eyes on her. Another brilliant piece of work by Tony.'

'Tony?'

'Chairman of the management committee. Got her appointed instead of Daryl Hopman. He was deputy when old Crosland retired. Good man, sound. Well, he didn't last long after Carrier arrived. Took early retirement, died. Inside a few years, all the old staff gone.'

'Did you know about Ian's pethidine problem?'

He glanced at me. 'Ian had a lot of problems. Not a well man.'

'Physically not well?'

'Mind, body, all the same. Not a well man.'

I had a stab in the dark. 'Someone said he might have had some sort of sexual aberration.'

He didn't reply. We walked in silence. At his gate, Dr Crewe said, 'Big word for a blacksmith, aberration. Well, Mr Blacksmith, I'd like to think that Ian didn't kill himself. But I can't. For your man, maybe you're right. I'll say good day.'

I said thank you.

He nodded, opened the gate and went down the path without looking back.

On the way home, in minutes, the day darkened and it poured, solid sheets like a monsoon rain. A freezing monsoon rain. Then it stopped, the clouds broke, the sun came out and all along the road the shallow pools were full of sky.

Ken Berglin was in his mid-thirties when I went to work for him, but to me he seemed to be of my father's generation. He was tall and gaunt, bony-faced, with colourless thinning hair combed straight back, and he always wore a dark suit with a white shirt and dark tie.

On my first day back from training in Chicago, waiting to go undercover, we met at the War Memorial at opening time. It was autumn in Canberra, cold, the flaming leaves changing the colour of the air. We were looking at a World War I biplane in a towering near-empty gallery when he said to me in his hoarse voice, 'So you seen all the shooting galleries and the crack shops?'

I nodded.

'They tell you you can't do this work without a sense of moral superiority?'

'They mentioned it in passing,' I said. 'Few hundred times. I'm shit-scared to tell you the truth.'

'Always will be. That's the job. Listen, Mac, this moral superiority, holding the line against the forces of darkness stuff, that's useful out there.

Like a swag full of arseholes. Believe me. I know.
I've been there. Let's have a smoke.'

We went out into a courtyard. I offered him a
Camel.

'There's some good comes from the Yanks,' he
said. The air was still and the blue-grey smoke
hung around us like a personal mist.

Berglin studied his cigarette. 'You live with the
scum,' he said. 'One of them, in their world, they
can buy anything, buy anyone. You forget what
you are. Some of them you even like after a while.
Then you start to think like them. The whole thing
starts to look normal. Like a business, really.
Ordinary business. Like being a man buys and
sells fucking meat. So the vegetarians don't like
the business. They don't even like to look in the
shop window. Half a chance, they'd put you out
of business. You think, what the fuck does that
matter? There's plenty who want a thick, juicy
steak. And all these friends of yours are doing is
selling it to them. Should that be a fucking crime?'

Berglin paused and looked at me inquiringly.
'Making sense to you, this?'

'So far.'

Something caught his eye. He pointed. 'Eagle,' he
said. We watched it for a while, bird all alone in the
vast blue emptiness, dreaming on the high winds.

'Anyway,' Berglin said, 'when you start thinking
like the other side, you're on the way to changing
sides. And that will make you a worthless, faithless person. Agree?'

It was hard not to. I nodded.

Berglin took a deep drag and blew a stream of perfect smoke rings, like a cannon firing tiny grey wreaths.

'Worthless, faithless, that's bad,' he said. 'But there's worse. Dead is worse.' He stood on his cigarette butt. 'Let's have a look at Gallipoli. My favourite.'

He led the way to a gallery that featured a huge diorama of the disastrous Gallipoli landing. Two young Japanese tourists in expensive ski wear were studying it, faces impassive.

'Always have a look at this,' Berglin said. 'Bloody marvellous, not so?'

We admired the huge scene.

'You think you're scared?' he said. 'Consider these poor bastards. Boys led to the slaughter.'

It occurred to me that our meeting place was more than a matter of convenience.

The Japanese left. They were holding hands. 'Dead, Mac,' Berglin said again. 'One inkling that you've moved across, you're just a picture in an album. And we'll know, believe me. You cross over, you can't go home anymore. Know that line? American book. This is like marriage except that when we say "Till death do us part", we mean it. And it's you who's dead. You religious?'

I shook my head.

'No. Me neither. They say it can help with the fear. I deeply fucking doubt that. Well, we've got to talk some details. Got a little room here I sometimes use.'

Later, before he sent me off, Berglin said, 'How to be a halfway decent person. That's the main question in life. The work, the job, it's on the side of the fourteen-year-olds. Get a few free tastes – two years later, they're in the cold filing cabinet, tracks all over 'em like a rash. This scum, they are way over on the other side. Across the dark river. Keep it in mind, Mac. Won't, of course. Wouldn't be any fucking use if you did.'

He was absolutely right. I never gave it a thought over the next few years, living under the gun, sweating on the moment of discovery. But I often thought about that meeting with Berglin later. And I thought about it again, driving home from talking to Dr Crewe.

I parked outside the smithy and went to have a piss in the bathroom alongside the office. Still thinking about Berglin, I was in the room before I heard the shower.

Allie was in the big open shower stall facing me. She had her head back under the spray, arms raised to shampoo her hair. Before I backed out, I registered sleek pubic hair, flattened breasts with prominent nipples, defined ribcage, long muscular thighs.

I was in the smithy, shaken, lustful, looking at a sketch of gateposts a hobby farmer outside Wallace wanted when Allie came in, shiny clean, spiky, no make-up.

'Sorry,' I said. 'No truck. Didn't occur to me you'd be showering.'

143

'That's okay,' she said without a trace of embarrassment. 'They told us at school to lock the cubicle. I was feeling filthy. Alarm didn't go off this morning, twenty minutes to get to the job.'

'Where's the truck?'

'Lent it to Mick. Met him in the pub at lunchtime. He's broken down other side Newstead.'

'Overloaded with furniture ripped off the rural poor,' I said. 'That's the first time I've seen you naked.'

She smiled. 'You only had to ask.'

We looked at each other for a moment, a trace of awkwardness.

'You working?' she said.

'Gateposts for a bloke at Wallace.' I handed her the sketch the man had given me.

She whistled. 'Gateposts? These are gateposts? What is the place? Some kind of agribrothel?'

'Hardiplank house on two acres. He says his wife saw gateposts like this in America. Went to Disneyland with her first husband.'

Allie scratched her head. 'Disneyland and Cape Kennedy, Cape Canaveral, whatever it's called. Does he see that they look like two giant wangers?'

'Wanger? That's the current term is it?'

She nodded. 'This week's term. Wanger.'

'He's under no illusions,' I said. 'I suggested to him that they looked like a pair of pricks and he said, there's been two of us. When my wife marries again, she can come around and get you to make a third prick.'

'No illusions,' Allie said.

'Any idea how you'd make something like this?'

She shrugged. 'You work behind closed doors. Then you transport them at night, under a tarp. And you don't have anything to do with their, ah, erection.'

When we stopped laughing, we went over to the office and worked out how to make the posts and what to charge.

'Add twenty per cent to cover embarrassment and possible prosecution,' Allie said.

'We may have priced ourselves out of the market here,' I said.

'For this kind of work,' Allie said, 'we *are* the market.'

I rang the man and gave him the quote. When I put the phone down, I said, 'Didn't blink. Wife wants them up in time for the Grand Final. They have a big gathering every year.'

Allie frowned.

'No,' I said. 'Stop now.'

We went out into the rapidly chilling day to inspect the steel store.

'**M**acArthur John Faraday,' Berglin said. 'Nothing for four years, then twice inside a month.'

I could picture the long, sardonic face, the narrow black shoes on the desk, the cigarette dangling from the jaundiced fingers.

'Twice?'

'Had your local jacks on the line about that special permit. Been firing the cowboy gun at the neighbours?'

'What'd you tell them?'

'Piss off. How've you been?'

'Fair. You?'

'So-so. Creeping age. What's on your mind?'

'Two things. One's a favour.'

'"And every favour has its price/paid not in coin/but in flesh/slice by slice." Know that poem?'

'Engraved on the mind,' I said. 'After two hundred hearings. I need to find someone.'

'We all do. It's the human condition.'

'Melanie Loreen Pavitt.' I spelled the surname. 'Born November 1966. Discharged from Kinross

Hall November 1983. No known family. No fixed address after 1979.'

I'd gone back to the Kinross Hall print-out after talking to Dr Crewe. It said that in October 1983, in the week that Simon Walsh found the naked girl on Colson's Road, a girl called Melanie Pavitt turned seventeen and reached the end of her two-year stay at Kinross Hall. It was a straw.

'Thirty-two now,' Berglin said. 'What's Kinross Hall?'

'Place of safety, girls' juvenile detention centre, whatever they call them now.'

'Out your way?'

'Yes.'

'So what line you in now? Blacksmith and missing persons?'

'It's personal.'

'And the second thing?'

'I hear Carlie Mance was in that pub in Deer Park with Bianchi close to the day.'

There was a long silence. I could hear smoke expelled. Then Berglin said, 'Bianchi's dead, you hear that?'

'Carlie's dead too.'

'I think this thing's pretty much closed, Mac.' Berglin's voice was as close to sympathetic as it got.

'Closed? Someone cuts Lefroy's throat, rapes Carlie Mance, cuts her throat, walks away with a few million bucks in smack. On my watch. It's

147

closed? It's a fucking unsolved crime. How does it get to be closed?'

Silence again. Then he said, 'Where'd you hear this Deer Park stuff?'

'Don't ask.'

'Jesus. And you want me to what?'

'Tell them to get out the file and start looking at Bianchi. Nobody looked at Bianchi.'

Berglin blew smoke. 'Mac, you look at Bianchi, who else are you looking at?'

'That's what I mean. I hear he's about to make deputy Pope.'

'You hear right. And you're suggesting I dump a bag of fresh dog shit in the Vatican air conditioning. I'll have to think about that. Give it a little thought. What's your number? This Pavitt, I'll tell you in the morning.'

I gave him the number. Then I said, 'I'm clean. You know that, don't you?'

Silence. A sigh. 'In so far as I can be said to know anything,' said Berglin. 'Yes.'

I was cutting twelve millimetre steel rods with the power hacksaw when the nose of a red Porsche appeared in my line of sight through the open smithy door. I cut the power, took off the helmet and went outside.

A big man, in his forties, overweight, bald, little ponytail, dark beard shadow, corduroy bomber jacket with leather collar, was getting out of the car. Another man was in the passenger seat. 'Afternoon,' he said. 'Mac Faraday?'

I said yes. He came over and put out a big hand. I shook it. Soft hand, gold chain around his wrist.

'Andrew Stephens,' he said. 'Sorry to butt in. Passing by. Can we talk for a minute?'

It took a second for the name to register. 'It's warmer inside,' I said.

We went into the smithy. He looked around like someone seeing for the first time a place where people worked with their hands.

'So what do you make here?' he said.

'Anything. Gates, fences, fighter aircraft.'

Stephens laughed, a girlish giggling laugh showing perfect teeth, capped. His head was pear-shaped. 'That's funny,' he said. He went over to the bench, took out a white handkerchief, wiped the bench, sat down, thighs wide apart.

'Saw Irene Barbie this morning,' he said. 'She told me you were interested in Ian's death, whether it was suicide.'

I nodded.

Stephens pulled at his ponytail. 'Great friend of mine, Ian,' he said. 'Can't believe he's gone.'

I didn't say anything.

He took a packet of cigarettes out of his jacket, waved it at me inquiringly, lit one with a slim gold lighter, blew smoke out of his nose. He was wearing a Rolex wristwatch. 'I'd like to think he didn't commit suicide,' he said. 'Irene said you asked about pethidine. What made you ask that?'

'Heard it somewhere,' I said.

Stephens took a drag, sighed smoke. 'It's true,'

he said. 'Poor bastard. Irene didn't know. Ian suffered from depression, came on him in his twenties. We all tried to help, all his friends. Wasn't anything you could do. Nothing. Out of anyone's control. Pethidine's the only reason he didn't kill himself years ago.'

He took out the handkerchief and blew his nose. 'I gather a friend of yours was found dead recently too,' he said. 'I'm sorry. You don't know what it's like until you lose someone like that. Rather bloody not know.'

'Yes.'

He stood up. 'Well,' he said, 'I was coming this way, thought I'd stop and say, you find out anything that makes you think Ian didn't kill himself, I'd be grateful if you'd tell me. We all would. I know Tony Crewe – y'know Tony Crewe, the Attorney General? Close friend of Ian's, of mine. Tony would appreciate hearing anything like that.'

'I'll do that,' I said. 'But I think he killed himself.'

'Yes. That's what's most likely. Wonderful bloke, lovely. Well. That's life.'

We went outside. The other man was out of the Porsche now, leaning against it, smoking a small cheroot. He was big, thick-necked, face like a ten-year-old on steroids.

'While I'm here,' Stephens said, 'I'm thinking of getting someone to look after the maintenance on my properties. Big job, mainly supervision. Well paid. Think something like that would suit you?'

'Not really,' I said.

He nodded, put out his hand. 'Anything makes you think Ian's death's other than the way it looks, you let me know. I mean first. Before you tell anyone else. That way, we make sure everything's properly investigated. Quickly, too, I can guarantee that. Tony Crewe will see to that. Okay? And I'll make sure you're not out of pocket for any expenses. My duty to the family.'

'You'll be the first to know,' I said.

'Good man.' He took out a wallet, gave me a card, tapped me on the arm.

They got into the car and drove off. I heard the engine note turn to a howl as they took the first hill.

I started at full forward, a position in the Brockley side where the ball was seen so rarely that a full forward had once gone home at the end of the third quarter and no-one noticed until the team was in the pub.

This Saturday was different. We were playing Bentham. I arrived about thirty seconds before the start, missing Mick Doolan's tactical briefing and inspirational rev-up. He got his motivational material from studying a six-pack of videos called *Modern-Meisters of Motivation* bought for $2.50 at a trash and trivia market. The players, many having their last cigarette before quarter-time, found messages such as *Sell the SIZZLE not the STEAK* and *Don't SEE to BELIEVE, BELIEVE to SEE* extremely powerful: aflame, the Brockley side would stroll out, tugging at their jocks. The usual result: five goals down at quarter-time.

Not today. Either a new video found or Mick had fed the men elephant juice. Billy Garrett was, without effort, leaping free of the earth's grip. Players who routinely handballed into the ground or to the other side were sending the ball to within metres of team-mates. Even Flannery seemed fresh from a Swiss rejuvenation clinic, backing into packs and coming out with the ball. From all over the field, players were kicking the ball in my direction. It was unnerving but I took four marks, kicked two goals and a behind. At quarter-time, we were four goals up.

As we trooped off, I saw Allie on the bonnet of her truck, leaning back against the windscreen, legs crossed at the ankle. She was wearing a red quilted jacket and a scarf, and you could see the colour in her cheeks from thirty metres. There was a man lounging next to her, floppy dark hair, sallow, young. She gave me the thumbs up, hand cocked forward. Three things went through my mind. One, she'd come to watch me play without being asked. Two, she'd come with another man. Three, don't be a stupid prick.

In the second quarter, Bentham put a man called String Woodly at fullback. He consisted almost entirely of thin rubbery arms that he wound around you like pipe cleaners while pretending to be interested in taking a mark. No-one had ever seen him take a mark, but very few opposing players had got one while wrapped in String. Carrying him around was exhausting. Billy complained to the umpire. This didn't work. I resorted to falling over in his embrace, trying to land on him with an elbow in some painful spot. This didn't work either. I kept landing on my elbow

153

with String on top of me. Finally, I had Flannery sent over and we had a chat.

The next time the ball came our way, coming down through the mist, Flannery got close behind the two of us, pulled out the back of String's shorts. Using the waistband elastic as a step, he ran up String's back and plucked the ball from the sky. String let me go, falling over forward, clutching at his shorts, now around his knees.

'That's not in the bloody game,' he said, offended, as Flannery landed on his right shoulder.

'Stick around, beanpole,' Flannery said, getting ready to kick. 'Show you lots not in the game.' He took two paces and kicked the ball through the middle. He looked around at me, astounded by his feat. 'Shit,' he said. 'Haven't kicked a goal since school.'

'That long,' I said. 'Since you were twelve.'

String wasn't the same after his experience, and Flannery and I saw off a few other Bentham spoilers before the day was over. We ran out ten-goal winners. No-one could remember Brockley winning by ten goals. We went back to the Oak in a state of high excitement, singing one another's praises. Nothing disturbed our joy until only the hard core remained.

'Was a time,' said Trevor Creedy, 'when Brockley won by bloody ten goals every second week.' He was a small man with close-set eyes, now murky, the kind of supporter who finds victory deeply unsatisfying. 'That was,' he said, 'before they starting pickin girls. And makin blokes coach never kicked a footy.'

'Trev,' Mick said, 'been meanin to ask ya. How'd ya like to share the coach's job? I mean, with a view to takin it over?'

Creedy's eyes narrowed. 'Ha,' he said. 'Tryin to bloody buy off ya critics. Won't bloody work with me.'

He left, now a happier man.

'Lovely fella,' said Flannery. 'Fixed his car for him, took it for a spin, see how it goes. When I give him the bill, he takes off fifty cents for petrol. Don't expect me to pay for your joyridin, he says.'

Mick's mobile trilled. He had a brief conversation, then he said, 'Vinnie, me own Gestapo's on the way. Let's have a lightnin round for the survivors.'

The dog joined me as I stepped out of the door, suddenly aware that no area of my body was without its own dull pain. A full moon gave a pale and cold daylight when the clouds parted. Both limping a bit, the dog and I walked down the road and down the lane.

I was in the office, going through Allie's work diary and writing up invoices, when I heard the car. Marcia Carrier was getting out of her BMW when I reached the door. She didn't look like an Olympic dressage contestant today. Today she looked like an Olympic skier *après ski*: dark hair loose, big cream polonecked sweater, camel-coloured pants. She looked healthy and fit, like someone who ran and swam and had a lot of wholehearted sex in front of open fires, followed by yoghurt milkshakes.

'Mac,' she said, 'I rang the number you gave me, no reply. So I drove over on the off-chance.'

'Nice to see you,' I said.

'Got a few minutes?'

'Hours. Days. Kitchen's the only warm room in the house.'

'I was hoping for the forge.'

'Forge's having a rest today. Sunday is forge's day of rest.'

The kitchen didn't look too bad. Spartan but clean. I pulled another captain's chair in front of the stove. Mick Doolan had sold me six for two hundred dollars: 'To you, Moc, a gift. What I paid for them. Less. I think about it now, less. Much less.'

'I'll make coffee,' I said.

'Mac, sit,' she said, lacing her fingers. 'I have to tell you something and I'm embarrassed about it . . .'

I sat down.

'When you came to see me about Ned Lowey, I think I said it was going to nag at me.' She was studying her left hand on the arm of the chair. It was older than her face.

'I remember.'

A spray of rain, like gravel thrown, hit the window. She tensed. Our eyes met.

'Well, it did. I went back to the files, looking for something that might have happened while Mr Lowey was working at Kinross. I found something. About an hour ago.'

'Happened to a girl?'

She nodded. 'Two girls.'

'When you were in charge?'

'I was new. Took over in 1983, into a nightmare. The place was run like a mini-kingdom, all these places were, minimal record-keeping, incompetent staff, all sorts of kickbacks with suppliers and contractors, ghosts on the payroll, you name it. My predecessor might have been a wonderful man but he was completely out of touch with what was going on around him. And to make things worse, Kinross wasn't even getting the funding it was entitled to. So I cleaned up the obvious rorts and got a proper reporting system going. Then I left the

157

day-to-day running to my deputy. He seemed to be an honest person. I devoted most of my time to working on the department and the minister to get Kinross's funding up to speed.'

'The girls,' I said.

She clasped her hands, face unhappy. 'Mac, I found a report in Daryl Hopman's confidential file. He was my deputy. I've never seen the file before, didn't know it existed. And I only found it by chance.'

'What kind of report?'

'It involves two girls. I should have been told about it and I wasn't.'

She paused. I waited.

She sighed again. 'It also involves Mr Lowey. I'm sorry to tell you that. I know how much he meant to you.'

'Involves?' I could feel the blood in my head.

Marcia put her hands through her hair. 'I'll just say it. The girls were caught coming back into the Kinross grounds shortly before four am one night in November 1985. They said they had been at Ned Lowey's house and had been given drugs, amphetamines, speed, for sex.'

I stood up. 'Not possible, a mistake. Not Ned. Absolutely not.'

'I'm sorry,' Marcia said. 'I'm really sorry. I felt I had to tell you.'

I went to the window, looked out, saw nothing. 'What was done?'

'Nothing. It's unbelievable. Nothing was done about a serious allegation of criminal conduct.

Nothing. It says everything about the way Kinross was run in the old days. I shudder to think what else may have been ignored like this. In the maintenance supervisor's file I found a note from Daryl saying that Ned was not to be employed again. I presume Daryl wrote the report as some kind of insurance if word leaked out.'

'Insurance?'

'He may have planned to say that he had made a report to me and that I was the one who failed to act.'

'The girls said Ned gave them drugs?' Ned having anything to do with any drug other than a stubbie of Vic Bitter was inconceivable. But my treacherous inner voice said: *What do you really know about Ned?*

Marcia unclasped her hands, pushed back her hair, started to speak, hesitated. 'I shouldn't tell you this, Mac,' she said, 'but that's not the whole story.'

I shook my head in disbelief. I didn't want to hear any more. I wanted to hold on to the Ned I loved.

'The girls said Dr Barbie was at Ned's house and had sex with them. Violent sex.'

Ned going to see Ian Barbie in Footscray.

Ned and Ian Barbie, both dead, hanged.

The girl's skeleton in the mine shaft. The newspapers Ned kept.

Melanie Pavitt, naked and bleeding in Colson's Road. About four kilometres from Ned's house.

'What are you going to do?' I said.

Marcia got up, tugged at her sweater. 'Nothing.

159

I'm not going to do anything. They're dead. Both men. What's the point of doing anything now? The families have had enough pain.'

She came over, put her hand on my arm. I could smell her hair, a rose garden far away.

'Mac, I've destroyed Daryl's report,' she said in a low voice. 'I think you and I are the only people who know about this. The two of us and the girls. They probably don't even remember it. I'm protecting myself, I can't deny that. I was in charge, I'm responsible for the girls' welfare. But I'm a victim here too. I knew nothing about what happened. Daryl left this thing behind like a time bomb.'

I didn't say anything.

Marcia squeezed my arm gently. 'Mac, I think I'm doing the right thing for everyone. Is it the right thing? If you think it isn't, I'll go public, take the consequences. If you think it is, we never speak of the matter again. To anyone.'

What else was there to say? 'Yes.' I said. 'It's the right thing.'

At her car, engine running, window down, she said, not looking at me, 'God, I'm glad that's over. Would you like to have a drink some time, dinner? Anything?'

I pulled myself together. 'Drink, dinner, followed by anything. And everything.'

'I'll call you,' she said, hint of a smile.

I watched the car go down the lane, turn, heard a little growl of acceleration. I didn't want to go inside, didn't know what to do with myself, got into the Land Rover and drove.

Stan Harrop and his son, David, were in the northwest corner of the field nursery on Stan's property, talking to the driver of a tip truck carrying a load of stones. I parked at the gate and made my way along the paths between raised north-south beds. David gave me a salute. He was about twenty-five, thin and sandy, with Stan's big hands. Stan had waited until he was nearly fifty to take his shot at immortality with David's mother.

'A wall, Mac,' Stan said. 'A drystone wall. Twenty metres of wall. Know anything about drystone walls?'

'Been a while,' I said. When I was sixteen my father and I built two hundred metres of drystone wall on a property called Arcadia near Wagga. In my mind I saw a man and a boy and a pile of stones in the burning day, and heard my father say: *Stone you need's at the bottom of the bloody pile. That's the way nature works. In bloody opposition to man.*

'So where d'ya want 'em?' the driver said. He was a fat, sad-looking man in overalls and a baseball cap with 'Toyota' across the front.

Stan scratched his head. 'Well, I suppose they can go just here.'

'Want my advice?' I said.

'Quick,' Stan said.

'What's the line of the wall?'

'North-south,' David said. He pointed. 'In line with that post.'

'Take it slow and tip 'em out down the line,' I said to the driver. 'You don't want any piles. Do that?'

'At the limit of the technology,' the man said. We got out of the way and he went into action.

'The right stone,' I said. 'Finding it's the problem. Much easier if they're spread out.'

'What about the footing?' said Stan.

'How high's the wall supposed to be?'

'Not high,' said David. 'Metre and half.'

'High enough,' I said. 'Needs a trench about half a metre deep, metre and a quarter wide. Then you taper the wall to about fifty centimetres at the top. Put a bit of cement in the bottom layers. Purists don't like that.'

'Purists be buggered,' Stan said. 'Get the machinery, lad.'

I got gloves out of the Land Rover, put on boots. David ripped the footing in half an hour. We shovelled out the earth, hard work, and then we got the strings up. I showed Stan how to arrange the bottom rocks, then David and I carried and Stan laid. It was punishing work, moving heavy objects not created with human hands in mind.

'Wanted to give the women a surprise,' Stan said.

'Gone to Melbourne. To shop. What kind of bloody activity is that?'

'I could learn to shop,' I said. 'Can't be that hard.'

I was glad to be there, glad that there was somewhere I could be, glad to be doing something that prevented me from thinking about Ned. I desperately didn't want to think about Ned.

We stopped when the light was almost gone, cold biting the face.

'I think I see a drink in your future,' Stan said, patting my shoulder. 'Thought metal was the area of expertise. Now you turn out to know a bit about stone.'

We sat in Stan's office next to the low whitewashed brick house he had built in the lee of the hill. A fire was burning in a Ned Kelly drum stove. David drank his beer and went off to feed the chooks. Stan took two more bottles of Boag out of the small fridge in the corner and opened them.

'Something on your mind,' he said.

I drank some beer out of the glass mug and looked at a botanical print on the wall. 'Heard a story about Ned today,' I said.

'Yes.' He was lighting his pipe with a big kitchen match.

I told him what Marcia had said.

Stan blew out smoke, drank beer, put the mug and pipe down. He didn't show any sign of shock.

'Ned. Drugs. Sex with teenage girls.' He looked at me over the big hairy knuckles of his clasped hands. 'Go to my grave not believing it.'

'Who'd invent something like that?' I said.

'You believe it?'

'Rather not think about it. Wouldn't have had to think about if I hadn't gone poking about.'

'What poking about?'

I told him about Ned's visit to Kinross Hall, how my questioning of Marcia Carrier had led to her finding of Daryl Hopman's report.

'Just her word for it, then,' Stan said. 'Could be trying to shift the blame from the doctor to Ned.'

'Then why mention the doctor at all?'

We sat in silence, Stan generating smoke. For a moment I had been going to tell him about the other things that haunted me: the skeleton in the mine shaft, Melanie Pavitt naked in Colson's Road, Ned's visit to Ian Barbie in Footscray. But Daryl Hopman's report offered an explanation for all of them that was too chilling to speak about.

'Better get moving,' I said, getting up. 'Boy's at home without food.'

'Boys find food,' Stan said. He walked to the vehicle with me. When I'd started it, he said: 'Learned a lot about men in the war. Scoundrels and saints, met 'em both. Don't believe this about Ned, so it's not going to change anything.'

We looked at each other, united in our desire to hold on to the Ned we knew.

'Another thing, Mac,' said Stan.

I could barely see his face.

'Ned was like a brother to your father. Something

like this, he would have known. See you to-morrow.'

As I drove away, I thought perhaps my father did know. Perhaps that was what he wanted to tell me on the night he shot himself.

W e'd put in five hours in the grounds of Harkness Park – me, Stan Harrop, Lew and Flannery – before Francis Keany's Discovery murmured down the driveway. What we were trying to do was uncover paths, using a large-scale plan Stan and I had drawn from exploration and aerial photographs and the old photographs I'd found.

'They're bloody there,' Stan said. 'Get the paths, we've got the garden.'

It was hard going: the place was one big muddy thicket. The elms in particular had embarked on world conquest, sending out armies of suckers, densely colonising large areas. Some of the suckers were mature trees, now spawning empires of their own.

'Dutch elm disease might be the answer,' Stan said. 'Nature's way of saying fuck off.'

Stan had assembled us at 8.30. We were armed with two chainsaws and a new thing, a brush-cutter with a circular chainsaw blade. Flannery liked the idea very much.

'Tremble, jungle,' he said.

I said, 'The point is, Flannery, we apply the technology with some purpose in mind. We don't apply it simply because we like laying waste to large areas of nature and seeing big things fall over.'

'Wimp,' said Flannery.

Stan went for a long walk through the muddy paddocks around the house. We were on smoko, sitting on Flannery's ute, when he came back. 'Major thing,' he said, hitching his buttocks onto the tray, 'major thing is, gardens like this, they're designed for vistas. Looking *from* the house and the garden, looking *at* the house and the garden. But if the bloody vista's gone, all brick-veneer slums crowding it, you can't see what the designer saw.'

'So you got it worked out,' Flannery said. He was eating a pie. A viscous fluid the colour of liquid fertiliser was leaking down his unshaven chin. This and the Geelong beanie pulled down to a centimetre above his eyebrows gave him a particularly fetching appearance.

'More or less,' Stan said. At that moment, Francis Keany's vehicle came into view.

Francis got out, the picture of an English country gentleman. He nodded to the peasants and said to Stan: 'Good morning, Stan. So what do we now know? Enough research to write an entry in the *Encyclopaedia Britannica*. Paid by the hour. Photographs taken from a great height. At a cost of about five dollars a metre. Charged both going up and coming down, as far as I can tell. So what do we now know about this garden?'

Francis had clearly been working on his opening lines during the drive from Melbourne.

Stan was patting pockets for his pipe. 'Not much,' he said, sadly.

Francis's face went tight. He pursed his full lips, lifted his chin and slowly turned his face away from us until he was in full profile. This was a mistake. Stan had a clipping of a magazine article in which Francis's profile was described as that of a Roman senator on a coin.

'What Roman senator do you think that magazine twat had in mind?' Stan said in a musing tone. 'Pompus? Was there a Priapus? What about Fartus?'

Francis came back into full face. He blinked several times, willing himself to remain composed. 'In a few minutes,' he said, voice edging on the tremulous, 'Mr and Mrs Karsh are going to drive. Through that gate. I'd like to have something to tell them. If that's at all possible.' Pause. 'Stan.'

Stan found the battered and blackened object resembling a piece of root rescued from a bonfire. He applied a yellow plastic lighter with an awesome flame. Smoke gathered around him until he looked like a smouldering scarecrow. Francis took two paces backwards to get away and was starting to speak when a black Mercedes station wagon with tinted windows nosed around the corner of the drive.

'Oh shit,' he said.

The car stopped next to Francis's Discovery. The front doors opened. The driver was a tall

168

woman, thirties, lightly tanned, sleek dark hair to her shoulders, minimal make-up. She was wearing a camelhair donkey jacket, thin cream sweater, jeans and walking boots. The passenger was in his late fifties, stocky, pale, small features, dark suit, tired eyes. He ran fingers the colour of chicken sausages through his thick grey hair and loosened his striped tie.

'Jesus,' he said. 'Why isn't it snowing?'

Francis coughed. 'Leon,' he said. 'Anne. Good to see you. Filthy weather, I'm afraid. I'd like to introduce Stan Harrop. He's one of my associates with a special knowledge . . .'

Leon Karsh ignored this and came around to shake hands with all of us, starting with Flannery. 'Leon Karsh. Thanks for your help here.' Soft voice, unusual accent, upper-class English over something else. When he got to Stan, he said, 'My wife tells me you were responsible for Faraway in Bowral. I knew the family. Wonderful garden.'

'Responsible, no,' Stan said. 'I was the maintenance man.'

Leon Karsh smiled. 'Excellent maintenance, then.'

'Thank you,' Stan said.

'What I'm trying to do here, Leon,' Francis said, 'is to recapture the essence of the original garden without necessarily being constrained by the more obvious limitations of the original designer's vision. To do that . . .'

'What limitations are those?' said Stan.

Francis gave him a look, a laser beam of hatred.

'To the trained eye,' he said, 'it's obvious that the absence of a central axis . . .'

'To the trained eye,' Stan said, 'there is a central axis. Mac, explain. I've got to get these expensive craftsmen back to work.'

It was amazing to me that Stan had managed to work for other people for so long. I fetched the plan and the copies of the photographs from the truck and laid them out on the tray. Anne Karsh was at my left elbow, Leon Karsh at my right. I could feel Francis behind me, trying to see over my shoulder. Anne smelled faintly of rosemary and cinnamon, a clean smell.

I said, 'The garden was designed around 1885 by an Englishman called Robert Barton Graham for the Peverell family. The Peverell brothers were on the Ballarat goldfields until they realised there was more money in supplying timber and then flour to the miners. They built a mill on the creek here in 1868 and the house later. It was in the family till the 1950s. Lots of them are buried down the road here, next to the church.'

I found the right photograph. 'This is dated December 1937. Two gardeners clipping a low circular hedge. It's box. If you look carefully, you can see there's a circle of hedge inside another circle. Paths run to the centre. A cross of paths.'

Anne Karsh leant forward to look at the photograph. 'A sort of double mandala,' she said. 'One path's wider than the others.' A breast touched my arm.

170

'Exactly,' Francis said. 'Mac has been very useful . . .'

'The luck here is the sundial,' I said, pointing at the photograph. 'It tells us this picture was taken looking north.'

'That's important,' Francis said. 'Obviously . . .'

'It also tells us the time of day,' I said. 'It's late afternoon. This dark at the top left of the photograph – we couldn't work that out. That's because we assumed that the wide path would be the key to the long sightline. You can see the path runs north–south, and that puts the house behind the photographer.'

'It's the shadow of the house,' Anne Karsh said, the pleasure of discovery in her voice. 'That's the big chimney.'

I said, 'That's right. It made Stan think that perhaps the long axis of garden ran across the front of the house.'

'Odd thing to do, isn't it?' Leon Karsh said. 'Not that I know anything about garden design.'

'You have an instinct for form, Leon,' Francis said. 'It's a gift.'

'It is odd,' I said, 'and unlikely, according to Stan. Then we got the aerial photographs.'

'I insisted on aerial photography,' Francis said. 'One of the most valuable tools in the armoury of the garden restoration architect.'

'Tools in an armoury, Francis?' Anne Karsh said. Stan was going to like her.

I unrolled the big enlargement. 'Here's the

171

house. Here's the creek. Here's the old mill. Now, from the length of the house shadow in the old photograph . . .'

'You can pinpoint the sundial,' Anne Karsh said, pointing. She had strong hands, no rings. 'God, it's just jungle.'

'We've found it,' I said. 'Box and yew trees now. Something else puzzled us.' I pointed to a large area, bare in comparison with the rest of the garden, to the right of the house.

'Not a natural shape,' Anne Karsh said. She bent over the photograph and her hair swung like a silk curtain and touched my cheek. I flicked a glance at her. I wished I'd shaved.

'Not at all natural, Anne,' Francis said. 'Very perceptive of you.'

'No-one had mentioned,' I said, 'that the original house burned to the ground in 1904.'

'The shape of a house,' Leon Karsh said. 'You fellows have done well.'

'Thank you, Leon,' Francis said, modestly.

'The mark of the house still shows because, for some reason, they didn't finally demolish the ruins until the late 1940s,' I said. 'They built the new house as a replica of the old one, but it was too late to change the main axis of the garden. You'll also have to live with it.'

'A pleasure,' Anne Karsh said. I didn't look at her. I wanted to.

'Stan's worked out the focal point of the main axis,' I said. 'The main sightline leads the eye to

172

the church steeple in Brixton. You can't see it now because of those pines planted about forty years ago. Stan found out that while Graham was working on the garden, he also designed the church. Colonel Peverell paid for it.'

'One cheque satisfied both man and God,' Leon Karsh said. 'In that order. Things don't change much.'

'So,' Francis said, 'you can now appreciate the enorm . . . the magnitude of my task here.'

'Can we see what's happened so far?' Leon Karsh said to me. I looked at Francis. He was not a pleased person.

'Go ahead, Mac,' he said. 'I have planning to do.' He turned to Anne Karsh. 'My dear, you have no idea – the logistics of a project like this resemble fighting the Gulf War.'

The Karshes put on gumboots and I showed them what we'd found so far, including paths, a sunken tennis court and a pond that was gravity-fed through a stone aqueduct from a spring on the hillside behind the house.

'Where does the water go from here?' Anne Karsh said.

'Haven't got to that yet,' I said. 'Probably chan-nelled down to join the creek above the pond that feeds the millrace.'

'There's a millrace?' She checked herself, delighted. 'Well, since there's a mill, I suppose there is.'

'In good shape,' I said. 'Locals say the mill

173

produced flour until World War II. The creek's dammed down there to create a millpond. You open a sluicegate to let water into the headrace.'

'I'd like to see that,' Anne Karsh said.

'Next time,' Leon Karsh said. 'The architect should be here. Should have been here before us.' He turned his weary eyes on me. 'So you're a landscape gardener?'

'No.'

Leon looked at me. Not a glance. A look. In his eyes you could see instinct and intelligence. I was being evaluated. God knows what he saw in my eyes. Attraction to his wife perhaps.

'No,' I said, 'I'm a blacksmith. I work for Stan when things are slow. Which is quite often.'

'But you haven't always been a blacksmith.'

'Leon,' Anne said, 'you're prying.'

'That's right,' Leon said. 'I'm prying. My whole life is spent prying.'

'I've done a few things.'

'And you're not easily pried. We'll need an estate manager here when we're finished. You might be interested.'

'Bit too independent these days,' I said. 'But that might change. I'll show you what's left of the walled garden on the way back.'

The architect was waiting at the house, a thin middle-aged man, wispy chicken-feather beard, dressed for an Atlantic crossing in an open boat. With him was a clone, cloned smaller, presumably the assistant architect. In my days among the rich, I'd observed that nothing they paid for came in ones: not lawyers, not gardeners, not architects, not whores. Even their women came with a mother or a sister or a friend, usually fat, often ugly, always resentful.

I excused myself to rejoin the labourers, to go back to my place. Leon shook my hand. Anne said, 'I'd like to see the mill some time if that can be arranged.'

'Any time you want to see it, it's down there,' I said. 'It's your mill.'

'Mac,' Leon said, 'I'll tell Francis to build in the time for showing Anne the mill. Keep her away from the dangerous places. These old buildings, everything's rotten.'

'Any time,' I said.

I found Flannery and Lew on their hands and knees looking for a path. 'Glad to see you're safe,' Flannery said. 'Thought you'd slipped over onto the managerial side. Notice that woman's mouth? Very powerful. Suck the grips off your handlebars. She give you an indication of anything?'

'Said she found the bloke with the pie gravy running down his chin irresistible. Turned her on.'

'I've heard it can do that,' Flannery said. 'Chittick's pie.'

At the end of the day, we had a few beers at the Heart of Oak and then I went home, dog-tired, still hurting from Saturday's football, sick at heart about Ned.

It was Lew's turn to make the meal. I poured a big glass of red wine and went out to the office to finish making out Allie's invoices. There was a note from her on the desk:

> You are my No 1 football hero. Can I wash your jumper, anything that has been close to you? On second thoughts, perhaps not anything. To business. You'll see I'm booked up tomorrow but can give you a hand with the, um, gateposts on Wednesday. See you tomorrow evening.
> Your devoted fan, Allie.

Something was nagging at me as I worked. November 1985. Ned and Dr Barbie. The depressed Dr Barbie. Barbie the skier.

Skiing.

I stopped writing mid-invoice and looked up Irene Barbie's number. She answered on the second ring.

'Irene, Mac Faraday. Sorry to bother you at night.'

'That's all right. I've been thinking about our conversation.'

'I want to ask you about Ian and skiing.'

'Yes.' Puzzled.

'When did he give it up?'

'When? Oh, I'll have to think— um, it would have been around 1986 or '87.'

'You said he went to Europe or Canada every year. What time of the year?'

'Usually from mid-November. He'd get back in time for the start of the school holidays.'

'You wouldn't be able to say whether he went in November 1985, would you?'

'I'm sure he did. I can find my diary if you want to hold on.'

'Take as long as you like.'

I drank some wine and waited, feeling the tension in my neck and shoulders.

Irene Barbie was back within three minutes.

'Mac? Still there?'

'Yes.'

'One second while I . . .'

I held my breath.

'Left for Canada on November 13, came back December 5.'

I breathed out. 'You're sure that's 1985?'

'Oh yes. This is from my diary. Can you tell me why you want to know this?'

'I'd like to talk to you again,' I said. 'If that's possible. And I'll tell you then.'

'Ring me,' she said.

I set off to get another glass of red. The pain had left my body. I felt a sense of relief and elation.

Marcia Carrier was lying about Ned and Ian Barbie.

B erglin traced Melanie Loreen Pavitt to an address in Shepparton, out where the neat town begins to fray. You drive past the restumped houses, disciplined yards, steam-cleaned driveways, tools hung on pegboard in swept garages, retired men in caps, full of empty purpose. Then the brick veneers, low, brown, ugly, lawns shaved, big windows blinded. At the end of the concrete drive, fixed to the two-car garage, a hoop. It waits for the sad boy to come home and throw the meaningless ball, pass the time until summoned to eat the processed food, watch the manufactured world, sleep.

Further out, on bigger blocks, windswept, tree-less, beyond mowing, stand exhausted weather-boards, at the end of their histories, all hope gone, boards sprung, stumps rotten, roofs rusted.

Melanie Pavitt's weatherboard house stood in a sea of long yellow grass, leaning with the prevailing wind, bright junk mail blowing around. The brick chimney on the right was bulging at the bottom and swaying inwards at the top. The windows' sash-cords had disintegrated and pieces of weatherboard fallen off the side of the house held up the top panes. I felt the verandah boards, grey, eroded like Ethiopian hillsides, sag under my weight. Next door was a work in progress, a long brick-veneer train carriage of a house with two window openings blocked with plywood and the end wall half-built. Silver insulation foil caught the light. Behind the house was a huge shed, more factory than garage. A newish red Nissan, dusty, stood at the end of a paved section of driveway facing the shed across a riverbed of bluestone dust.

There was no response to my knocks. Inside a radio was on at full volume. Country and western. I thought of going around the back, then a vertical blind in the unfinished house moved. I went over and knocked on the unpainted front door. It opened instantly, on a chain. A woman in her forties, pretty face, plump, long dyed auburn hair, sleep in her eyes, lipstick a little smudged, said, 'Yes.'

'Sorry to bother you,' I said. 'I'm looking for Melanie Pavitt. Does she still live next door?'

There was a wary silence. Finally, she said, 'Police?'

'No. I'm not selling and I'm not collecting either. It's a personal matter.'

She put a finger to the corner of her right eye, pulled the skin back. 'Yeah, she's next door.'

'She doesn't seem to be home. Any idea when she might be back?'

The woman closed the door briefly to take off

the chain. She was wearing a purple dressing gown. 'Didn't hear her go,' she said. 'The car makes a helluva noise, exhaust shot. She might be in the back. Let me put something on, I'll come with you.'

I waited on the verandah. It was quiet here, just a faraway hum of traffic. The woman came out wearing tight jeans, a fluffy blue mohair-like top with three-quarter sleeves and black pumps. She had repaired her make-up. She walked ahead of me, buttocks jiggling.

'Doesn't go out much, Mel,' she said. 'Not since the boyfriend moved in. Nice bloke. Used to be in and out of my place. Not anymore.'

We tried knocking again. Nothing. Just the music.

'Try the back,' said the woman. 'By the way, my name's Lee-Anne, two words with a hyphen.'

'John,' I said. We walked down the car tracks beside the house. The kitchen was a lean-to at the back, younger than the main house.

Lee-Anne knocked on the back door. The music was louder here. 'Stand by Your Man'.

'Won't hear anything over that racket,' Lee-Anne said. She tried the doorknob. The door opened. She took a step inside.

'Mel? You there? Someone for you.'

Nothing. Just the music.

Lee-Anne took another step in. I followed. The kitchen was neat, a smell in the air of something burnt. 'Mel!' Lee-Anne shouted. 'Barry!'

The door to the rest of the house was closed. Lee-Anne opened it and called out again.

We went down a short, dark passage, past a door on the left, towards a closed door and the music. At the door, Lee-Anne paused, turned to me. 'You go first,' she said. She bit her lower lip.

I opened the door.

It was a sitting room, also dark, curtains drawn, old blond-wood furniture, a big television, radio on top of it. A fairground barker's voice was saying, 'Wangaratta Ford. Where the best deals are waiting for you.' The burnt smell was gone now. Replaced by something else.

I knew what it was. Before I saw the man.

Lee-Anne came in behind me and screamed.

He was sitting in the chair facing the television. A big part of his face was missing, a black, congealing cavity, and his whole chest was dark with dried blood. Behind his head what looked like a gallon of blood had seeped into the chair upholstery.

That was the other smell: the salty, sickening slaughterhouse smell of blood.

I stepped forward for a closer look at the man. He was holding a revolver in his right hand.

'Barry?' I said.

Lee-Anne nodded, face chalk-white, lipstick startling against it.

'Don't touch anything,' I said.

Two other doors, closed, led from the room. I opened the left-hand one: a small bedroom, empty.

I turned. Lee-Anne was looking at the floor. 'Through there?' I said, pointing.

'Mel's bedroom,' she said softly, without looking up.

I opened the door. Double bed, made. Wardrobe, dresser. No-one there.

I went back, down the dark passage, to the other door.

'Bathroom,' said Lee-Anne from close behind me.

I opened the door.

The bath was directly in front of me. A woman was in it, naked, floating in dark water. Shot once, through the left eye. She had been sitting upright and the bullet had sprayed the contents of her head over the wall behind and beside her.

'Don't look,' I said. 'Call the cops from your place.'

I heard her run down the passage. Then I had a look around. An old suitcase was on top of the wardrobe in Melanie's bedroom. I took it down, gripping the handle in a tissue from the dressing table, and opened it on the bed: perhaps a dozen letters, an empty perfume bottle, a pair of gold high heels, a gold chain belt, three packets of photographs, a bead purse with some Fijian coins, a small velvet box that had held a ring, a black-covered book.

I opened the book. On the *first* page was written large: *My Life. By Melanie Loreen Pavitt.*

I put the letters, the photographs and the book into my shirt, replaced the suitcase, left the house.

182

At the car, I made sure Lee-Anne wasn't watching and put the stolen goods under the front seat. Then I drove the car into Lee-Anne's yard, over the bluestone dust and parked behind the house. I found the emergency cigarettes and went round the front and sat on the front step.

'Get a smoke off you?' she said from behind me, voice tremulous. 'I'm shakin.'

'Natural,' I said, offering her the packet and the matches. She lit up and sat down beside me. We sat there smoking, not saying anything, waiting for the sirens and the police. When I heard the first wail, I said, 'Inside's better. There'll be television people and other journos coming. They tip them off.'

We went in and stood at the breakfast bar in Lee-Anne's kitchen. This room was finished, all pale gleaming wood and stainless steel.

'Nice room,' I said. 'Listen, I'll explain afterwards but I'm going to arrange it with the cops that they tell them the bodies were found by a neighbour. They'll want you on camera. You want to do that? It'll get rid of them.'

She nodded. The idea didn't displease her.

'Okay. Don't say anything about what you saw. Don't mention me. Just say something like, "I've lost a good friend and neighbour and I'd appreciate being left alone to grieve".'

She nodded again, eyes brighter. Then the cops knocked.

I was lucky. I got an intelligent plainclothes cop straight off. He listened to me, wrote down my name and the number I gave him to ring, rang his station commander, gave him the number. The superior rang back inside five minutes, they exchanged a few words, the cop came over.

'That'll be in order, Mr Faraday. Mrs Vinovic's giving a statement in the sitting room. I'll take yours here.'

We heard the sound of a helicopter. 'Vultures here,' the man said. I looked out of the window. The helicopter was above Melanie's house, camera protruding like a gun.

It was dark before the circus was over. We stood in the sitting room. 'Helluva way to spend an afternoon,' I said. 'Anyway, it's over. Time to get moving.'

'A drink,' she said. 'Have a drink.' The high colour brought on by the television appearances was fading. She tried out the name. 'John.'

'I've got a long way to go.'

'Just a drink. One drink. What d'ya drink? Beer? I've got beer. Wine? Lots of wine. Bobo didn't drink anything except wine. All kinds of wine. There's a cellar y'know. Proper cellar. Bobo had to have a cellar.'

'Beer would be good.'

'Beer. I'll have a beer too. Don't often drink beer. Fattening. What the fuck.'

At six thirty, we watched the news on television. Melanie's house from the air, the voice-over. 'A thirty-two-year-old Shepparton woman and her de facto husband were found dead of gunshot wounds in their house outside the town today.'

We saw a lot of police coming and going and a young male reporter with receding hair identified the dead man as Barry James Field, twenty-seven, an unemployed building worker. Lee-Anne came on and said her dignified piece. The camera liked her.

'Good,' I said. 'Just right.'

'Police are treating the deaths as a murder–suicide,' the reporter said.

At eight o'clock, I rang Lew. 'I'm held up here,' I said. 'Back tomorrow.'

Lee-Anne came into the kitchen with a bottle of champagne. The heating was on high, she'd taken off the fluffy top to reveal a Club Med T-shirt strained to its limits, her colour was back. 'Perrier Something,' she said. 'Fucking case of it down there. All right, y'reckon?'

'I reckon.'

I opened it gently. I'd have to get a cab to a motel.

'Bobo had the cleaning contract at my work,' Lee-Anne said. 'Clean, clean, clean, it was like a religion. First place we lived in, rental, you won't believe this, he used to get in the roof with this industrial vacuum. Huge fucking thing, noise like a Boeing, suck a rat out of a drain.'

I poured. Lee-Anne drank half a glass.

'Dust in the ceiling. Couldn't bear the idea. Can you credit that? I mean, who cares you don't even know it's there? Mind you, look at this place now. Bobo'll be spinning.'

'Looks fine,' I said. Somehow I'd forgotten that we were twenty metres from a house where we'd found two people dead.

'Light's too bright.' She went to the door and turned a knob. 'Better. Dimmers in every room. Toilet, even. I thought dimmers were about bloody romance. Shouldn't talk like this about Bobo. Drove the ute under a semi outside Wang. Horror crash, the paper said. Could've posted it. What I want to know is what the fuck he's doing outside Wang when he tells me he's in Bendigo overnight, big cleaning contract coming up?'

Lee-Anne came back to her seat opposite me. She put her elbows on the counter, held out her glass and looked into my eyes. She was looking startlingly attractive. 'Bobo was number two. First was Steve. Don't even think about him. Photographer. Just a kid when I met him. Coburg girl. Very strict family. My God, strict. You don't know strict. You have to be Coburg Lebanese to know strict.'

I filled her glass, added Perrier Jouet to mine. Very good drop. Howard James Lefroy liked Perrier Jouet. Not the drink you'd expect to be having outside Shepparton on a freezing night in June, wind coming up outside, silver foil insulation on the unfinished wall vibrating like a drum skin, blood still on the tiles in the shaky weatherboard next door.

'Not that it kept you fucking pure,' said Lee-Anne. She put her hands on the counter. They were good hands, long fingers, nails not painted. 'Not when you met a photographer. Called himself a photographer. Not what a lot of people called him.'

Lee-Anne put an arm up her T-shirt to adjust her bra. I was hypnotised.

'Wedding pictures. Half the time they didn't come out. Whole fuckin weddings, excuse me. Vanished like they never happened. Steve was always on the run from fathers, brothers, uncles. I donta wanta my money back, I wanta my daughter's pictures, watta fuck you do with them? Not a street he could walk in safety, Steve, that many people lookin for him.'

We opened another bottle of the French. It seemed to last five minutes.

'Listen, Lee-Anne,' I said. 'Reckon we can get a taxi out here? Take me to a motel?'

She put her glass down, got up, took off her T-shirt, threw it over her shoulder, put her hand behind her back, unclipped her virgin-white bra, tossed it away. It landed in the sink.

'I don't suppose you'd have a spare bed,' I said, mouth dry.

'It's been four years,' she said, coming around the counter. 'I've still got Bobo's condoms.'

In the night, she woke me and asked, 'You seen dead people before?'

What do you say?

I left before dawn, kissed her on the mouth.

The title of Melanie Pavitt's handwritten autobiography promised more than it delivered. It didn't go beyond the age of thirteen. She stopped in the middle of a page with the words: *I did not see Mum again. I herd she went to Perth with a man but I dont no if its true. She never loved me so it dosent matter.*

All the letters except one were from a man called Kevin, written from Darwin and Kalgoorlie, never more than a page: weather, job, miss you, love. The most recent one was five years old.

The other letter was brief, too, in a sloping female hand, signed by someone called Gaby, dated 12 July 1995. No address. It read:

Mel!!! You rememberd my Mums adress!!! She sent the letter to me here in Cairns. Im living here with a man called Otto, hes a German mechanic and very nice and kind altho a bit old. Still you cant have everything can you. I was really shocked to see the things you wrote. The barstards shoud be locked up!!! You are pretty lucky to be

188

alive I reckon, its like those backpackers mudered near Sydney, Otto new one of them, a girl. Id never have said that Ken woud do something like that, they are people you are suposed to be abel to trust!!! I suppose they think there money makes it alrite. Now you now where I am come and stay, theres lots of room. Otto wont mind. Its hot all year here. To warm a lot. Write soon.

Love Gaby.

I read the letter twice.

Ken?

That was the name Dot Walsh said the naked girl in Colson's Road had said over and over.

. . . saying the name Ken over and over again.

I read Gaby's letter a third time. I was in the kitchen, sitting near the fired-up stove, but I felt a chill, as if a window had been opened, letting in a gust of freezing air.

I opened the stove's firebox and fed in the letters from Kevin. If he was Melanie's killer, he was probably going to go unpunished, courtesy of me. Then I went out and got the Kinross Hall records. They listed a girl called Gabriele Elaine Makin, age sixteen, at Kinross Hall at the same time as Melanie Pavitt in 1985.

I found the staff list and went through it. No Ken.

At least two people knew who Ken was and what

happened on the night Sim Walsh, World War II fighter pilot and drunk, found Melanie Pavitt naked in Colson's Road.

One of them was dead, one bullet through the left eye from a .38 Ruger from at least two metres away. If my judgment was worth anything, Melanie Pavitt had not been shot by her boyfriend, Barry James Field, unemployed building worker. Lee-Anne described Barry as a calm, sensible person who was the best thing that had ever happened to Melanie. He also seemed an unlikely owner of a weapon the cops had in ten minutes identified as stolen from a Sydney gun shop in 1994.

The other person who knew what happened to Melanie in 1985 was Gaby Makin.

I went over to the pub and rang inquiries. Then I rang Berglin. I gave them my name, we went through the rigmarole and they connected me.

'Wanting to ask you,' he said without preamble. 'What is it with you and dead people?'

'Raised the subject of Bianchi?' I could see Flannery at the bar, hunched, staring into a glass of beer, just a shadow of Saturday's hero.

'I mentioned it, yes.'

'So what's going to happen?'

'Don't think it's going on the priority list.'

'It should.'

Berglin sighed. 'Mac, listen. We talked about this before. Things blow up on you, it happens. The smack lost, the woman in the wrong place. Lefroy, that was a plus. Nailed him, he'd own the whole fucking prison system now, living like King Farouk, meals from Paul Bocuse, hot and cold running bumboys. Do a line anytime he likes. You've got another life now. Forget about the shit. Any brains, if I had them, I'd ask you can I join you out there in chilblain country, making candle-sticks, whatever the fuck it is you do.'

I let the subject lie. 'I need another trace.'

'Jesus, I don't know about you.' Pause. 'Who?'

I spelled it out: Gabriele Elaine Makin, born Frankston 1967, juvenile offender last known in Cairns. Not in the phone book.

'Hope she survives your interest in her,' Berglin said. 'Don't call me.'

'Something else.'

Silence.

I changed my mind. I had been going to ask about Bianchi's widow.

'Forget it, not important.'

'I'm glad.'

I went to the bar and sat down next to Flannery.

'I like the next day more when we lose,' he said. 'Whole week more. I don't think we should win again this Satdee.'

'Three in a row?' I said. 'In another life.'

'Beer's on the house,' Vinnie the publican said. 'Few more Satdees like that, I'm takin the place off the market.'

'Didn't know it was on the market,' Flannery said.

'Pub without pokies?' Vinnie said. 'Pokieless pub is on the market.'

'Tabletop dancers,' Flannery said. 'That's the go. Uni girls shakin their titties, showin us the business. Have a pickin-up-the-spud competition.'

Vinnie looked over to where two elderly male customers were grumbling at each other. 'Tabletop dancers? Need a bloody ambulance on standby outside. Mind you, that fuckin' cook'll need an ambulance if he doesn't come in the door in two minutes.'

When the cook arrived, Flannery and I ate steak and onion sandwiches. From where we were sitting, I could see the wet road and the entrance to my lane. I was washing down the last bite when Allie's truck turned in. We had work to do on the gateposts.

I woke early, stood in the shower thinking about the heft of Lee-Anne's breasts, the sight of Allie naked. Then I thought about being fifteen, digging out rotten stumps from grey rock and unyielding clay, face down in fifty centimetres of damp and cold crawl space, breathing the dank, dead air under a farmhouse near Yass. Crawling out, hearing footsteps on the boards above me, turning over and looking up through a gap between old floorboards, parched boards, tongues shrunk, parted from their grooves, unmated. Seeing from below a woman, a naked woman, mature woman, my eyes going up the sturdy legs, parted legs, pink from the bath, seeing at the junction the secret hair, the dark, curly, springy, water-beaded hair that marked the place, the little folds of belly, the plump wet undersides of breasts, a glimpse of chin, of nose. Of seeing her move her buttocks against a towel, run it over her breasts, breasts swaying, long nipples, of seeing her open her legs, wipe the towel casually between the thighs, wipe the dark, intimate folds of skin . . .

Time for breakfast. I was sitting in a patch of

weak sunlight eating breakfast, grilled bacon and a poached egg, when the phone rang. It was Berglin.

'That inquiry,' he said. 'Party's no longer with us. Motor accident in 1993, dead on arrival.'

I swallowed my mouthful. 'Sure about that?'

There was silence, then he said, 'As sure as one can be on the basis of the information supplied and the absence on all available records of anyone else with identical particulars. Yes.'

'Sorry. Thanks.'

'One more thing. The person in the Vatican we spoke of. You with me?'

'Yes.'

'Extremely resistant on a number of grounds to revisiting the matter in question.'

'So?'

'So the future of this course of action is uncertain.'

I went back to my breakfast. A cloud extinguished the sunlight like a door closing on a lit room.

When I'd finished, I got Gaby Makin's letter out again. It was dated 12 July 1995.

Written from beyond the grave. Either that or Berglin was lying to me. Everything was starting to remind me of the old days.

I drove into town and consulted the Cairns Yellow Pages. I tried the Mercedes dealership first, asking for the workshop.

'Have you got a mechanic called Otto?' I said. 'German?'

'Otto the Hun. Otto Klinger. Not any more. He's at Winlaton Motors in Brissy. Couple of years now. Miss him, too.'

He gave me a number.

The workshop office at Winlaton Motors got Otto Klinger on the line inside a minute.

'Ja, Klinger,' he said.

'Otto, I'm a friend of Gaby Makin . . .'

'Gaby and I are no longer together,' Otto said. 'She has gone with another person.'

'I heard she was killed in a car accident in 1993.'

'Gaby? Incorrect. She has only gone approximately one year.'

'Any idea where?'

'No. It is no concern of mine.'

'Do you know anyone who would know?'

Otto sighed. 'I suppose her girlfriend down the road would know. This is important, yes?'

'Otto,' I said, 'it could be a matter of life and death, yes.'

He sighed again. 'Give me a number for you and I will speak to the woman today if I can find her.'

I gave him a name and number. On the way home, I thought about how I'd got Melanie Pavitt's address from Berglin. Would Melanie be alive now if I hadn't? It wasn't a thought I wanted to entertain. Why would Berglin lie to me about Gaby? He had never heard of Kinross Hall until I rang him to trace Melanie.

But, before that, why had Marcia lied to me about Ian Barbie and Ned?

Allie was dampening the green coal in the forge when I came in the door. The dog was watching her. She was wearing jeans, a leather apron and one of her shirts with canvas sleeves.

'Okay to fire it when you're not here?' she said. 'We didn't discuss that.'

I gave the question some thought. It had meaning. Significance. 'You mean, can you play with my toy when I'm not here. Is that it?'

'Pretty much,' she said. 'I should have raised it. Some smithies are like petrolheads, only the forge is the car. One vehicle, one driver. One toy, one boy.'

'The toy can be played with,' I said. 'Day and night. And the bits in between.'

She gave me her slow, one-sided smile. 'Day'll be fine. I've got till four. Reckon we can get these giant wangers out of the way?'

We finished the things just before three pm, no feeling of achievement, just relief. I made corned beef and cheese sandwiches and we ate them sitting on the office step, reading bits of the paper, not saying much.

'That vet,' I said. 'Rottweiler or Jack Russell?'

Allie frowned. 'Labrador, it turned out. Nice but not too bright.'

'Sometimes,' I said, standing up and taking her plate, 'that's what you want in a dog.'

She looked up at me from under her straight eyebrows. 'Maybe it's a mongrel I'm looking for.'

'Flannery's between engagements.'

'Then again, maybe it's not. Do we have to deliver these monstrosities?'

'No. Spared that. He's picking them up. Feel like a beer later?'

She pulled a face. 'Would be good but I'm heading way over the other side of town. Tomorrow?'

I suddenly remembered it was Friday. Football tomorrow. No, thank God, we had a bye. 'Tomorrow.'

'I'll ring,' she said.

I worked on a chef's knife until the drink called. Mick Doolan and Flannery were at the bar.

'Tactics, Moc, we're talkin tactics,' Mick said. 'Just a couple more wins and we'll be bookin a finals berth. Wouldn't that be grand?'

Flannery groaned. 'Extra games,' he said. 'We'll be playin on cortisone. Can they test for that?'

I was watching the Saints beating the Eagles in Perth when the phone rang.

'Klinger,' Otto said. 'This stupid girlfriend of Gaby's wishes to telephone Gaby and to tell her why you wish to speak with her, and to get permission to give you Gaby's telephone number. I think she thinks that it is I who wishes to find out Gaby's number. That is a very foolish thing to think, I can tell you.'

'Thanks, Otto. Can you tell the friend I want to talk to Gaby about someone called Melanie Pavitt.' I spelt the name.

'I will call again,' Otto said.

He rang back in twenty minutes.

'That is all okay. Here is Gaby's telephone number.'

I thanked him, wrote it down. It was in Victoria. I dialled it. A woman answered: 'Yes.' Wary.

'Tony Mason,' I said. 'I sent you the message through Otto. I'd like to talk to you about Melanie Pavitt.'

'What about her?'

'About her experiences after leaving Kinross Hall. Immediately after she left.'

She thought about this for a while. 'Who are you?' she said.

'Investigator for the Department of Community Services.'

'Why doesn't she tell you?'

Gaby didn't know that Melanie was dead. This wasn't the time to tell her.

'She has, but I'd like to talk to someone who was at Kinross at the same time and who heard about what happened directly from Melanie. It won't take long.'

'On the phone?'

'No. I'll come and see you. Or we can meet somewhere, whatever suits you.'

'Well,' she said, 'I suppose so. But I'm out in the country.'

'That's not a problem.'

I left long before dawn in the freezing and wet dark, trees stirring in the wind, huddled sheep caught by my lights on the bends. By 9.15 am I was in the high country, in Mansfield, eating a toasted egg-and-bacon sandwich and drinking black coffee. It was cold up here, hard light, pale-blue cloudless sky. The coffee shop was full of people on their way to ski, groups of rich-looking people: sleek but slightly hungover men, just edging pudgy; women with tight smiles and lots of blonde hair; vicious children, all snarls and demands, woken early for the trip. The women had a way of tossing their heads and flicking their hair from below with their fingertips as if it were tickling their necks. In the street, it was all four-wheel-drives, BMWs and Saabs.

I wasn't going towards Mount Buller. I was going north-east. On the way to Whitfield, following Gaby's instructions, I turned right onto a dirt road, turned again, again, thought I'd missed the place, found it, a brick, stone and weatherboard house, low, sprawling, expensive, a long way from the road, at the end of a long curving avenue of poplars, bare. Off to the right was a corrugated-iron barn and beyond that what looked like stables. Gaby had done well for herself.

Going through the gate either triggered something or sound travelled long distances in this air. A woman was waiting near the barn when I came around the final bend. She pointed to the road that led to the stables and turned to walk in that direction. She was big, tall, not fat yet, pale hair in a ponytail, dark glasses, sleeveless quilted jacket.

There was a house beyond the stables, an old stone building with a weatherboard extension. It said *Manager's House*. Gaby hadn't done as well as I'd thought. I parked next to a clean Toyota ute and got out.

Gaby took her dark glasses off. She was reaching the end of pretty, face not sure what to become. No make-up, eyes that had seen things. You wouldn't want to mess with her.

'Tony Mason,' I said, putting out my hand.

She shook, no grip, ladylike. No smile.

'Let's go inside,' she said. 'I have to be in town in an hour.'

She took off her boots at the front door. 'You don't have to,' she said. 'Been in the stables. You smell it in the warm.'

The house was warm, uncluttered, smelling pleasantly of something I couldn't recognise.

I followed her down a passage lit by two skylights into a sitting room full of light, foothills in the windows, pale grey hills beyond.

201

A baby cried, small sound, pulling power of a regimental bugle.

Gaby said. 'Feedin time. Sit down.' She was taking off her waistcoat as she left.

I sat down in the most upright chair in the room. She came back with something wrapped in a pink blanket, sat down opposite me, unbuttoned her checked shirt, fiddled and produced a breast, aureole the colour of milky instant coffee and the size of a small saucer. She revealed the baby's head. It was a big head, covered in fuzz.

'Never thought I'd just take out a tit in front of a stranger,' she said, no expression. The child ship docked with the mother ship. Gaby's expression softened.

'Well,' she said, little smile, not looking at me. 'Not just one tit anyway.'

I laughed. She looked at me, her smile opened and we were both laughing.

I said: 'Melanie's dead. I think she was murdered.'

The smile went. We sat in silence for a moment. Gaby had the look of someone who'd had a new and untrue and malicious charge levelled at her.

'Dead?'

I told her how.

She pulled the baby closer. 'You're not from the fucking department,' she said, matter-of-fact, not alarmed. 'That was all bullshit.'

'No,' I said. 'Gaby, I'm a friend of someone who

sometimes worked at Kinross. They're trying to shaft him with molesting girls.'

'Who?' she said.

'He was a handyman. Ned Lowey.'

She said, 'No, I never heard that. Barbie, yes.'

'Tell me about Melanie's letter. What happened to her?'

She shifted in the chair, adjusted the baby. 'Didn't keep the letter. She came to see me, y'know? In Cairns.'

'No, I didn't know.'

'Yeah. After the letter.' She tilted her head, thoughtful. 'How'd you get my letter?'

'I found it in her bedroom.'

'Before she . . .'

'After. I found the body. Me and the woman next door.'

She nodded.

'So she came to see you?'

'In Cairns. Stayed for a week. Was going to be longer. Otto started playin up, so she left.'

'You talked about what happened?'

'Yeah.'

'Someone called Ken was involved. Who's he?'

Gaby looked down at the suckling. 'I don't want to get in any trouble,' she said. 'Had enough trouble.'

'There'll be no trouble,' I said. 'No-one's going to hear anything you tell me.'

'Well.' She sighed. 'We were pretty pissed when she told me. Don't remember all that much.

203

Couldn't hear a lot of what she said anyway. Cryin and sniffin.'

'Ken,' I said. 'Who's he?'

'The doctor.'

'Dr Barbie?'

'Yeah.'

'Why do you call him Ken?'

'The dolls? Barbie and Ken. There was Barbie and Ken.'

'Right. Barbie and Ken. How was Ken involved?'

Gaby sighed again. 'Day Mel was leavin, he examined her. Said he was goin to Melbourne, he'd give her a lift, save her goin by train. Only she mustn't tell anyone cause he'd get into trouble. She thought he was a nice bloke. We all did. Anyway, they took her to the station and dropped her and Ken picked her up. Gave her a can of Coke.'

She stopped and fiddled with her breast, shifted the baby. 'Mel said she remembered drivin along, gettin dark. Next thing she woke up, she was bein dressed in schoolgirl clothes, y'know, a gym and that.'

'Who was doing that? Ken?'

'She wasn't sure. Two men. They did all kinds of sex things to her. Not normal, know what I mean? Tied her up. Hit her with something. Made her do things to them. She cried when she told me.'

'She saw their faces?'

'Not properly. They didn't hide their faces. That's why she knew they were going to kill her. But she didn't get a real good look at them. The room was dark and she felt dizzy. And they had a light in her eyes all the time.'

'She couldn't describe them at all?'

'Not really.'

'So one could have been Dr Barbie?'

'Well, he's the one gave her the Coke.'

'How'd she get away?'

'They went off. The one man goes, "Back soon, slut, with a friend for you. She's been looking forward to this."'

'She?'

'Yeah. She. Anyway, Mel's in this room, stone room, bars on the window, it's upstairs. There was a bed and she stood it up on its end, got on it and she ripped a hole in the ceiling. There was a small hole and she made it bigger. Got into the roof, pulled off some tiles and got out onto the roof and climbed down a drainpipe. Pretty incredible, hey? She's just a little thing but really strong. Barbie liked the little ones.' She stopped. 'She was. Really strong.'

'And she got away.'

'She said she ran for ages, like through some kind of forest. Pitch-dark and she was dead scared they were coming after her. She got to a road and she hid from cars. Then it was so cold she thought she'd die, so she started walking along the road. Naked. Then an old man stopped and took her to his house.'

'I know what happened from then,' I said.

I went over the story with her. There wasn't any

more to tell. Outside, cold a shock after the warm house, Gaby said, 'I don't want any trouble. Really. I've got a good bloke now and the baby.'

'Don't worry,' I said. 'You won't hear anything about this again. But if you remember anything else, ring me.'

I wrote my number on the back of an automatic teller machine receipt.

In the rear-view mirror, I saw her watching me go, standing in the universal stance of mothers, baby on hip, pelvis tilted, knees slightly bent. I thought, what right have I to give her any assurances?

The last person I had given assurances to was Carlie Mance.

Driving back, my mind drifted over what I knew and what I didn't know. The two men who assaulted Melanie could be the killers of the girl in the mine shaft. Who were they? Ian Barbie and someone else.

Barbie the delivery man. Had he delivered other Kinross Hall girls? How could he do that without the girls being reported missing?

And that raised the issue that I didn't much want to think about. Had my inquiry about Melanie led to her death? How could that be? I ask Berglin to trace someone and then I find the person shot dead. Melanie Pavitt, not shot dead in the messy way of domestic killings everywhere. No. Shot dead with fussy precision. One shot in the eye. Was this the work of her gentle unemployed builders' labourer? This I could not believe. Then Berglin lies to me about Gaby Makin. Why? What conceivable interest could Berglin have in my inquiries? He was a federal drug cop and drugs didn't seem to enter this puzzle.

Berglin lie to me? Of all the things he said to me over the years, when I thought of him, two sentences spoken in his hoarse voice at our first meeting always echoed in the mind: *How to be a halfway decent person. That's the main question in life.*

In the shitstorm after the Lefroy and Mance killings, when all fingers pointed at me, Berglin had been impassive. He never said the words I wanted him to say, never patted my arm, never invited me to confide in him. You could read nothing in his eyes. One morning, suspended from duty, wife gone, unshaven, hungover, I went to his office. He looked at me with interest while I shouted at him: abuse, recriminations, accusations of betrayal. When I ran out of things to say, Berglin said, no expression, 'Mac, if I think you've moved across, you'll be the first to know. I'll come around and kill you. Enjoy the vacation. Now fuck off.'

I left, feeling much better.

Now I'd have to see him, confront him with the lie he'd told me. I hoped very much that he could explain it away, but I couldn't see how.

I was still brooding on this as I drove down the damp and overgrown driveway at Harkness Park. Stan had rung to say that Francis wanted him to put on extra hands, presumably so that he could send out his bills sooner. Stan was reluctant: he didn't like big crews. I'd suggested that instead of bringing in more workers we draw up a work schedule that provided incentives for meeting targets early. Flannery and Lew liked the idea. They were to have spent the morning clearing the main path down the sightline. Stan had estimated hours for the job and I wanted to see how far they'd got.

They'd done well, pushing at least thirty metres beyond Stan's expectation, neat work, greenery piled ready for chipping. I was admiring the elaborate brick and cut stone path uncovered, thinking about where to establish the compost heaps, when I heard a vehicle in the driveway, just a hum. I didn't think about it, backed into the dense overgrown box hedge beside the path, looked back towards the house. A month earlier, I wouldn't have done this. Fear had come back into my life, uninvited.

I waited.

Anne Karsh, hair pulled back today, jeans, battered short Drizabone, looking around. I stepped out of hiding. We walked towards each other down the path, eyes meeting, looking away, coming back.

'Checking on progress,' I said when we were close enough.

'You or me?'

'Both?'

'No, not me,' she said. She smiled. 'Just wanted to be here, really. In love with it. What were you doing in the hedge? If that's a hedge.'

'Hedge examination. How about this path?'

'This is an unbelievable path. It's so ornate.'

I turned and we walked to the edge of the known garden. Beyond was wilderness. 'It's like archaeology,' she said. 'For the first time, I can understand the thrill.'

'Thrill time next week,' I said. 'The pines come down. Then we see the steeple. See what the man wanted us to see.'

'Who cuts them down?' We were on our way back.

'A professional. The biggest one's nine metres around at the base. Death to amateurs. We could bring in a portable sawmill, turn them into planks. You could have something made out of them. Terrible waste otherwise. All those years of growing.'

She looked at me. 'Leon'll like that. Could you do it?'

'If you tell Francis that's what you want.'

She held out her right hand. We stopped. 'I'll tell him now.' She took out a small leatherbound book, found a page, took a mobile telephone, minute, from another pocket, punched numbers. After a short wait, she said. 'Francis, Anne Karsh . . . Well, thank you. Francis, the pines blocking the view to the church steeple are coming down next week. Can you arrange to have them turned into usable timber? . . . Leon will be thrilled. Stan will arrange it, I'm sure. Thank you, Francis . . . I look forward to that too. Bye.'

We walked, explored the thicket around the site of the original house, forced our way through to the old orchard, desperate-looking fruit trees but the least overgrown place because of the deep mulch of fallen fruit.

'You can prune these buggers back to life,' I said. 'If you want them.'

'I want them,' she said. 'I want everything the way it was.'

I looked at her.

'I've got a flask of coffee,' Anne said. A thorn had scratched her cheekbone, delicate serration, line of blood like the teeth of a tiny saw. 'Drink coffee?'

'Got enough?'

'I've got enough.'

The Mercedes boot held a wicker basket with a stainless-steel flask and stainless-steel cups. We sat side by side on the front steps of the house, huge, dangerously aged poised portico above us, drinking coffee, talking about the garden. She had an easy manner, sense of humour, no hint of rich lady about her. A weak sun emerged, touched her hair.

'Nice,' she said.

'Good coffee.'

'The day, the place, the moment.'

'Those too.'

We didn't look at each other, something in the air. Then our eyes met for a moment.

'Mr Karsh working today?' I said, regretted the question.

'No. He's in Noosa for the weekend. His new girlfriend goes to Noosa for the winter.'

I looked at her. 'I understand it's wall-to-wall girlfriends in Noosa.'

She leaned sideways, studied me, smiled a wry smile. 'I've been a girlfriend. There's no moral high ground left for me.'

'Not for any of us,' I said.

'Leon's a charming person,' she said. 'His problem is chronic envy. Non-specific envy. His greatest fear is that he's missing something, that there's something he should be doing, that there's something he doesn't know about or hasn't got that will make him happy and complete. If he saw a man leading a duck down the road on a piece of string and looking at peace, Leon would send someone out to buy a duck and give it a try for fifteen minutes. Then he'd say, fuck this duck, why's that woman on the bicycle look so pleased?'

'Why did you?'

'What?'

'Look so pleased?'

'So,' Anne said. 'Blacksmiths are not without insight. I worked for a merchant bank that was hired by a company to fight off a takeover bid by one of Leon's companies. Very messy business, went on for months, working seventeen, eighteen hours a day, seven days. One Sunday I got home and my husband had gone off with my best friend. Anyway, we fought off Leon and we had a no-hard-feelings drink with the other side and Leon showed up. I think he then began to see me as a substitute for the company he couldn't have. Anything Leon can't have leaps in value in his eyes.'

'So he took you over.'

She smiled. 'Well, as I said, he's a charming person. He has the gift of charm. It was a totally uncontested takeover. But as I found out, for Leon, you conquer the peak, another peak beckons. More coffee?'

'Just a drop.'

'There's plenty.' She poured. 'That's me. And I'm not complaining. What about you?'

'My wife didn't like my hours either.'

'Blacksmiths work long hours?'

'Pre-blacksmith.' I stood up. 'Time to go. Thanks for the coffee.'

She stood up too. Standing on the step above me put her eyes level with mine. We looked at each other. 'Let me know when you'd like to see the mill,' I said.

Anne nodded. 'Can you give me a number?' She wrote it in her leather-bound book.

'Well,' I said. 'See you soon then.'

She put out a hand and straightened my shirt collar, pulled her hand back. 'Thank you,' I said. I thought she blushed a little.

'Terrible urge to straighten pictures,' she said. 'I'll call you. Next week.'

I drove home in the waning day. Towering dark clouds on all horizons made it seem as if I were crossing a valley floor. It was dark by the time I stopped outside the Heart of Oak to see if Flannery was there. He wasn't.

'Car went in your drive just before dark,' Vinnie said.

I left the vehicle where it was, walked up the road, climbed the paddock gate in the far corner and crossed the sodden field so that I could come at the house from the back, from behind the smithy.

The caller was still there: a car was parked in front of the office. I went across the gravel, slowly, my gravel, gravel put down so that I could hear it crunch. All senses on high-beam, I looked into the kitchen window.

Something touched my leg. I froze.

The dog, puzzled.

Inside, Lew was feeding the stove. He turned and said something to someone out of my field of view. The person laughed.

I let out my pent-up breath and opened the back door.

Berglin was in my favourite chair, long shoes on the table, cigarette dangling from a hand.

'MacArthur John Faraday,' he said. 'Home is the hunter.'

There was no other way to do this. 'Lew,' I said, 'I need to talk to this gentleman alone.' When he'd gone, I said, 'You lied to me.'

'Come again?' Berglin's eyebrows went up in the middle.

'That trace. Gabriele Makin.'

'Yeah. Dead.'

'Not dead. Undead. Not a million fucking kilometres from here.'

He blew smoke towards me, eyes narrowed. 'You sure?'

'Of course I'm fucking sure.'

'How'd you find her?'

'Phone book. What the fuck did you use?'

'Contractor.'

'Why?'

He blew smoke. 'Why? I'm going to put some personal request through the system? I'm going to do that? I put that Melanie Pavitt through the system, Canberra'd be asking me why I wanted to find a person turns up dead. Make sense to you? Fresh air's slowing the brain out here.'

'Who's the contractor?'

Berglin mashed his cigarette into the ashtray Lew had found for him. 'It's my worry. I'll talk to him. Believe me, I'll talk to him.'

From nowhere the thought came to me. 'Alex Rickard,' I said. 'You're using Alex Rickard.'

Berglin was lighting another cigarette, lighter poised. He lowered it. 'I'll stand on the cunt's head,' he said. 'We'll know why in quick time.'

'What about a beer?' I said, slack with relief. Not Berglin to blame but Alex Rickard.

'Thought you'd never ask.'

I opened two Boags, found two glasses, sat down at the table.

Berglin took a big draught from the bottle. 'Listen,' he said, 'two reasons I'm out here in the fucking tundra. One is, from your time on the Lefroy fuck-up, the name Algie mean anything?'

'Algae? As in blue-green slime?'

'Don't know. Could be. Not likely. Could be A-L-G-I-E. Could be two parts: Al G, like a first name and a surname initial. Maybe Al Gee.'

'No. Never heard it. It's someone's name?'

'Calls himself that, yeah.'

'How's this come up?'

'Run-through last night, Bulleen of all fucking places. Nothing's sacred. Person we had an interest in last year. Local jacks turned over this low-level garbage in Footscray, he tells them this weed bloke's grown overnight. Now he's a smack supplier, found some fucking original channel – big, not your arse full of condoms at all. Scully's cockbrains wire the place up like a recording studio, move in across the road. Nothing to report. So they say. Stereo-quality farting, got the man mango-kissing his sister-in-law, very vocal perform-ance, that's about it. Waste of public money.'

He drank some more beer. 'This is good,' he said, looking at the bottle. 'The pointyheads can make beer. Anyway, subject closed until last night. Then the serene Bulleen household is severely disrupted. Man alone at home, wife at the Chadstone shop-ping centre. He's beaten, badly knocked about, teeth dislodged, flogged. Worse. Throat cut.' He paused. 'Don't say anything, the thought occurs.'

We sat in silence for a few seconds. Berglin drank most of his beer, wiped his thin lips. I got out two more.

'Good dog,' he said. 'Now the reason for all this unpleasantness might have remained ob-scure, MacArthur. But for one thing. False wall in the back of the house, space about a metre between the kitchen and the laundry. Get into it through the ceiling. Up the ladder in the garage, through the inspection hole. Last night, half the fucking kitchen wall kicked in.'

Berglin put out the cigarette, more gently this time, found another one, looked at it, put it down on the table. 'Christ knows what these cunts went off with,' he said, 'but they left behind, down there in a corner, up against the plasterboard, a quarter kilo of outstanding, medal-winning-purity product. Melbourne Show quality.'

217

'How come?'

'Just bad light, they reckon. Pricks in a hurry, got plenty, never saw it.'

'Algie,' I said. 'Where's that come in?'

'The wife says, she is a very scared person, that the deceased said to another man, person she doesn't know, she was near them in a public place, he said, "Algie's on, the lot".'

'That's it?'

'She heard that. Algie.'

'Four words. What public place? Street? Shopping centre? Lots of noise?'

'Noisy, but Algie, yeah. She says, she said to him in the car, who's Algie? He said, just a bloke I'm doing business with.'

'Could have been clearing his throat. Said it fast? *Algiesonthelot*. Native English speakers these Bulleen people?'

'Since your departure,' said Berglin, 'we find ourselves bereft of ideas. But we stumble on. He's Turkish, old man's a Turk. We've run Algie by umpteen Turks. More Turks than Gallipoli. Doesn't make sense in Turkish.'

'But it's come up before.'

'What?' He was studying the beer bottle again.

'Algie. Algie – the word in question.'

He shrugged. 'It's been around.'

'Around? Well, familiar word. Algie. Since when? Since before Lefroy?'

'No. That's why I'm here. Asking you.'

'So when's it come up? How long after Lefroy?'

'Not long. Soon. On some drug bug, these spiders are talking. Appears to be about Lefroy. The one says, heard it was Algie.'

'I've never heard that,' I said. 'How come I don't know that?'

'Mac, no-one needs to know everything.'

'What does that mean? Exactly?' I said.

'What it says.'

I took a deep breath. 'Soon after Lefroy I had a definite need to know about anything like that, Berg,' I said. 'But moving on, you're here because you're in some kind of shit, second Lefroy-style run-through, new boys in Canberra think it's time you kicked on to that block at Batemans Bay. That it?'

'Third,' said Berglin.

'Third?'

'Third Lefroy-style run-through. There's lots of them go on but not killing. Three years ago, we had two Chinese blokes, property investment advisors for Hong Kong syndicates, that's the story. Rent a flat in St Kilda, ground floor, beachfront, big flat, four bedrooms, gold taps, that sort of thing. They come and go, Hong Kong, Taiwan, Bangkok, Hawaii, Sydney, Brisbane. Never stop for more than a few days, real estate people show them around buildings. Hong Kong clears them, Scully's people give them a clean bill. Operation terminated. I had a bad feeling, but we couldn't go on without the local jacks.'

Berglin lit his cigarette. 'About eighteen months ago, the lady lives upstairs looks down from her balcony, sees a pool of blood on the balcony below.

From under the door. It's all tiles, inside and out. Blood runs free. She calls jacks. Chinese bloke's taped up, throat cut.'

He looked at me in silence for a while.

'What?' I said.

'Woman there too. A hooker. In the bathroom. Same treatment as the bloke. And worse. Much worse. We kept the details quiet.'

I swallowed. 'This means what?'

He shrugged. 'Don't know. Stuff, money, probably money. Pick-up, pay off. Someone knew.'

'Algie?'

'Yesterday was a big day for shit floating up. There was another hooker these Chinese blokes liked. Hired by the day on other visits. Woman called Lurleen. We couldn't ever find her. Yesterday she rings a number we gave this other hooker, her friend, back then, Lurleen's back in town and she's scared. I had a little walk and talk with her. Guess what?'

'No.'

'She's in the flat too on the night. She's got a key, been there all afternoon. Now she's in the kitchen, hears the doorbell, hears the Chinese open the door, he says something and then she hears him scream. She doesn't fuck around, knows shit when she hears it coming, out the door to the garage, gone. Next day she reads the bit in the paper, moves interstate. Wollongong. She reckons anyone looking for her, they won't look there. I reckon she's right.'

'How does she help?'

'Algie,' Berglin said. 'That's what the Chinese

said at the front door. He said, "You are Algie?" A question.'

'She heard that from the kitchen?'

'He had a high voice, the Chinese, she says. Clear voice. And there was a half-open door to the hallway and the sitting room. Open-plan place.'

'You give her the name before she told you what she heard?'

'Don't be a dork. This woman's kosher. Lefroy and the Chinese, same visitors. And if this Algie in Bulleen is Lefroy's Algie . . .'

I finished my beer, fetched two more. 'So that would just about get you to the second thing that brings you here,' I said.

'Yes,' said Berglin. 'Bianchi and Mance at the pub in Deer Park. You need to tell me who told you that.'

'No,' I said. 'My telling days are over. Anyway, person can't take it any further. Just heard it.'

Berglin nodded, drank some beer, scratched his head. 'Need a pee,' he said. 'Let's go outside. I like an open-air pee when I'm in the country. Pee, a cigarette and a look around. The stockman's breakfast.'

We went into the night, over to the paddock fence and pissed on the weeds.

'Wouldn't want to expose the pork out here too long,' Berglin said. 'Lose it to frostbite. Listen, should be clear to you if Mance was playing both you and Bianchi, the idea came from Scully. Bianchi was just a cockbrain, messenger, fetch the hamburgers, get us a pie.'

'And then,' I said, 'you have to begin to think the unthinkable.'

He zipped his fly. 'A possibility, no more.'

'Here's another possibility. Three separate surveillance operations, three targets dead, stuff gone. And it's all got nothing to do with the surveillance.'

'Odds higher there,' Berglin said. 'It gives me the same worry you had and that makes doing anything very difficult.'

'And I hear the surveillance records vaporised.'

Berglin looked at me, head tilted. 'For a bloke way out of the loop, you hear a lot.'

'What about the spring cleaning after I left?'

'Did that, but houses get dirty again. Christ, let's get inside.'

At the back door Berglin stopped, tapped my arm, took out a cigarette. 'Mrs Bianchi, she went on protection, new name, new everything, new tits even if I read the expenses right. Got a bloke looking for her now, reliable bloke, one hundred per cent, reports only to me. He says he's warm. We find her, you want to talk to her?'

'You know an expression I always hated in the old days?' I said. 'The loop. Well, I don't want to be back in the loop.'

Berglin lit the cigarette, flame cupped, eyes narrow in the flare. 'This loop is you and me, Mac,' he said. 'You don't come into it, you want to think about sending that nice young fella away, put the dog in the kennels, sleep under the bed with the big gun. The old days aren't over yet.'

Alex Rickard was a creature of habit and that is not a wise thing to be when people you may not want to see want to see you. The habit meant he would be at Flemington Racecourse on Wednesday afternoon. On another day, it might have been Moonee Valley or Caulfield. What was certain was that on a Wednesday afternoon Alex would be at the city races.

I got there early and found a place where I could watch the turnstiles. It wasn't going to be hard to spot Alex in the crowd. There wasn't a crowd, just a trickle of depressed-looking men in jail-release clothes. Ten minutes before the first race, Alex and a short, bald man in a raincoat who looked like Elmer Fudd came through. Alex raised the standard of dress by a few hundred points. He was very Members' Enclosure: grey flannels, a grey tweed sports jacket, blue shirt, red tie.

The pair stopped off for a quick hot dog and read their race books. Elmer Fudd had two quick hot dogs. He talked a lot, waving the race book and the hot dogs around. Alex found him amusing, smiling as he ate, and then carefully wiped his lips and hands on the little paper napkin.

I kept a good distance from them in the betting ring. They favoured different bookies. Alex knew his firm well: he got a pat on the arm from the man with the laptop computer and the slip writer whispered something in his ear. Alex had a good laugh, Fudd came over and the pair went onto the grandstand. I found something to lean against and settled in.

After the first race, the two came down, pleased with themselves, visited their bookies. Same after the second race, not as pleased now. It was going to be difficult to talk to Alex if he went everywhere with Fudd.

I almost missed Alex after the third race. He was alone and I was looking for the pair of them.

He wasn't going to his bookie this time. When I realised he was heading for the toilets, I picked up speed, got too close to him, prayed he wouldn't look around.

But he didn't. And there was more luck in the toilet. Only one cubicle door was closed and Alex was alone at the urinal, in the right-hand corner, getting his prick out.

He didn't see me coming.

I ran the three steps, slammed him into the stainless steel with my left shoulder, punched him in the kidneys three times, one full shot with everything, two short chops.

Alex made a vomiting noise and sagged. I held

him up by his left shoulder, took a handful of his smooth hair at the crown and smashed his head into the wall several times.

I let him go and he dropped to his knees. There was blood on the stainless steel at head height. I put a knee between his shoulder blades and jerked his head back by his long front lock until he was looking up into my eyes.

'Alex,' I said. 'Didn't keep my inquiry confidential. Who'd you tell? Quick, they'll find you dead here.'

He opened his mouth wide. Blood from his forehead ran into it and he coughed, spraying red onto the stainless steel. 'No, Mac, no . . .'

I heard a sound behind me. A tall man with black rimmed glasses had come out of one of the cubicles.

'Back in the dunny or I'll kill you,' I said.

He went back like a film in reverse. The lock clicked.

'Quickly, Alex,' I said, banged his head against the urinal again. Blood dropped onto the white disinfectant balls in the trough.

'Mac, no . . .'

I banged his head again, took his ears in my hands, small ears, not easily grasped, and began to twist them off. It was difficult. They were slippery.

'Last chance, Alex. Who?'

'Bobby Hill,' he said, barely audible. 'Didn't think it mattered, thought you were out of it.'

I let go of his ears, pulled his head back by the hair, strong hair, and looked into his eyes from close range. 'Alex,' I said, 'who told you to tell Berglin that Gaby Makin was dead?'

'I'm dead.'

I bounced his head off the urinal again, once, twice, blood spattering. 'Right, you prick,' I said. 'Dead now if you don't tell me.'

Alex groaned. I gave him one more smash. Harder.

'Bobby.'

'Why? Quick.' I pulled his head back again.

'Anything you or Berglin wanted to know, pass it on.'

'Listen carefully, Alex,' I said, jerking his head back again so that he could look at me. 'You're a little man in deep shit. Tell Bobby Hill you've told me, Bobby kills you. Then I dig you up and kill you. Repeatedly. Then it's Berglin's turn. No matter what happens, you tell Bobby, you die. Painfully. Understand me?'

I let him go. Alex's head hit the urinal again and he collapsed sideways, slowly. I pushed his head into the trough with my right foot and pressed the flush button. A gentle spray of water dampened his face and hair. Trickles ran down his bleeding forehead and the trough turned bright pink.

'"Let the water and the blood from his riven side which flowed be of sin the double cure",' I said. Was that the way it went? It just came to me.

Four men, different sizes, all wide-eyed, were blocking the passage.

'Gentlemen,' I said, 'an emergency. Need St John Ambulance here. This man has had a serious pissing accident.'

They flattened themselves against the walls. I passed between them, left the racecourse, went home, fed the dog, made supper, played Scrabble with Lew, got beaten again.

I was washing up, thinking: open another bottle, go to bed. Lew appeared in the door.

'Mac,' he said, moved his shoulders, looked at the floor. 'Think I'll go back to school. That's what Ned wanted.'

I looked at the boy: father unknown, mother unknowable, grandfather allegedly something I didn't want to think about. And nothing bad in this quiet and gentle person.

I wished I could hug him.

'I'll take you to the bus,' I said. 'That's easy.'

He did a ceiling examination.

'Down the road,' he said. 'The girl. They go in every day. I asked. Will you talk to the school? And tell Stan I'll work at weekends?'

'Sure. Talk to them tomorrow.' There was a new family down the road. I'd seen the girl on a horse from a distance. Perhaps both Ned and I and the girl all wanted Lew to go back to school. I had a feeling dawning about which one had had the deciding influence.

Before I went to bed, I put the Colt Python,

227

safety catch off, in a Blundstone boot next to the right back leg of the bed.

I lay on my back for a long time, thinking about Bobby Hill, thin and handsome Bobby Hill, straight dark hair combed back, metal-rimmed dark glasses. Of the trio of Scully, Hill and Bianchi, Hill had been the watchful one, little disbelieving smile never far from his lips. He was Scully's offsider but managed to give the impression without saying anything that pudgy Scully worked with him.

Bobby's making lots of money in the baboon hire business. Those were Brendan Burrows's words. What interest would Hill have in my Kinross Hall inquiries? Something Berglin once said came to mind: *He who says Hill says Scully.* Would that still be the case? Could it be Scully who was interested in me? I was history, he was about to be made deputy commissioner.

Was I history? What had Berglin said?

The old days aren't over yet.

Not a thought to fall asleep on.

I dreamt I was in the old factory in Footscray, Dr Barbie's point of exit. It was cold, dark in the corners spreading out. I was walking from cavernous space to cavernous space, looking for something in the gloom, uneasy. I pushed open a huge sliding door and I was in a room filled with light, the ceiling seemed to glow, one huge skylight. People were standing in groups, talking and drinking, laughing. The nearest group had their backs to me. As I approached, one by one they turned, smiling, greeting me: my father, that shy smile, Ned, Alex, forehead bloody, Brendan Burrows, Berglin, Scully, Hill, Bianchi, Lefroy. The group parted and Carlie Mance appeared, radiant, took my arm, tucked it under hers. We walked together to the centre of the chamber and she pointed. A body, elongated, was dangling from the roof, slowly turning. I waited, full of dread, to see the face. It came around slowly, slowly, familiar profile . . .

I woke, sweating, still filled with the dream's apprehension. Just like the old days, I thought.

It was almost five am. I got up, no point in

staying in bed, washed my face, revved up the kitchen stove, made a pot of tea, read *The Plant Hunter* till it was time to shower, cook, eat and start work. Today was committed to finishing Frank Cullen's contraption, long overdue. But Frank was a patient man. He never hurried the realisation of his inventions because it gave him time to think about modifications. Not big ones: tweaks of the brilliant concept.

I was tidying up the welds with the anglegrinder when Allie arrived. I switched off and lifted the helmet. She knew about the contraption.

'What I don't understand,' she said, 'is why you wouldn't simply put whatever it is you want to load onto the back of the ute. Why would you put it on this thing and haul it up with a winch?'

'The idea, as I understand it, and I may be utterly wrong here, is that you can take this thing where utes fear to go. Reach the parts ordinary utes cannot reach. Then you haul it back and wham! It's on board.'

She rolled her eyes. 'Haul it back? How much cable is there going to be?'

'Brilliant idea or scrapmetal in the making,' I said, 'the man doesn't blink at the bill, writes out the cheque right here in front of me, very neat and legible hand, and the bank doesn't blink either. Which is a lot more that can be said for many of our clients.'

'Which is why I'm glad I don't have to send out my own bills anymore.'

'Not gladder than I am,' I said. 'Listen, this extensive training of yours equip you to make a knife blade?'

'You don't have to be a Rhodes scholar,' she said, 'to make a blade. All you have to do is take pains.'

I put up my gloved hand. 'Point taken, to the hilt. I'm weeks behind with the knives. Fit it in? I'll show you what's needed.'

'Let's look at the diary,' she said. 'Has to be time this week.'

I was fitting the wheels when Frank Cullen and Jim Caswell arrived, today in full squatter's uniform. Jim took his seat on the bench, Frank came over to inspect the work.

'Nice wheels, Mac,' Frank said. 'Where'd you get 'em?'

'Place in town sells bearings,' I said. 'Cost a fair bit.'

'Quality,' Frank said. 'Remembered when price is forgotten.'

'Very true,' I said. 'Motto of this workshop.'

'Now these tracks,' Frank said. 'Bin givin 'em some thought, woke up this mornin with the answer.' He took a folded piece of paper from his shirt pocket and carefully opened it. 'This diagram shows what I've come up with.'

I looked at it. The tracks now had angled projections at each end.

'Beauty of it,' Frank said, 'is these top bits. They slide into these housings you bolt to the tray. What d'ya think?'

231

'Like all the best ideas,' I said, 'you wonder why you didn't think of it earlier.'

Frank took a seat, lit a cigarette, had a good cough.

'Don't know how you can do it,' Jim said, shaking his head.

'Do what?' Frank said.

'Smoke. You know what the doctor said.'

'Bloody doctors,' Frank said. 'What do they know? Know buggerall, that's why they blame the fags. Could be somethin else entirely. Could be— could be bloody potatoes kills ya. Carrots. I read where everybody in China smokes, from babies upwards, they don't bloody die any more than anyone else. Look at that Mao Tsebloodytung, used to smoke in his sleep, couldn't get him to die. Same with the other bloke, whatsisname, thingummy, shot them students, eighty fags a day, still runnin the place at ninety, whatever.'

'The Veenes,' I said. 'What do you know about the Veenes?'

'Veenes,' Frank said. 'Don't talk to me about Veenes. I know Veenes. Worked for bloody old Clarrie Veene, the most miserable bastard ever to walk God's earth, bar none. Used to look at you like you were a sick dog he wouldn't waste a bullet on, kill it with a spade. Little bastard used to come up to me, didn't reach my top button, course I was six-three then . . .'

'You were never six-three,' Jim said.

'You bloody dwarf, what would you know? You

232

couldn't see that high. Come up to me, the old bastard, wasn't all that old then either, come right up to me, under me nose, say something like, whining bloody voice, "Cullen, when you going to do something about that slate you're running over at Meagher's?" Coulda killed him right there, one blow.'

'A Veene had some land near Milstead,' I said. 'Pine forest now.'

'That was Ernest's,' Frank said. 'Clarrie's brother. Another miserable bastard. Went to his son. Donald.'

'Some Melbourne company owns it now,' I said.

'Rick Veene's got a share in the company,' Frank said. 'Heard that. He's Donald's boy. Looks a lot like Ernest. Rick's tied up with that Stefanidis from over near Daylesford. RSPCA went there, heard he was shooting pigeons. Bloke behind a wall throws 'em in the air, Greek shoots 'em with a twelve bore from about four yards. Sticks it up their arses practically. Couldn't prove it. Not a feather to be found.'

'What's on the land apart from trees?'

'Old house. Bluestone place. Solid. Never lived in I don't think after Donald moved to town.'

'When was that?'

'Oh, donkey's. Died about twenty years ago.'

Just before noon, I finished the contraption. We fitted the housings to Frank's ute, attached the tracks and ran the tray up them, not without difficulty.

'Good work,' Frank said. 'Excellent work. Craftsmanship of the highest order.'

We went over to the pub for a sandwich. I had a beer. Jim had a glass of milk. Frank had three brandies.

The phone was ringing as we came up the lane. I ran for it.

Irene Barbie.

'Mac,' she said, 'I've had a call from my daughter. From London. She's just got back from Italy and Greece and she found a letter from Ian waiting for her. It's been to about five of her previous addresses.'

I was still panting.

'Are you all right, Mac?'

'Fine. Been running. Go on.'

'Well, I think it puts Ian's suicide beyond doubt. Alice was in tears and the letter sounds a bit disjointed, but Ian says he's leaving a note explaining everything and apologises for the pain he's caused.'

'Leaving a note where?'

'He doesn't say.'

'Police ever mention a note to you?'

'No. Well, they asked me if I knew of any note Ian might have left. They didn't know of one.'

Ian's wristwatch. Brendan Burrows on the station platform.

Well, watch's gone, clear mark of watch on left wrist. Probably nicked by the deros.

Could they have taken anything else?

'It'll probably turn up. Thanks for telling me, Irene.'

'About Ian and pethidine . . .'

'Yes.'

'You were right. Andrew Stephens told me. I never knew. Must have been blind.'

'Most of us are blind some of the time,' I said. 'Some of us most of the time. There wasn't anything you could have done.'

'No, well, I suppose not. Thanks, Mac.'

I went out to see Frank and Jim off. Frank said: 'Gettin the winch tomorrow. Big bugger. More pull than a scout-master. I'll come round, you can bolt it on for me, we'll settle up.'

Frank and Jim had to wait at the entrance to the lane to let another vehicle in. A silver Holden. I stood where I was outside the smithy and Detective Sergeant Shea drove the car to within twenty-five centimetres of my kneecaps.

D etective Shea was alone, the lovable Cotter presumably engaged in bringing cheer elsewhere. He got out of the car, looked at me, looked around, not approving. 'Bloody freezing as usual,' he said.

'I'm stuck here,' I said. 'You on the other hand are free to leave for warmer parts any time you like.'

'Don't take it personal,' he said. 'Talk inside?'

We went into the office. It wasn't much warmer there. I sat behind the desk, Shea looked at the kitchen chair disdainfully and sat on the filing cabinet.

'Suppose you thought we weren't doin anything,' he said.

'No,' I said. 'Thought you weren't achieving anything.'

He smiled his bleak smile. 'Takes time,' he said. 'You'd know. That complaint you told me about. One Ned made. About Kinross Hall, 1985. I looked that up. Investigated and found to be without substance. No further action taken.'

'What was the complaint?'

Shea looked awkward. 'Well,' he said, 'y'know I'm not allowed to divulge this kind of stuff. Lots of complaints, they've got no basis in fact, cause innocent people harm if the word got around . . .'

'Ned's dead,' I said. 'And it's a long time ago.'

He rubbed his jaw with a big red hand. 'This's off the record, I never told you this, flat denial from me.'

'I never heard it from you.'

'Ned said a girl at Kinross told him the director, her name's Marcia something . . .'

'Carrier.' A sick feeling was coming over me.

'That's right. The girl said this Marcia got her alone and made sexual, y'know, advances to her. She didn't want to and the woman slapped her up, blood nose, hit her on the body with somethin she said, stick, cane.'

I kept my voice neutral. 'This was investigated?'

Shea nodded. 'Oh yeah, two officers investigated. No substance. Girl said she'd made up the story to get some smokes from Ned. Marcia whatshername, she said the girl was always makin up stories, been to her with wild stories, fantasy artist, something like that.'

'Fantasist.'

'That. So end of story. Scully and the other officer said no grounds to do anythin.'

The light from the window seemed suddenly brighter. I had difficulty seeing Shea's features. 'Scully?' I said.

'Yeah. Big noise now. You'd know him. In drugs.

They say he's going to be deputy commissioner. Stationed here for three, four years in the eighties.'

'I know him,' I said. 'Who's the other officer?'

Shea got out his notebook, found the place. 'Bloke called Hill,' he said.

I nodded, got up. We went out into the rain. At the car, I put out my hand. We shook.

'Not finished with Ned,' he said. 'There's stuff I'm workin on. Be in touch.'

I went back to the office, sat down, stared at the desktop: Scully and Hill at Kinross Hall investigating Ned's complaint about Marcia Carrier.

I thought about the paintings in Marcia's office, small paintings of what looked like primitive sacrifice or torture.

The skeleton in the mine shaft. A girl. Around sixteen.

Ned's work diary, that was where it all began. I got out the box holding everything from Ned's desk: the newspapers, the marbles, the old wooden ruler from the grocer in Wagga, the big yellow envelope full of stuff.

I read the diary again. It was 1985 that had started me on Kinross Hall. As I went through it, I was thinking about Berglin. Berglin on making sense of scraps of information, on knowing people:

What you ask yourself is: what will this stuff I'm hearing about look like in hindsight? What kind of sense will it make then? You've got to think like an archaeologist, digs up this bit of something, fragment, could be bit of ancient pisspot, could be bit of the Holy Grail. The archaeologist's got to see the whole pot in the fragment. It's called using your imagination. They don't pick you people for this kind of ability, so we're working against type.

Same thing with targets. You think you know them. Seen the pictures, maybe watched them in the street, public places, read the file, know their histories. But you don't know them until you can predict what they'll do in given circumstances. Till then, they're just cardboard people to you. That's why you've got to listen to the tapes. Everything. Every boring word, never mind it's about who's picking up the kids from school or who did what at fucking golf. You don't know a target until every grunt has meaning for you. And lots of it, it's just grunts. People just grunt at each other. Grunts with meaning.

It came out of the page in Ned's diary, lifted out at me, 1987: *March 12. Veene house, Colson's Road. Fix gutters, new downpipes. Six hours. $100.00. Materials $45.60. Found silver chain.*

Under this entry, Ned had written: *Forgot to put with invoice.*

Silver chain. I remembered something about a silver chain. In the newspapers from Ned's drawer. I got them out. Page three, a Thursday in June, a photograph of a chain with a small silver star and a broken catch. An ankle chain.

Was the chain Ned found at the Veene house an ankle chain? He hadn't returned it with the invoice. Had he handed it in later?

Perhaps he forgot to. Perhaps he still had it when he saw the picture in the newspaper.

My eye fell on the big yellow envelope. I'd looked in that.

Hadn't I? I remembered seeing staples and string. I took the envelope out of the box and tipped its contents onto the desk.

Staples, a bulldog clip, box of rubber bands, neatly coiled length of string, small penknife.

And then the chain slid out like a thin silver snake. A silver chain, broken catch.

I shook the envelope.

Something dropped out, fell onto the newspaper, bounced, came to rest a few centimetres from the photograph.

A small silver star, the twin of the one in the picture.

I hadn't noticed the message on the answering machine, left while we were having lunch at the pub. It was Anne Karsh.

Mac, hi. Anne Karsh. I've got nothing on this afternoon. I'll be at the house from about three pm if you're free to show me the mill. If you can't make it, don't worry, we'll do it another day.

Ned thought he knew where the girl in the mine shaft was killed: the Veene house, where he'd found the ankle chain. He didn't trust the police, so he went to see Marcia. Then he went to see Dr Ian Barbie. And then he was murdered.

Marcia Carrier, Dr Marcia Carrier, Director of Kinross Hall, attacking a girl . . . *blood nose, hit her on the body with somethin she said, stick, cane.*

One of the men who abused Melanie Pavitt told her: *Back soon, slut, with a lady friend for you. She's been looking forward to this.*

Was it possible?

I thought about these things, dark things, on my

way to Harkness Park, slit-eyed streamlined dog face in the outside rear-view mirror, wind baring the fangs.

Anne Karsh's small black Mercedes was parked in front of the house and she was sitting on the steps where we'd sat drinking coffee. She got up at my approach, walked to meet me. Not the outdoor look today: hair down, long black and green tartan skirt with pleats, green shirt, black V-necked sweater.

'Mac,' she said.

We were close. I moved back.

'Thought you wouldn't come,' she said. 'I had business things, they fell through. Suddenly couldn't bear the city. I'm on my way to becoming a country person.'

'I'm glad,' I said.

'Are you? Ripped away from the blazing heat of the forge?'

I hadn't registered her eyes before. Hazel.

'Not blazing today,' I said. 'Today was welding, grinding and fiddling.'

She smiled. 'Oh, is that the blacksmith's burden? To weld, grind and fiddle.'

'By and large,' I said, 'I'd rather blaze.'

Silence for a moment, looking at each other. I wished I was better dressed.

'Have you seen the house?' she said.

'No,' I said. 'What entrance do I have to go in?'

She appraised me, serious face. 'Take your boots off, you can come in the front.'

We went through the front door, boots and all.

'Almost everything's here except the clothes and the pictures,' she said. 'It's as if they went on holiday and never came back.'

We started downstairs, went from huge room to huge room, looked out of the dirty windows at a dim day growing duller. Everywhere, we bumped into each other; in big spaces, we bumped into each other, sorry, sorry, hands unsure of where to go.

Upstairs. More bedrooms than a country pub, beds in all of them, clean coir mattresses, striped, some with neatly folded blankets on them.

In a large bedroom, not the master bedroom but big, wooden double bed, we looked out of the window, down at the newly cleared garden.

'It's going to look beautiful from here,' Anne said. We turned inward at the same moment, looked at each other.

'Beautiful,' I said. She was beautiful.

There was a moment of decision, indecision.

I put out a finger and touched her lips, in the centre.

'Oh Christ,' she said, reaching up and taking my head in her hands.

I put my hands on her waist, long, strong waist, drew her to me. As our mouths and our bodies met, she tilted her hips and pushed her pelvis against me. My hands slid down over her buttocks, lifted her, pulled her.

When our mouths parted, I said, close to her skin, 'Terrible urge to take off your clothes.'

'Terrible urge,' she said, 'to have you take them off.'

Kissing again, lost in her mouth, my hands on the bottom of her sweater, pulled it up. We broke free just long enough for it to pass over her head. I started unbuttoning her shirt from the collar, she took her fingers out of my hair and unbuttoned her cuffs, pulled the shirt over her head.

White lacy bra. I held her by the shoulders, looked, kissed the round tops of her breasts, put my tongue into the half cups, felt the nipples, risen, insistent.

'Oh sweet Jesus,' she said. Her hand went behind her back and the bra fell away, trembling breasts, not small, not big, lolling in my hands, mouth torn between three places, more, nipples, hollows of the throat, ears, eyes.

She loosened my belt, waistband, silky hand sliding over my stomach, gripping me, chamois grip, pulling, squeezing. I groaned.

The bed drew us, shoes, socks, pants, underpants went. I was naked first, five-limbed. Cold, hot. Anne was on her back, mouth open, loose, lovely. I pushed up her long skirt, pulled her pantyhose down her legs, over the long thighs, tense, the curve of calves, delicate ankles. Small white lace knickers, dark and springy promise beneath. Off. Pale stomach, hollow. I rubbed my face against it, kissed it, felt a pulse against my lips, buried my face in her dense pubic hair, thighs opening, sweet musk, the place, moist, salty,

244

impossibly delicate rose petals of flesh, my hands under her buttocks lifting her, feeling the muscles clench, her hands in my hair pushing me down, hips moving.

Anne brought me up, my tongue tracing a line to her belly-button, tip pushing into the whorl, turned me over, tartan skirt off and in the air, floating to the ground, knelt above me, pushing her hair back with one hand, holding the engorged thing with the other, leaning forward, shoulders, breasts bigger, flushed with blood, kissing me, sucking my lips, her lips pulling mine in, her hand drawing the thin foreskin back, down, slowly, tight, drum tight, edge of pain, exquisite. And then the instant beyond pleasure, the touch, the warm, wet, tight, yielding, nipping, teasing, enfolding, gripping.

'Yes,' she said, sliding down, sitting on me to the hilt, ecstatic pubic junction. Beautiful, abandoned, impaled jockey, grinding, bending backwards, breasts flattening, nipples, ribs, hipbones, tendons in her neck sticking out, 'Yes. Yes. Yes. Oh fuck, Jesus Christ, yes.'

We didn't do the mill inspection; it would have to wait. We kissed goodbye outside, against her car, lingering kiss, kisses, almost started the whole thing up again.

I was about ten kilometres from home, happy, at peace for a moment, driving in the dark down a winding lonely stretch without farmhouses. A siren came on behind me, harsh, braying sound, happiness disrupted, rear-view mirror full of flashing orange light.

I slowed, went onto the verge, stopped.

The car pulled up close behind me but much further off the road.

I rolled down the window, waited.

A middle-aged cop, moustache, leather jacket, no cap, appeared at the window.

'Licence,' he said, tired voice.

'What's this about?' I said. 'I wasn't speeding.'

'Licence, please,' he repeated.

I found it in my wallet, handed it over.

He shone his torch on it. 'MacArthur J. Faraday?'

'Yes.'

'This your current address?'

'Yes.'

'Mind stepping out of the vehicle. Sir.'

'Jesus,' I said, got out. Bitter cold outside, no moon, north wind humming in the trees. The dog made his warning sound.

'Quiet,' I said 'Stay.'

'Turn and face the vehicle, please, hands on top,' the cop said.

'What's going on here?' I said. 'There's no . . .'

'Do as I say, please. This'll only take a minute. We're looking for stolen goods.'

I turned and assumed the position.

'Pace back, please.'

I took the pace, weight on my hands, un-balanced, leaning on the freezing vehicle.

A second cop came around the back of the Land Rover, short, pale hair slicked down, head just an extension of his thick neck. He had no visible eyebrows and a nose like the teat of a baby's dummy.

He walked straight to me, swung his left leg, kicked my left leg out backwards, hit me in the back of the neck with a round side-on swing of his fist.

Everything went red, black, white, unbearable pain behind the eyes, in the bones of my head. I didn't even feel myself fall, land on the wet tarmac.

The next thing I registered was a heavy weight, a foot between my shoulder blades, something cold and hard pressing against the cavity under my left ear.

The muzzle of a revolver.

The pain seemed to dissolve. Cold and rough tarmac against the face, chill wind down here at ground level, smell of Anne on my shirt, French perfume, delicious Anne. I registered that but all I felt was sad. Sad and stupid. The watchful years, the looking for the signs, the ingrained disbelief about everything. For nothing. This is a stupid way to go, I thought. Careless. What would Berglin say?

'Bobby said to say goodbye,' said the middle-aged cop. 'Be here to say it himself, only he's got better things to do.'

He pulled my head back by the hair, painful, changed the angle of the muzzle to make sure he blew my brain away.

Headlights. Coming the way I'd come.

'Fuck,' said the man. 'Don't move.' He took the barrel away from my ear, pushed down harder on my spine with his foot.

A vehicle slowed, slowed, almost stopping. Went past us. Stopped.

I turned my head, saw the driver's door of a ute open, stocky frame come out, curly hair.

Flannery. On his way to the pub.

'What's this?' he said. 'What the fuck's this?'

'It's an arrest, sunshine,' the neckheaded cop said. 'Get back in your vehicle and drive on immediately. Now. Or you're under arrest for obstructing a police officer.'

I couldn't see the expression on Flannery's face but I could see the shrug.

'Okay, okay, I'm going,' he said. 'You could've asked nicely.'

He got back into the ute. Trouble getting it into gear, clutch grating.

'He ID us?' the middle-aged cop said.

'This light?' Neckhead said. 'No fucking way. He gets round the bend, buzz this cunt.'

Flannery revved his engine.

Hope gone.

And then Flannery's ute was coming at us in reverse, engine screaming.

'Jesuschrist!' the cop standing on me shouted.

His foot came off my spine.

I tucked my legs in, rolled to my right, heard Flannery's ute hit flesh and bone, brakes squeal, shouting.

I got around the front of the Land Rover, stood up. Flannery in first gear, coming back past me.

The cop he'd bumped was up, walking towards the police car, holding his left arm up by the elbow, screaming, 'Kill the fucking cunts!'

Neckhead, where?

I was backing off in Flannery's direction.

Neckhead popped up behind the Land Rover tray, revolver combat grip, two-handed, steadied himself to shoot me.

The dog jumped three metres onto Neckhead's out-stretched arms, jaws lunging for his throat, silent.

Neckhead made a shrill sound, went over backwards, rolled, knocked the dog off with the revolver barrel, tried a shot at it, two shots, missed, lead singing off the tarmac.

I screamed for the dog, ran for Flannery's ute, wrenched open the door, ute moving, half-in, foot dragging, heard the dog land on the back.

Flannery put his foot flat.

There was sound like a hard doorknock on the back window, followed by a smack on the roof above the rearview mirror.

I ducked, looked at the window: neat bullet hole, spider-web of cracks around it.

'Fuck,' said Flannery. 'Couldn't they just give you a ticket?'

I breathed heavily for a while, got my breath back. 'One tail light out,' I said. 'Attracts the death penalty. They coming?'

'No,' he said. 'Reversed over, attacked by dog, probably think, shit, let him off this time.'

I got out the mobile phone Berglin had insisted on leaving with me, found the number he'd written on a blank card, punched it in. Berglin answered immediately.

'Listen,' I said, 'that loop you were talking about.'

'Yeah?'

'Count me in. Two blokes in cop uniforms just tried to kill me. Told me Bobby said to say goodbye.'

'Bobby? That's our Bobby, is it?'

'I only know one Bobby.'

'Yeah. One Bobby's enough. Bears thinking about this. Good timing though. We've found the lady in question. Today. This afternoon.'

'Far?'

'From you? Five, five and a half hours.'

'Let's have it.'

When I'd put the phone away, Flannery said, 'What was it you said you did before you took up the metal?'

You couldn't lie to a man who would reverse over a policeman for you.

'I didn't say. Federal cop. Drug cop.'

'That's was, is it?'

'Very was. But there's stuff left over, unfinished stuff. Some stuff's never finished. Glad you came along then. Thanks.'

'Done it for a blind bloke,' Flannery said. 'What now?'

Home wasn't safe anymore. The only real home I'd ever had. My father's house, his workshop, his forge, his tools. The only place he'd ever felt settled, his demons banished. For a while at least. And bit by bit, over the years I'd lived there, I'd banished my demons too. Found a life that wasn't based on watching and lying and plotting, on using people, laying traps, practising deceit. But I'd brought a virus with me, carried it like a refugee from some plague city, a carrier of a disease, hiding symptoms, hoping against hope they would go away. And for a time they had. And I was happy.

But that life was over. Men in police uniforms came to execute you on the roadside beside dark potato fields. That was a definite sign the new life was over.

'Reckon you could drive me and Lew over to Stan's? I want him to stay there. We can pick up the Land Rover on the way back?'

'If I get a drink after that.'

'For you, Flannery,' I said, 'it's a possibility. I'm considering rewarding you with a few bottles of Boag's. Tasmania's finest.'

'Foreign piss,' Flannery said.

I didn't go into the house until I'd stood in the dark and watched Lew moving around, making supper, normal behaviour. Then I went in and made the arrangements.

B eachport in winter would be a hard thing to sell: dirty grey sky, icy wind off white-capped Rivoli Bay whipping the tall pines, seven cars, two dogs, and a man on a bicycle in half an hour. But no-one had to sell the little boomerang-shaped town to Darren Bianchi's widow. She chose it.

I slept in a motel in Penola, little place out on the flats, vine country, turning on the too-soft mattress, half-awake, feeling the gun behind my ear, hearing the man say *Bobby said to say goodbye*.

I got up early, feeling as if I'd never been to bed, put on a suit and tie, ate eggs and fatty bacon at a truck stop, got to Beachport in time to see the former Cindy Taylor, former Mrs Cindy Bianchi, present Marie Lachlan, open her hairdressing salon. It was called Hair Today and it was a one-person show.

Marie was dressed for the climate: red ski pants, boots, big red top with a hood. I gave her twenty minutes to settle in, walked across the road, opened the door.

It was warm inside, clean-smelling, hint of

coffee. Marie was in a sort of uniform now, pale pink, talking on the phone, back to me, didn't seem to hear me come in. She put the phone down, half turned and caught sight of me in the mirror. Her head jerked around. She was in her late thirties, short dark hair, pretty in a catlike way, little too much make-up.

Her eyes said *Oh shit*.

'G'day,' I said. 'Do men's haircuts? Got a meeting in Adelaide this afternoon, looking pretty scruffy.'

She was going to say no but she hesitated, changed her mind. 'Sure do,' she said. 'Come and sit down at the basin.'

I went over and sat in a low chair, back to a basin.

'You're out early,' she said.

'Too early. Drove from Geelong yesterday, stayed over in Mount Gambier. Thought I'd come down, have a look at the coast along here. First time I've been this way.'

'Pretty ordinary in winter,' she said. 'Lean your head back.'

She wet my hair with warm water, began to shampoo it, a kind of scalp massage with finger-tips, soothing.

'Mind you,' she said, 'it's pretty ordinary in summer too.'

She was relaxing. I could hear it in her voice. People who come to kill you don't take time out for you to give them a shampoo and haircut first.

'So what do you do?' she said.

'Liquor rep,' I said. 'Well, wine rep these days. Mostly wine. Like wine?'

'Don't mind a few wines,' she said, fingers working in my hair. 'Like champagne. You carry champagne?'

'We're agents for Thierry Boussain, French. Terrific drop. No-one's ever heard of it, small firm. All people know is the Moët, Bollinger, that stuff, produce it in the millions of bottles. Thierry's exclusive, few thousand cases.'

'Never heard of it,' she said. 'Might try it one day.'

She dried my hair with a towel. 'Cutting time. Sit in the first chair. Warmest place.'

I changed chairs.

'Now,' she said, 'how do you want it?'

'Actually,' I said, looking at her in the mirror, 'I think I'll give the cutting part a miss, Cindy.'

Cindy froze. Terror in her eyes, tiny step backwards.

'No,' I said, 'I'm not bad news. Bad news doesn't have a shampoo first, anyone can come in, see me in the chair, get a good look at me.'

'Who are you?' she said, voice controlled, scared but under control.

'A friend,' I said. 'Someone who wants you to stay alive. We want to talk to you about Darren. You talked to the police, I know. This is different.'

'How different?' She wasn't looking at me, looking towards the door, possibly calculating her chances of reaching it.

'Cindy,' I said. 'Look at me, look at me. Don't be a dork, think you can run out the door, that'll save you. Nothing to fear from me. I'm your best chance of staying alive. Forget witness protection, that number they gave you to ring. Rang it now, you'd be saved, would you? Batman, out of the sky, saves you?'

She swallowed. 'That's Superman. Batman comes in the Batmobile.'

'Superheroes. Can't get my superheroes straight. Darren had a big trust in cops, did he? Did he?'

'No,' she said, meeting my eyes in the mirror. 'Didn't trust anyone. Specially not cops.'

'Wise man,' I said. 'Wisdom of an ex-cop.'

'So wise he's dead.'

'No-one's wise enough. Unfortunately.'

Cindy hugged herself. 'What more can I tell?'

'Things you didn't tell the cops, right?'

'Maybe. Some. I don't know?'

'Darren ever talk about someone called Algie?'

'Algie? Didn't say it like that.'

'Didn't say it like what?

'Algie. Said it like El G.'

'El G?'

'Yeah, y'know, like El Torro?'

'I get it. El G. Darren talk about El G?'

She shrugged. 'Well, after the burg . . .'

'What burg's that?'

'More like a hurricane than a burg,' she said.

'Place destroyed. Fifteen grand's worth of damage.'

'Darren said what?'

'I dunno, El G. He said, fucking El G.'

'He said, fucking El G. Like El G did it? You tell the cops that?'

'No.'

'What else didn't you tell them?'

She hesitated.

Two cars went by in quick succession. Rush hour in Beachport.

'Cindy,' I said, 'they've done the show. This is the tell.'

'He said – Darren said – don't worry, what they want, the lawyer's got.'

'The lawyer. Who's the lawyer?'

'In Melbourne. Fielding something, they used to write. I don't know. I was out the house so quick. Fielding, three names. You want some coffee?'

'Coffee would be nice, Cindy,' I said. 'Black.'

'Sugar?'

'Just the one. Thank you.'

There was a glass percolator on a warmer at the back of the room. She came back with coffee in glass cups.

'Want to move?' she said.

'This is comfortable. Nice chair. You happy standing?'

'Stand all day.'

We drank coffee. 'Good, this,' I said.

'Real coffee,' Cindy said. 'Miss coffee places. Nescafé, that's what they give you around here.'

'Darren ever talk about someone called Lefroy?'

She didn't hesitate. 'Yeah. Saw him killed. Throat cut.'

My skin seemed to shrink, pull tight around my mouth, eyes. 'Darren saw him killed?' I said.

Cindy had a sip of coffee. 'Video. This bloke showed them a video. Girl killed too.'

Never change your tone. Berglin's rule. Start with it, stay with it. Want another tone, get someone else. 'What bloke is this?'

'El G. Took them to this place, big house, with like a little cinema.'

'Who's they?'

'I dunno. Darren and his mates, I dunno. Cops. We stayed in a hotel after the burg, Darren got so pissed, just talked. I didn't ask questions. Didn't know about that part of his life.'

'So they saw a video of a man called Lefroy and a woman being killed? That's what you're saying?'

'Yeah. Darren told me that. Said it made him sick. The man laughed.'

'El G?'

'Yeah. El G laughed. Showed it twice, Darren said. Funny name that. Stuck in my mind.'

'El G?'

'No. Lefroy. Spell it how?'

'Wouldn't have a clue,' I said.

A customer came in the door, elderly lady, head wrapped in a woollen scarf.

'Not late am I, Marie?' she said. 'Lovely and warm in here.'

'Have a seat, Gwen,' Cindy said. 'Won't be a moment.'

'On the night,' I said, 'Darren went out to the boat, never came back. That's it?'

'Where'd you hear that?' Astonishment. 'Cop said it must've gone on for an hour, more. Cut his ears off, burnt his hair off, don't you know that?'

'Yes,' I said. 'Just testing. The lawyers – Fielding, Something, Something?'

'Yes.' She picked up a comb and combed my hair. 'Nice hair.'

'My father's hair,' I said. 'Couldn't give him anything back.'

I had plenty of time to think on the trip back. El G, Scully, Hill and Bianchi watching a video of the killing of Howard Lefroy and Carlie Mance. A quick video, home movie really. Made while I was telling Mackie there wasn't any point in tailing Howard's brother when he left. El G enjoying it, laughing, showing it again. Did it show the moment of Carlie's execution? The man in rut behind her, between her legs, her head pulled back, blood squirting up the tiles?

One to do the killing, one to film it. Was that the way it had worked? Was the killer the driver, the man made up to look like Dennis Lefroy? Or was it the man who must have been in the boot when Dennis drove into the garage? Perhaps there were two men in the boot?

Years later, Bianchi burgled, then tortured and killed. Tortured for what? Pleasure? Something else?

Don't worry, what they want, the lawyer's got.

The killers Bobby sent had come up behind me on a country road. How could they know where I'd be?

I had a hamburger at a McDonald's on the outskirts of Geelong, read the *Age* I'd bought in Hamilton, rang inquiries for the Law Institute of Victoria on Berglin's mobile. An obliging woman took about two minutes to find the only three-name law firm in Melbourne beginning with Fielding: Fielding, Perez, Radomsky. She gave me an address in Rathdowne Street, Carlton.

I found a park across the street, outside a book-shop. As I crossed, the sun came out, took the edge off the wind. The gang of three had a shopfront office, two women behind a little counter. I said I'd like to see one of the lawyers. A five-minute wait produced a man who looked like the young Groucho Marx.

'Alan Perez,' he said, hand outstretched. 'Come into my office.'

It was a very basic office, desk, computer, two client chairs, degree certificate.

'Now. How may I help you?' he said. 'Mr . . . ?'

'Bianchi,' I said, 'Craig Bianchi. I'm helping my sister-in-law tie up the loose ends of her husband's estate. He was a client of your firm.'

'Who was that?' he said, furry black eyebrows coming together.

'Darren Bianchi.'

'Not a client of mine. I'll just look him up. Spell it how?'

He swivelled his chair, did some computer tapping, peering at the screen. He needed glasses. 'Bianchi. Yes. Client of Geoff Radomsky's.' He swivelled back to look at me. 'Deceased, did you say?'

'Dead, yes.'

'Well, both of them.'

'Both of them?'

'Geoff's dead too. Here, in his office.'

'Heart?' I said. But I knew what was coming.

'No. Abducted at his house, just around the corner, Drummond Street. Parking his car, garage's off the lane. They, well, no-one knows, could be one person, brought him here, made him open the safe. Shot him. In the eye.'

Melanie Pavitt, lying there in her bath, gaping wound where her eye had been.

'Nothing of value in the safe,' Perez said. 'Druggies, they think. Thought we kept money here.'

'Things taken from the safe?'

Uncomfortable, pulling at a ring on the little finger of his left hand. 'Don't think so. Safe's register of contents wasn't up to date. Oversight, happens in a busy office. Everything thrown around, of course.'

'When was this?'

'More than a year ago now.'

'And you wouldn't know if there was anything concerning Darren in the safe. Right?'

Perez gave me a reassuring smile. 'We can check that. I'll get Mr Bianchi's file.'

He went away. I got up and looked out the window. Two men, both balding and bearded, expensive clothes, were leaning on cars, BMW, Saab, parked next to each other on the median strip. They were talking across the gleaming metal, lots of gestures.

Alan Perez came back with a folder, sat down, went through it, eyebrows again trying to merge. There were only two pages as far as I could see.

'Yes,' he said, eyes down. 'That's unfortunate.'

'What?'

'File's confidential, obviously, but there is a record here of a tape, audio tape, left with Geoff for safekeeping.'

'Where would that be kept?'

'Well, in the safe I imagine. In the absence of other instructions.'

'Are there other instructions?'

Perez drew his furry upper lip down. 'No. So that's where it would have been put. I'm sure.'

'Still there?'

'I'll check,' he said, left again.

He was back inside a minute.

'No. Not there. No tapes.'

'So it could have been taken?'

Eyebrows again, black slugs trying to mate. 'If it was in the safe. Where we would expect it to have been. But we don't know. Yes. It could have been.'

I tried him on. 'My sister-in-law says my brother left clear instructions with you about something. That would be about the tape, would it?'

He wasn't happy. 'Client's instructions are confidential, we can't . . .'

'Client's dead,' I said. 'And you don't know what you had in your safe. Followed his instructions, have you? I'm happy to have the Law Institute take this up.'

I got up.

Perez said, 'Mr Bianchi, you'll appreciate our problem here. With Geoff dead, no-one was aware of his client's instructions. We could hardly go through all his files to see . . .'

'He's my brother,' I said. 'All I want to know is what he wanted you to do. There's something says you can't tell me that?'

Pause. Perez shrugged. 'Well, I suppose not. He wanted the tape handed over to the Director of Public Prosecutions. With copies to the media.'

'In the event of what? When was this to be done?'

He couldn't back off now.

'In the event of his death from other than natural causes.'

'He's dead. Of unnatural causes.'

'We didn't know that. Unfortunately.'

'Followed the instructions?'

He shrugged, crossed his legs. 'You'll understand our position, Mr Bianchi. The circumstances are such that we find ourselves . . . it would be un-reasonable . . . we didn't even know he was dead.'

'Okay, I'll accept that. Is there a Mrs Radomsky?'

'Yes.'

'I'd like to talk to her. He may have said some-thing to her about the tape.'

'Very unlikely. And I'm not sure that she . . .'

'Alan,' I said, 'you owe this to Darren's widow. You were negligent in your handling of a client's affairs. You did not have procedures for ensuring that a client's instructions were followed and . . .'

'I'll ring her,' he said. 'Would you excuse me for a moment?'

I went out and sat in the waiting area for a few minutes. Perez came out and beckoned me back into his office.

'Helen Radomsky says she knows absolutely nothing about any tape. Geoff never talked about clients' affairs – never.'

'What about his secretary? She here?'

'No. She took Geoff's death badly. Both secretaries did. They both resigned. You can understand . . .'

'Got a number for her?'

Perez looked unhappy again.

'Ring her,' I said. 'Explain what it's about.'

I didn't have to leave the room this time. He got out the phone book. 'I got a call from some solicitors in Hawthorn asking about Karen,' he said. 'Blandford something. Here we go.'

He dialled a number. 'Alan Perez, Fielding, Perez, Radomsky. Do you have a Karen Chee? Yes, thank you . . . Karen, Alan Perez. Good thank you. You're well, settling in? . . . It was a pleasure. Karen, we're trying to find out about a tape that should have been in the safe. Audio tape.'

He listened for several minutes, saying 'Yes. Right'. Finally, he said, 'Didn't see them again.

Sure about that? . . . Yes. Well, thanks. Look after yourself . . . I'll certainly pass that on. Bye.'

He put the phone down.

I held my breath.

'She says Geoff asked her to get the tape copied, two copies. There was some urgency about it. The copying was done by DocSecure – they do confidential copying. She went into the city by taxi, the job was done, she came back and put the master tape in the safe.'

'She had a key?'

'No, there's a slot. Anyway, she then dropped the copies off at Geoff's house. It was after five. The arrangement was for a courier to pick up the package at Geoff's to deliver to Darren Bianchi in Noosa. She assumed both copies were being sent.'

'I'd like to talk to Mrs Radomsky.'

Perez sighed, hesitated, caught my look, dialled. 'Helen, Alan, sorry to disturb you again. Look, it really would be a great help if Mr Bianchi could talk to you for a few minutes . . . I know, I know. It'll put his mind at rest. I'd appreciate it . . . Great, fine, yes. Thanks, Helen.'

The Radomsky house was a minute away, a free-standing brick two-storey, lace ironwork in need of paint. But not for much longer: a panel van with Ivan De Groot, Painter written on the side was parked outside. I pushed a brass button on the front door. It was opened by a short blonde woman, chubby, in her early forties.

'Mr Bianchi? Helen Radomsky. Come in. We'll have to go into the kitchen, everything else is being painted.'

We went down a wide passage and turned left into a kitchen, a big room with windows looking onto a walled garden.

'Sit down,' she said. I sat down at a scrubbed table. She leant against the counter under the windows.

'I'm sorry about your husband,' I said.

'Thank you. The most senseless thing.'

I nodded. 'Mrs Radomsky, Alan Perez may have explained. My brother left an audiotape with your husband and it's gone, not in the safe.'

She nodded.

'His secretary says she had the tape copied late one afternoon and dropped off two copies here. A courier was going to pick them up.'

'I remember a courier coming one evening. About six thirty. That's two or three weeks before Geoff . . . I didn't see what Geoff gave him.'

I put my elbows on the table, palms together. 'It's most likely Geoff sent off both copies. But I'd like to ask you something, just to be certain.'

'Yes?'

'If Geoff didn't give the courier both tapes, where would he have put the second one?'

She smiled. 'Well, he'd have put it on the side table in the study to take to work, forgotten all about it, put a newspaper on top of it the next day. Six weeks later there would be a panic search and we'd find it under sixteen copies of the *Age*, three books and four old *Football Records*.'

'Is it possible?'

She pulled a face. 'I haven't been into the study for more than ten seconds since the night. Actually, I haven't been into it for more than ten seconds in years. And Geoff wouldn't let the cleaning lady near it. He attacked the mess himself about twice a year.'

'Could you bear to . . .'

'Of course,' she said. 'Come.'

We went back down the passage. She opened the second door on the left, went in, pulled open heavy red curtains. It was not the study of a tidy person: books, newspapers, files on all surfaces, two bags of golf clubs leaning against the fireplace, a filing cabinet with the bottom drawer pulled out, two full wastepaper baskets, a team of old cricket bats meeting in a corner, empty wine bottles and several wine glasses and mugs on the mantelpiece.

The side table was to the left of the door, no centimetre of its surface visible under a haystack of printed material.

I looked at it. 'So far the hypothesis holds,' I said.

Helen Radomsky began clearing the table, dropping the material on the carpet. She got down to a final layer of newspapers.

'Well,' she said, 'if it was put here . . .' She lifted the stack.

A Game Boy, paperback entitled *The Mind of Golf*, gloves, set of keys, dictation machine, coins, ballpoints, two Lotto tickets, window envelopes, dark glasses, a small silver torch, a pocket diary, small dark-coloured plastic box.

Helen Radomsky picked up the box. It had a sticker on the side. She read: 'DocSecure.'

I said, 'Anything in it?'

She shook it. It rattled.

She opened it: one tape.

I said, '"And when it seemed that destiny sought them slain/Came from the legion's throat one joyous sigh/All eyes gazed up from that bloodstained plain/To see a white dove beneath a salamandrine sky."'

'What's that?' she said.

'Some poem,' I said. 'All I remember. It's about salvation.'

I fought against it and then I did it: I rang Anne Karsh. If Leon answered, I'd say Francis wasn't answering and we needed instructions about the pine trees at Harkness Park.

It rang and rang. I was about to give up when she said, 'Hello. Anne Karsh.' Short of breath.

I didn't have much breath either. 'Mac. If this is a bad idea, for any reason, say wrong number and put it down.'

She laughed. I knew the laugh. 'It's a good idea. It's the kind of idea you desperately hope someone else will have because you're too uncertain to have it yourself. And you're walking around feeling like a schoolgirl with a crush. A thirty-four-year-old schoolgirl.'

'I'm in the city,' I said. 'Business.'

I could hear her breathing.

'Is that in the city staying over or in the city going back?'

'In the city staying over. Not sure where yet.'

'I can suggest somewhere,' she said.

'I'm open to suggestion.'

'I still have my flat in East Melbourne. It could

269

use an airing. We could meet there, cook something, eat out, order a pizza, not eat anything.'

'I think eating's important,' I said. 'Not so much
what but the social act.'

'So do I. I think social acts are very important.
We'll think about the social act when we're there.
Make a joint social act decision.'

'You're free this evening then?'

'I'm free for the next two hours, then I've got a
brief engagement, then I'm free again. Leon came
back from Queensland last night, flew to Europe
this afternoon. In hot pursuit of something.
Possibly a small European country. Smaller than
Belgium, bigger than Andorra.'

'So we could meet quite soon?'

'I think we should get off the phone now,' she
said, 'and make our separate ways to East
Melbourne at the maximum speed the law allows.
Slightly over the maximum speed. When you get
there, press the button for A. Lennox.'

'Give me the address,' I said. It was unusual for
me to become aroused while talking on the telephone in a car parked outside a newsagency.

The address was a Victorian building, a huge
house, three storeys, converted to apartments. I
parked across the road, waited. Quiet street. It
began to drizzle.

The black Mercedes took ten minutes to arrive,
went down the driveway beside the house. I waited
two minutes, got out.

I pressed the button next to the name A. Lennox.

Anne Lennox. Her name before she took Karsh. There was a lift to the third floor. I walked up, glad to stretch after a day of driving, found the elegant door.

Before I rang, I unsnapped the shoulder-holster button under my right arm. The door opened instantly.

Anne was wearing a trenchcoat over jeans and a camel-coloured top, hair pulled back, dark-rimmed spectacles. I hadn't seen her in glasses.

She brushed my lips with the fingertips of her right hand.

'Suit,' she said. 'Sexy in a suit, Mr Faraday.'

Inside, door closed, we looked at each other.

'Sexy in the glasses,' I said.

'Thank you. For driving.' She took them off, put them in an inside pocket.

I touched her hair. 'Wet,' I said.

'Everywhere. I was in the shower.'

'Rang and rang. Almost gave up.'

'Pays to wait the extra second.'

'Pays like Tattslotto,' I said.

She took off the trenchcoat, hung it on a hook behind the front door, adjusted the central heating dial on the wall.

She kicked off her shoes, unbuttoned her top at the throat and pulled it over her head.

'Pays better than Tattslotto,' she said.

She was naked underneath, nipples alert. She cupped her breasts for me. I bent to kiss them, feverish.

271

'Didn't have time to get dressed properly,' she said.

'Like you dressed improperly. Very much.'

Kissing, undressing, touching, we found our way down the passage and into a bedroom. I managed to get my jacket and the shoulder holster off together.

'First in quick time, I think,' Anne said, voice blurred. 'Then in slow. Very slow.'

Later, lying naked, sated, in the warm room, Anne side on to me, head on my chest, my hand between her thighs, she said, 'Leon tells me you have an unusual background for a blacksmith, Mr Faraday.'

I felt the sweat on my neck chilling. 'What does Leon know about my background, Ms Karsh?'

She laughed. 'When you turned down Leon's job offer, you became an unobtainable object. And therefore an object of interest.'

'A man with a duck on a string.'

'Exactly.' She bit my right nipple gently, worried it, put her fingertips in my pubic hair, scratched gently.

'And so he made inquiries about me. Is that it?'

'That's it. He couldn't bear not to know.'

'What did he say about my background?'

'Unusual. That's all. Leon never reveals everything he knows. Not at once. He likes you to know he knows and to tell you what he knows when it suits him.'

'And how does Leon find out what he knows?'

'Oh, I think Leon could find out what toothpaste the Pope uses.'

'Would you say,' I said, 'that Leon was a jealous man?'

'No, not jealous. Envious. Of everything he doesn't have.'

'If he thought you were having an affair, would he want to know the details?'

'Probably. Not out of jealousy. Just for the knowledge. Knowledge for its own sake.' She moved her lips onto my ribs. 'Talking of knowledge,' she said, 'carnal knowledge of you is nice. And not just for its own sake.'

She reached over and got her watch off the bedside table, looked at it with her head on my stomach. 'Christ!' She sat upright. 'Have to postpone the learning for a while. I'm due to represent Leon at this charity thing . . .'

I lay on the bed and thought while she showered. She came back into the room, unselfconsciously naked, walked around, found clothes.

'Suspender belt tonight, what do you think? Black or white?'

'White. I like the virginal associations.'

She was wearing just the suspender belt and stockings, towelling her hair, breasts jiggling, when she said, 'Leon's got a man called Bobby who can find out anything. I think he called in Bobby to give the once-over when he decided he fancied me.'

I went cold everywhere now. 'What's Bobby's full name?'

'Never heard it. Leon calls him Bobby the Wonder Dog.'

I swung my legs off the bed, reached for my clothes.

'Mac? What? What's wrong?' Alarm in her voice.

I said, 'Anne, it's complicated. Leon's Bobby is likely to be a man called Bobby Hill. After I left you last night, two men sent by Bobby tried to kill me.'

'Kill you? Kill you? Why?'

'Goes back a long way,' I said, putting on my shirt. I sat down to put on my shoes. 'Sordid stuff. Couldn't work out how they knew where I'd be last night. Now I think I know.'

Anne came around the bed, put her hands on my shoulders, kissed me on the lips. 'I'm out of my depth here, Mac,' she said. 'Who are you?'

I kissed her back. 'When it's over,' I said, 'tell you the whole sad story. I have to get out of here. The best thing is for you to leave and then I'll wait a while and go. Is there a back door?'

'To the building? Yes.'

'To this flat?'

'To the fire escape. Yes.' She sat down next to me, put her hand on my thigh. 'Going to be all right, isn't it?'

I kissed her again, soft, hard, hand on her silky neck. 'Has to be. Haven't got to the very slow part yet.'

I stood, found the shoulder holster in my jacket and put it on.

Anne looked at the revolver, looked at me, bit her lower lip. 'Tell me I shouldn't be regretting this,' she said.

I touched her lips. 'No regrets,' I said. 'I'm flying with the angels. Scout's honour.'

While she was putting on lipstick, I said, 'If I'm right, the flat is being watched. If you leave alone, they'll wait for me to come out, jump me outside. If I don't come out and there's still a light on in the flat, they'll think I'm planning to stay here overnight and they'll come to get me later. So I'll leave a light on when I go.'

She was ready. I took her face in my hands, kissed her. She kissed me back, took a hand and kissed it. 'It isn't just lust – you know that, don't you?'

I nodded. 'Yes. I know that. This thing, it's almost over.'

I didn't believe that. Not for one instant.

Anne went out the front door. In the kitchen, by the light from the passage, I found a dark dish-cloth, tied it around my neck like a napkin to hide my white shirt. I went out the door, quietly closed on the latch, stood against the wall on the steel fire escape landing and looked down on the parking area.

It was dark, half moon hidden by cloud, the only light coming from a long open-fronted tenants' garage at the back of the property. There were only a few lights on in the building, most people not home yet. In this area, they'd all be working fourteen hours a day to pay for the flat and the BMW and the holiday in Tuscany.

Music coming from one of the flats: Miles Davis.

Anne came into sight briefly, long legs, walking

briskly towards her car. Moments later, she reversed out, bathing the yard in blood red light, drove around the corner of the building.

Bobby's boys would not touch Anne, had no reason to. It was me Bobby wanted.

I unclipped the holster, drew the Colt. Time to go.

I took a step towards the stairs, hesitated, moved to the landing rail, back and right cheekbone against the wall, looked down at the landing below.

Nothing. I leaned my head a little further over . . .

The tip of a shoe, a black running shoe, in the doorway.

Can't go down. Can't go back. The man below's partner would be in the building now, possibly already in the flat.

I opened the back door, thankful that I'd put it on the latch, backed into the kitchen.

No sound in the flat.

I looked around. Espresso machine on the counter. I holstered the Colt, unplugged the machine, picked it up, solid, heavy, cradled it in one arm, stepped out the door again, closed it quietly.

I stepped carefully to the front edge of the landing, coffee machine held above my head, leant forward until I could see both shoes below.

'Hey,' I said, gruffly, urgently.

He came out of the doorway fast, in a crouch, looking up, silenced weapon coming up in the two-handed grip.

Neckhead. I saw his face for a split second before

I threw the coffee machine at him with all the force I could muster. He fired, just a 'phut' noise, no louder than a clap with cupped hands.

But I was already on my way down, one jump to the intermediate landing, painful contact with the railing, left turn . . .

Neckhead was on his knees. The coffee machine appeared to have struck him full in the face, blood down the right cheek, the appliance lying in front of him.

He brought the pistol up – one-handed now, not fast, puzzled look on his face – as I dived at him.

Another phut.

I felt nothing, just the impact of crashing into him, knocking him backwards. I was feeling for his throat, found the hand holding the pistol, forced the barrel back towards him, back, back, tried to find the trigger. He was making a strangling noise, I could smell his hot breath: cigarette smoke and meat.

Close up, the sound was loud, I felt the heat, smelt the acrid cordite. His body went limp instantly.

I pulled away, stood up. The bullet had gone in under his left nostril, the back of Neckhead's head was gone. Even in the dark, I could see the blood spreading out from him onto the steel deck.

It had all taken a few seconds. No-one was shouting. Miles was still playing. Probably a tape on a time switch to deter burglars.

Above me, I heard Anne's kitchen door open.

I took the silenced pistol out of Neckhead's

hand, shrank back against the door of the second floor flat. Where Neckhead had waited.

Waited.

Heard the soft feet on the steps. Rubber soles.

Saw the shoes, big, the trousers, dark, the waistband of the ski jacket.

No more.

The legs stopped. He had seen Neckhead's legs.

'Jesus,' he said, came down the steps in a rush, swung onto the landing, sawn-off shotgun in his right hand, its ugly pignostril muzzles coming around to face me.

I shot him in the chest, twice, a third time. His eyes registered something, he bounced against the railing, mouth open, made a sound, cheerful, surprised sound, fell over sideways, slid.

I stood there, pistol in hand, feeling sick. The dishcloth was still around my neck. I took it off, used it to wipe the pistol, put it back in Neckhead's hands again, pressed his fingers, utmost care.

I listened. Nothing but the growl of traffic on Hoddle and Victoria and Wellington Parades, and Miles Davis.

I left the scene of the crimes. Left carefully, in case Bobby had sent more than two people to get me. Not that taking care would make any difference in the long run, the short run even.

He who says Hill says Scully.

I couldn't kill armies of people.

I went out on the Tullamarine freeway, suddenly hungry, bought a hamburger in the drive-through at a McDonald's in Keilor, sat in the car park, appetite gone, system flooded with adrenalin, mind lurching between clear and blank.

I hadn't listened to the Bianchi tape.

I didn't want to listen to it. I'd left the Radomsky house with it in my hand and what I had done was to telephone Anne Karsh. All the effort to find it, lying to decent people, and then I put it in my pocket, put it out of my mind.

I took the slim plastic box out of my coat pocket, took out the cassette, slid it into the tape player, hit the buttons.

A voice, counting, humming, whistling. Darren Bianchi's voice.

Silence.

What was he doing?

Testing a wire, that's what he was doing.

Noise, traffic noise, tinny music, scratchy sounds.

So what's she supposed to know, I mean, what do I . . . Bianchi's voice again. Barely audible against the background sounds.

Know the absolute fucking minimum, anything goes wrong, she knows close to fuckall. Scully's voice.

Bianchi is wearing a wire, sitting in a car with Scully. His boss, Scully.

Dennis will ring . . . Bianchi's voice.

Then Scully: *If Howie goes for his walk, only if he's out of there. Doesn't go, we wait till he goes somewhere. He goes, we see him, Dennis rings, says he's coming round. At eight thirty. Now she's got to wipe that from the tape, get it? Howie hears it, we're fucked. It's for fucking Faraday's benefit.*

So Howie doesn't know. He's gonna think, who's at the door?

Darren, don't worry about that, right? My department. Just one thing the bitch's got to do, right. Open the garage door at eight thirty on the fucking nail. You make sure she understands that. No fucking margin for error.

Yeah, eight thirty.

Yeah, eight thirty. It's just a run-through. She keeps her mouth shut, she gets wrapped up, they'll be out of there, five fucking minutes, less. No way Dennis will know she's not as surprised as he is. Okay?

Okay.

Something else. You make sure she knows, change of mind now, she's meat. Too fucking late for that. She's fucking in. Doesn't want to do it, she's seen fucking Daimaru for the last time. She's fucking sushi. Doesn't do it right, same thing. Applies to you, too. And me. And fucking Bobby. You don't know this fucking El G, fucking mad. I know him from way back, kill anything, kill anyone, come in his pants while he's doing it. Totally fucking crazy, makes snuff movies. Fuck it up, we'll be fucking snuff stars.

Scuffling noises, car door slamming, Scully saying something inaudible.

The next five minutes of the tape were recorded somewhere noisy with background voices, laughter, scratchings, scrapings, bangings. The pub in Deer Park? Bianchi, low voice, giving Carlie Mance her instructions.

I listened with my head back on the seat, mouth dry, wishing I had something to drink, a cigarette.

Carlie showed no signs of fear, no desire to call it off. Bianchi told her what would happen to her anyway. Her last words were: *Darren, tell 'em make sure they don't put anything over my nose – can't bear that, can't even have a pillow over my nose.*

Bianchi said: *Not a problem. Won't happen. I'll tell 'em.*

I ejected the tape, put it in its box, put it in my pocket.

Scully. The bastard. Scully and El G. Scully, the deputy commissioner-to-be. Scully, the man who investigated Ned's complaint. Sitting in that car, talking to Bianchi, he knew that someone – El G, someone – was going to murder Lefroy and Carlie. Murder them, rape Carlie, enjoy it. Film it for future pleasure.

The tape might be enough to nail Scully, but I doubted it. I sat motionless for a while, uneaten hamburger on my lap, staring sightless.

Unfinished business.

I shook myself. Ian Barbie's suicide was unfinished business. His letter to his daughter said he'd left a suicide note. Where? At his surgery? He hadn't. Where he lived? He hadn't. Where he committed suicide? People often did.

I got out the Melways, put on the inside light and found the quickest way to Footscray.

Varley Street, Footscray: one streetlight, icy wind pinning the newspaper pages against the container depot fence, somewhere a door banging in the wind, lonely sound.

I thought I heard them as soon as I stepped into the old loading bay: the sound of a classroom where the teacher has stepped out for a minute, not loud, but unruly, a jostling of voices.

I knew where the sound was coming from. I went across the loading bay, out into the courtyard, turned right and walked towards the glow coming out of a big doorway.

There were four of them upright, around a smoky, spitting fire. Other bodies lay as dead outside the circle, one face down. The fire cast a cruel russet light on wrecked faces, shapeless clothes, a swollen blood-filled eye. Two men who could have been a hundred years old were fighting weakly over the silver bladder of a wine cask, speaking incomprehensible words, neither strong enough to win possession. Someone who could have been a woman was nursing another person's head in her lap, drinking beer from a can, golden liquid running down a cracked chin, dripping onto the long, greasy grey hair.

'Robbo here?' I said.

Only two heads turned, looked at me without interest, looked away.

I went a few steps closer. The smell was over-powering, smoke, wet clothes, other animal odours.

'Boris here?' I shouted.

This time a figure to the right of the fire looked at me, dirty bearded face under a beanie, filthy matted jumper like an animal skin. He was drinking a can of Vic Bitter, two more held between his thighs.

'Fuck you want?' he said.

I went over to him. No-one paid any attention to me. 'You Boris?'

He drank some beer, looked into the fire, spat. It ran down his chin. 'Fucksit you?' he said, rocking back.

'You found the bloke hanged himself here?'

He looked at me, trouble focusing. He wasn't more than thirty years old. 'Course I fuckin did,' he said. 'Fuckin hangin.'

I knelt down. 'Boris, you took his watch.'

He blinked, looked away, put the can to his mouth, half missed it. 'Fuckin,' he said.

'Boris,' I said, 'I don't care about the watch. Did you take anything else? From the man? From the car?'

His eyes came back to me. 'Whar?'

'Did you take anything else from the hanging man? Understand?'

'Fuckin,' he said, looked away, head lolled.

I stood up. Some other time perhaps. Not tonight.

I was on my way out when Boris said, quite distinctly, 'Pay me.'

I stopped and turned, went back. 'Pay you for what?'

He was holding himself together with great effort. 'Pay me 'n' I'll show you.'

I got out my wallet, found a twenty-dollar note, waved it at him. 'Show me and I'll give you this.'

Boris focused on the note, craned his neck towards it, fell back. 'Fifty,' he said. 'Gotta be fifty.'

I offered him the twenty. 'Show me and I'll give you another thirty if it's worth it.'

He put out a hand, black with dirt, fresh blood on the inside of the thumb, and took the note, stuck it somewhere under his jumper. Then he lost interest, studied the beer can.

'Boris!' I shouted. 'Show me!'

His head jerked around, some life in his eyes, drained the beer can, threw it over his shoulder, put the other cans under a coat on the floor. 'Gimme hand,' he said, trying to get up.

I gripped the shoulders of his jumper and lifted him onto his feet. He weighed as much as a six-year-old.

'Over there,' he said and began to stumble towards the dark left corner of the big space.

I walked behind him. He fell once. I picked him up.

There was nothing in the corner except a rusted sheet of corrugated iron lying on the concrete.

'Under,' Boris said, swaying. He put out a hand to steady himself against the wall, misjudged the distance and fell over onto the corrugated iron.

I picked him up again, propped him against the wall.

'Lift,' he said, waving vaguely.

I bent down and lifted the corrugated iron, shifted it. Under it I could make out some clothes, two Coles plastic bags, a pair of shoes.

'Bag,' Boris said. 'Gimme.'

I picked up both bags, offered them to him. He focused, put out a hand and knocked one away, almost fell over, took the other one.

He couldn't get it open, fumbling at the plastic. I helped him. 'Thangyou,' he said, put his hand in, couldn't get hold of what was inside, turned the bag upside down and tipped the contents onto the concrete.

An envelope, A4 cartridge envelope.

I picked it up. It was unsealed. I walked back to the ambit of the firelight. Behind me Boris was making sounds of protest. I opened the flap, took out four or five pages, paper-clipped, top page handwritten. I held it up to the light. It began: *I am writing this because I can no longer bear to go on living . . .*

I put the pages back in the envelope, went back to Boris, found two twenty-dollar notes, gave them to him.

'Thank you,' I said.

'Gennelman,' said Boris.

I was in the pub in Streeton, in front of the same fireplace where I'd talked to Ian Barbie's wife. A tired and dirty man who began the day coming out of fitful sleep in a motel in Penola, out there in the flat vine country, far from home. Sitting in the warm country pub, I could smell myself: sweat, sex, cordite, wood smoke. All curdled by fear. I drank three neat whiskies, dark thoughts.

'Listen, Mac, I'm closin.'

It was the publican. I knew him, welded his trailer for nothing.

'Finish this,' I said.

'No,' he said, coming over and putting a half-full bottle of Johnny Walker on the table. 'Just closin the doors. Sit long as you like, fix it up later. Put the light out, give the door a good slam when you go. Lock doesn't go in easy.'

'Thanks, mate.'

'Back roads, right.'

'Back roads.'

I drank some more whisky, thought about Lew, Ned asking me to look after him. Lew and the dog, my responsibilities. Lew: mother gone, grandfather gone, just me now. I thought about my life, what it had been for so many years: the job and nothing but the job. Utter waste of time. I didn't even remember whether I'd loved my wife. Couldn't remember what it felt like to love her. Remembered that she could give me an erection with one look. What I did know was that all the self-respect that I had lost with one bad judgment had been slowly given back to me by my ordinary life in my father's house. A simple life in a simple weatherboard house. Working with my father's tools in my father's workshop. Feeling his hand in the hammer handles worn by his grip. Walking in his steps down the sodden lane and across the road to the pub and the football field. And knowing his friends. Ned, Stan, Lew, Flannery, Mick, Vinnie – they were all responsible for giving me a life with some meaning. A life that was connected to a place, connected to people, connected to the past.

But now I was back in the old life, worse than the old life because then it wasn't just me and Berglin. It was me, Berglin and the massed forces of law and order.

It was highly unlikely that my life was connected to the future.

For an hour or so, I slumped in the armchair, drinking whisky, clock ticking somewhere in the pub, lulling sound, sad sound. Fire just a glow of gold through grey. Putting off reading Ian Barbie's last testament in the same way I'd put off listening to Bianchi's tape.

Berglin. I needed to talk to Berglin. I got up, stretched, moved my shoulders, pain from tackling Neckhead on the fire escape. I got out the mobile, switched it on, pressed the numbers.

'Berglin.'

'Mac.'

'Mac, where the fucking hell have you been? Point of having a mobile is to have the fucking thing switched on.'

'Sorry,' I said. 'Been busy. This line secure?'

'Well, as secure as any fucking line is these days.'

'Got a tape. Bianchi, Scully, Mance. Before Lefroy. Bianchi had a wire on him. Insurance.'

Berglin whistled. 'Fuck,' he said. 'Where are you?'

'In the sticks. People are trying to kill me.'

'Again?'

'Yeah.'

'Must be learners. I'll meet you. Where?'

I thought for a while, gave him directions. It was as good a place as any.

I took cigarettes, matches from the bar and the bottle of whisky.

Back roads, route avoiding anything resembling a main road.

As I turned the corner of the drive, the clouds parted for a few seconds, the half moon lighting up the house at Harkness Park. It didn't look ghostly or forbidding, looked like a big old house with everyone asleep. I parked around the side, settled down to wait. It would take Berglin another half an hour. I had a sip of whisky, hunched my shoulders against the cold. Tired.

I jerked awake, got out, yawned, stretched, lit a cigarette. It tasted foul, stood on it.

Car on the road. Berglin? Quick driving.

Stopped. At the entrance to the drive.

Typical Berglin. I'd told him to drive up to the house. But Berglin didn't do the expected. He didn't drive the same way to work two days running.

I went to the corner of house, looked out between the wall and the gutter downpipe. Hunter's moon, high clouds running south, gaps appearing, closing, white moonlight, dark. Waited for Berglin.

He was no more than fifty metres from me when the clouds tore apart.

A coldness that had nothing to do with the freezing night came over me.

Bobby Hill, slim and handsome as ever, dark clothing, long-barrelled revolver, man wants a job done properly, has to go out and do it himself.

And behind him, a few paces back, another man, short man, wearing some sort of camouflaged combat outfit, carrying a short automatic weapon at high port, big tube on top.

Clouds covered the moon. Too dark to see the man's face.

Moonlight again.

Beret on the second man's head. Turned his head.

Little pigtail swinging.

Andrew Stephens. My visitor in the Porsche.

How did he fit in?

No time to think about that.

The car door was open. I found the box of cartridges under the front seat, moved into the heavy, damp, jungle-smelling vegetation beyond the rotten toolshed.

How many? Just Hill and Andrew Stephens?

It wasn't going to be only two again.

Escape. Which way?

Down to the mill would be best. Cross the stream above the headrace pond, follow the stream down to the sluice-gates. Go around behind the mill, up the wooded embankment. Places to hide there, wait for dawn, ring Stan.

The mobile. I'd left it on the passenger seat.

No going back. I was moving in the direction of the site of the house that burnt down, the first house. But the growth here was impenetrable, I'd end up like a goat caught in a thicket.

I had to veer left, pass in front of the sunken tennis court. But to do that I would have to cross the top of the area we had so painfully cleared. In darkness, that wouldn't be a problem. But if moonlight persisted, I'd have to wait. And they'd be coming . . .

Steady. They didn't know which way I'd gone. They'd have found the car by now. It was coal dark. I could be anywhere.

Scully's words on the tape came into my head:

You don't know this fucking El G, fucking mad. I know him from way back . . .

Way back? How far back? From Scully's days in the country?

El G? El Torro, The Bull. El Greco, The Greek.

The Greek? Who had said something about a Greek recently? Greek. Recently. In the past few days. The past few days were blurred into one long day.

Frank Cullen, man of contraptions: *Rick's tied up with that Stefanidis from over near Daylesford. RSPCA went there, heard he was shootin pigeons. Bloke behind a wall throws 'em in the air, Greek shoots 'em with a twelve bore from about two yards. Sticks it up their arses practically.*

Andrew Stephens. Andrew Stefanidis?

Andrew's father was a good man, fine man, fought with the Greek partisans in the war. Dr Crewe, walking around the lake, talking about Ian and Tony and Rick and Andrew.

Sudden chilling clarity. Andrew Stephens's father was Greek. He'd anglicised his name.

Andrew Stephens was El Greco, The Greek, close-range shooter of pigeons, maker of snuff movies, organiser of murderous run-throughs.

And then the realisation.

Berglin had always known who El Greco was. Berglin had toyed with me. Berglin had given me to Scully, Hill and El Greco.

Naive. You only know about naive when it's too late.

Absolute silence.

I walked into something, old fence, some obstacle, small screeching noise.

Something landed in the vegetation near me, sound like an overripe peach falling. And then a thump, no more than the sound of a hard tennis forehand.

Whop.

The night turned to day.

Blinded.

Flare grenade. I backed away, left arm shielding my eyes.

The bullet plucked at my collar, red hot, like being touched by an iron from the forge.

I fell over backwards, twisted, crawled into the undergrowth, hands and knees, through the thicket, thorns grabbing, scratching face and hands, reached a sparser patch, got to my feet, ran into the dark, into something solid, forehead first.

I didn't fall over, stood bent, stunned, looked back. The flare was dying, white coal.

'Mac.' Shout.

Bobby.

'Mac. Deal. The tape, you walk. Don't need you dead.'

What hope did I have?

'Okay,' I said, 'I'm coming.'

I ran left, northeast, hindered by wet, clinging, growing things, hampered but not blocked. I reached the fringe of the cleared area, exhausted. Knew where I was.

Clouds opened. Moonlight.

The bullet hit something in front of me. Something solid, tree trunk.

Night-vision scope.

That was the fat tube on El Greco's rifle. Light-enhancing nightscope.

He could see in the dark.

I threw myself into the denser growth to my right, crawled deeper, deeper, desperate, no breath left, ten metres, fifteen, more. Into, over plants, roots, through ditches of rotten leaves, mud, scrabbling, don't want to die like this . . .

I fell into the sunken tennis court, fell a metre, head over heels, got up, dazed, winded, pitch-dark, sense of direction gone, ran, ran a long way, length of the court perhaps, knee-high weeds, swimming in porridge, fell, crawled, a barrier, a wall, the other side of the court, bits of rusted wire, hands hurting, sodden soil, tufts of grass coming away in my hands.

I was out of the court, on my stomach, all strength gone.

The end.

Fuck that.

I was being hunted. I was their victim. They'd had lots of victims. They knew about victims: they run, you find them, you kill them.

Dangerous is what you want to be. Go mad. Nobody wants to fight a mad person. Nobody wants fingers stuck up his nose.

A father's words to a small and scared ten-year-old son.

Yes. I found the strength, crawled around the perimeter of the sunken court, turned north. Waited in the undergrowth.

Whop.

Fireball. In the tennis court. Night sun. Cold, white night sun.

I buried my head in the dank, wet weeds. Flare thrown from the edge of the tennis court, somewhere near where I'd toppled into the court.

Flare dying, fading.

Dark.

Dark.

And then light, cold silver moonlight through the flying clouds.

Bobby Hill, ten metres away, moving through the knee-high weeds, long-barrelled revolver at his side, not anxious, not hurrying, man out for a walk in difficult conditions.

Dark again. Lying on my face, I reached under my chest, found the gun butt, comforting feel, drew the Colt from the shoulder holster. Safety off. Hammer back.

Whop.

In the air, above me, intense sodium-like light.

I cringed, pushed myself down, didn't move, Mother Earth, breathed wet soil, waited for the pain. You bowl these things, I realised, throw them, they float for a few seconds. Not parachute flares.

No pain. White glare dying away. Slowly, slowly. Dark.

I got up. Walked to the edge of the sunken court,

slid down on my backside, stayed down, drew up my knees, rested my outstretched arms on them. Waited.

Look down. Another flare goes off, don't look at the light.

Pitch dark.

The clouds tore, moon revealed.

Bobby Hill.

The length of a ute from me.

I saw him.

He saw me.

Handsome man, Bobby Hill: dense black hair combed back, nice smile, standing in knee-high weeds on a forgotten tennis court.

He was smiling as he brought the long-barrelled revolver up.

I fired first, at his middle, big bang.

The bullet hit him somewhere near the bottom of his fly, massive punch in the groin. His lower body went backwards, feet leaving the ground.

For an instant, I saw the expression on his face. It said: *This is odd.*

In my head, I said, *Goodbye, Bobby.*

From close by, from the thicket above the tennis court, El Greco said, 'Bobby. Got him?'

I went up the side of the court again, crawled through the vegetation, Colt in hand, dark again, ground sloping, stopped for a second, heard the creek below me, full this time of year.

Flare behind me, to my left. El Greco had misjudged my direction. He was looking further up, thought I'd turned north. I holstered the Colt, lay still, crawled again, mud in my mouth.

Creek close, few metres, rushing water, making a noise no problem. I was in the thicket of poplars that lined the creek, dead branches poking at me, cheek torn open.

I fell head-first down the bank into the stream. Freezing water, couldn't find my feet, taken downstream, banged into a fallen tree trunk, turned around, use of only one hand, swallowed water, Jesus Christ, I couldn't drown after all this . . .

My feet found the oozy bottom, I got a hold on a branch stump, pulled myself along the tree trunk. Island in the middle of the creek, some moonlight. Hid behind the trunk until it went.

Another flare, even further over. El Greco thought I was trying to get back to the house, to the car.

Relief. I lay on a cold carpet of moss and caught my breath: I could get out of this.

I waded the second half of the stream, much shallower there, up the bank, into another poplar jungle, blundered into a barbed-wire fence, sound of sleeve ripping, climbed through it, caught, jacket ripped.

I knew where I was. I'd walked down here from the mill. The millpond was about two hundred metres downstream and there was a path of sorts along the creek. I could walk upright. El Greco couldn't see me here, poplar thickets on both banks too dense.

It took me about five minutes to reach the brimming millpond. The moon came out and I could see what I had been hearing: water spilling over the dam wall, small waterfall.

Panting, I went over to the rusting sluicegates, looked down into the empty brick-lined millrace. It ran straight to the old mill, slight fall, disappeared around a corner to where the mill-wheel was.

If I dropped into it, I could run the hundred-odd metres to the shelter of the mill unseen, climb out, cross the bluestone-paved loading area and climb the embankment, get deep into the trees.

Safe.

Whop.

Sodium daylight.

In the poplars on the other side of the race pond, not thirty metres away.

El Greco.

Changed direction, come back. Probably seen me in the nightscope.

Frozen, I couldn't move, reflexes not working. Tired. Tired.

I sank to the ground slowly, lay full length, felt for the Colt.

Gone. No Colt. In the stream. Oh Jesus.

The flare died. The millrace. Get into the millrace. I said this to myself. Get into the millrace and run.

I crawled to the edge of the sluicegate.

Just do this and you're safe. He'll have to go upstream or downstream to cross.

I turned and put a leg over, found a foothold, looked to see how far the drop was . . .

Whop.

Flare over the middle of the race pond, white light intensified by the reflection.

El Greco in the poplars, weapon at the shoulder, looking through the nightscope.

Drop. About to let go, fall into the millrace.

Bang, wink of red light at the mill end of the race. Bang on the metal sluicegate, felt the tremor of the metal in my hand.

Someone in the millrace. Shooting at me. Of course, two down the drive, two come from below. I knew there'd be more than two.

Bang, red wink, sound of bullet over my head.

I heaved myself back over the top.

Trapped. Finished.

My hand was on the sluicegate lever. Jesus. Heard Flannery's voice in my head: *Sluicegate'll still work. Someone's been greasing it.*

I grabbed it with both hands, pulled.

Nothing. No give.

Pulled. Oh Jesus.

Moonlight. Two men in the millrace, thirty metres from me. Bang, barrel flame.

Pull!

The lever gave, I fell to my knees. Sound of rushing, falling water, sluicegate half a metre open.

Not caring where El Greco was, I watched the wall of foaming water barrel down the millrace. The men were on either side, trying to climb out, when it hit them, ripped them off the walls, tumbled them down towards the wheel, sweet Jesus . . .

'Hands in the air, Mr Faraday.'

El Greco, behind me, five metres away, pear-shaped head behind the fat nightscope. I raised my tired arms. Berglin, you treacherous bastard. All those years.

'I think we have to do a deal,' I said.

He laughed, delighted.

'A deal. What a wonderful idea. Selling something, are we? Gates? Fighter aircraft?'

Laugh again, the girlish laugh.

'Haven't got the tape on me,' I said. 'Somewhere safe.'

'That's not true, John. For telling me lies, I'm going to punish you. Before I kill you.'

The bullet hit me in the left thigh, like a hard blow from a stick, spun me around, knocked me over.

Pain. Intense, burning pain.

I could see him from where I lay. He came closer, weapon still at the shoulder.

'That was the first part of the punishment, John,' he said. 'Now I want you to ask me not to punish you any more.'

Has to be some dignity at the end.

'Fuck off,' I said. 'You disgust me.'

El Greco lifted his eyes from the sight. 'That was a mistake, Johnny. This is going to take much longer now . . .'

He sighted again.

He was going to shoot me low down in the body.

Moon free of cloud, silver light, sound of water. You bastard, Berglin.

How to be a halfway decent person. That's the main question in life.

What would you know, Berglin, you worthless, faithless bastard?

'Wait for it, Johnny,' El Greco said. He laughed, the light, little-girlish laugh. 'It's going to hurt, really hurt. And there's more. Much more.'

A shot. Close. Loud. Another shot.

El Greco looked up from the rifle. His mouth opened. I could see his tongue lolling in his mouth.

He fell over forward, rifle barrel digging into the ground, chest resting on the butt, slowly toppling sideways.

Someone came out of the shadows, wet to the waist, arms at his sides, big automatic pistol pointing at the ground.

'Fuck,' Berglin said. His long foot moved El Greco's rifle away from the body. 'Flare grenades, night sight. Think bloody technology's the answer to everything.'

I tried to get up, got to one knee. Pain. Whole left thigh on fire. 'Why'd you do that?' I said. 'Just going to leap at him, knock the rifle away, strangle him.'

'Got bored waiting,' Berglin said. 'Who's he?'

'Algie. El G. El Greco.'

He reached down, turned the body over, licked fingertips, held them to El Greco's nostrils. 'Won't be standing trial,' he said, straightening up. 'Just as well. Guilty fuckers get off half the time.'

I was in the smithy getting ready to temper a knife blade when Detective Michael Shea drove up, again without Cotter. He came in and sat on the bench.

I had a thick iron plate on the fire, just about ready, almost red.

'Can't talk,' I said. 'Got to get this right.'

It was red enough. I took tongs and moved it to the cooler side of the fire, picked up the knife blade and put it on the plate. The important thing now was to quench the blade when it showed the right colour.

Shea came over to watch. The blade absorbed heat from the plate, turned strawy yellow, went through orange into brown, began to turn a redder brown.

I picked it up with heated tongs and put it in the quenching bath of water under a layer of clean olive oil, moved it about.

'What's that do?' Shea said.

'Hard steel's too brittle, snaps. Get rid of some brittleness this way,' I said. 'First you have to harden it, then you temper it like this. What's happening?'

'Big morning. They found more bones. Marcia's rolled, Veene's decided to give us Crewe.'

'That's big.'

'Crewe got pulled this morning. Steps of Parliament. Do it that way down there. Tip off Channel Nine, get your face on camera. Excellent for the career. They ran Marcia through the Canadian databases. No Marcia Carrier. But a Marcia Lyons did time for assaulting girls at a girls' home in Montreal. Turns out it's her. That's her married name, Lyons. She says Crewe found out before she got the job, didn't say a word, made sure she got it. Then he had her.'

'Took part?'

'Admits. Very distressed. Blames her old man. Says he used to beat her and her sister. Says she didn't know the girls were killed after she left. Guilty only of assault.'

Gaby Makin had said something. She was talking about Melanie Pavitt, how strong she was for a small person. What was it?

Barbie liked the little ones.

She hadn't been talking about Ian Barbie, she'd been talking about Marcia. Marcia was Barbie to Barbie's Ken.

'What's Rick say?' I said.

'Gone to water. Says he had sex with the girls at the farm, left them with Andrew and Tony. Only found out later that Andrew killed them. On video. We got the videos. In the basement at Andrew's mansion. Safe buried in the floor.

Found it with a metal detector. Make you puke, tell you.'

'Crewe's in the picture?'

'Not. But there's enough. Got dates, times from Barbie's last letter. Crewe was up here for all of them. They picked girls being discharged, nowhere to go, no family. So they just vanished, no-one looked for them.'

He came around and looked at the cool blade, picked it up. 'Nice,' he said. 'You do good work. There's something else. Ned. Been waiting for people to get back to me. Cop in Brisbane, he's been trying to nail a bloke called Martin Gilbert for years, reckons he's Mr Rent-a-Rope, priors for assault, attempted murder. Smart guy. Joe Cool. Three hangins up there, all got the smell, plus one in Sydney, one in Melbourne. One Brisbane one, car belongs to mate of Gilbert's, bloke's interstate at the time, car's a block from the scene at the right time.'

'That takes us where?'

'Got a picture of Gilbert,' Shea said. 'Nice colour picture. Had the troops takin it around the motels. Slow business.'

He had something to tell me.

'Motel up the top of Royal Parade had two blokes come in on the night, just before midnight. One's Gilbert, bloke's a hundred per cent on it. The two got pissed in the room, made a lot of noise, manager had to get up, copped a lot of abuse from Gilbert. I'm goin down tomorrow, show him the pictures come today. Some of Gilbert's mates.'

I'd got this large, pale, sad-looking man very wrong. 'You do good work too,' I said.

Shea said, 'There's more. We done the car rentals for the day, ran the IDs, got a rental, cash, false ID. Brisbane troops seen it before, think it's used by Gilbert.'

I started to say something.

Shea held up his hand. 'Small rental place this,' he said, 'not too many paying cash these days. They remember this roll of plastic tape, black plastic tape, found in the boot of the rental when they cleaned it. Still got it too, lyin there in the office. Thought it'd come in useful, says the bloke.'

Shea shifted his buttocks, couldn't get comfortable, got up and went over to stand in the doorway. 'Forensic's had another look at Ned's pyjamas, Brissie cops told 'em what to look for. Now they reckon there was tape on the pyjama sleeves, on the pants.'

'You do more than good work,' I said. 'You do excellent work.'

He looked away. 'Forensic think they might have missed some acetone stuff, like nail varnish remover, used to clean Ned's face, round the mouth. Same on two hangins up in Brissie. Reckon this Gilbert knows his stuff.'

'The plastic tape,' I said. 'Match it with the glue?'

'Tomorrow, we'll hear tomorrow, next day. Soon.'

'Be enough?'

He shrugged. 'Get a positive ID from the motel on Gilbert's mate, he might shake loose.'

He looked out of the door. It had started to rain. 'Got to go,' he said. 'Be in touch.'

I went out with him, put out my hand, 'Glad we drew you on the night.'

He shook my hand. 'Gettin there. Any luck, we get the bastards. Then they get a smart lawyer and they walk.'

I was finishing up for the day when the phone rang in the office.

'Gather your local Member's the first item on the news tonight.' Berglin. No greeting.

'So I hear. What's with our friend in the Vatican?'

'That's why I'm calling. Scully resigned this morning.'

'They going to prosecute?'

'No.'

'No? The bastards. He's a murderer, how many times over.'

'Can't prosecute.'

'Can't? Can't? What kind of . . .'

'Can't prosecute the dead. He shot himself. In his garage at home.'

I sat in silence for a while, telephone forgotten, looking out of the window at the tattered clouds blowing south, at the willows down at the winter creek sending out the first pale green signal of spring.

Berglin cleared his throat. 'Well,' he said, 'there endeth the lesson.'

I said, 'Amen.'

We limped off after the third quarter, six goals down, our supporters – now grown by about ten thousand per cent – giving us a sad little cheer. Kingstead got a roar, hooting, small boys jumping and punching one another.

Mick tried his best in the break. 'Six goals is nuthin, fellas. Knock 'em off in the first ten minutes, cruise away to a magnificent victory. Make it all the sweeter, that's all . . .'

'You goin to play Lew or not?' Billy Garrett said. 'What's the bloody point of him sittin on the bench?'

'Keeps 'em guessin, Billy, keeps 'em off balance. Expectin any minute we'll bring on the young fella, brilliant talent, legs of steel . . .'

'They're not bloody guessin,' Billy said. 'They're not off bloody balance. They're bloody kickin our arses, that's what they're doin. You gonna play him or not?'

Mick put his hands in his anorak pockets, looked around for understanding. 'Can't, Billy, boy's in the golf tournament of his life tomorrer. Tiger

Woods in the makin, how kin I put him out there, some great lump kicks him in the leg, stands on his head? Great career ruined. My fault. Swore I wouldn't play him except in an emergency.'

'Emergency?' said Billy. 'You think a bloody emergency is like what? Only bloody Grand Final I'll ever play in, thirty-six points behind, side's absolutely bloody knackered. Not an emergency? You off your bloody head?'

'No need to shout, Billy,' Mick said. 'Don't want 'em to think we're not of one mind, gives 'em a psychological hold over us . . .'

'They don't need a bloody psychological hold over us, you mad Irish prick,' Billy said. 'They've got a hold on our actual balls, squeezin.'

I was at full forward, second game back after four weeks out, leg almost healed. Garrett and company had got along fine without me, winning three out of four.

Flannery and I walked on together. 'Christ, be glad when this is over,' he said. 'It's not the losin I mind, it's havin to play so long after you know you've lost.'

'No time for defeatism, Flannery,' I said. 'We mature players are supposed to set an example.'

Flannery was walking in the direction of his opponent. Over his shoulder, he said, 'You'll see an example if this cockbrain doesn't stop puttin his elbow in my ribs. Example of how to get a two-hundred-game suspension.'

For the first five minutes, Kingstead were all

over us, winning the ball everywhere, four shots at goal, four behinds.

Then something happened to them. Billy Garrett won the ball from four consecutive ball-ups, everyone seemed to have found some speed.

Three goals in four minutes.

At the centre bounce, Billy knocked it out to Gary Weaver, who ran twenty metres, kicked the ball to Flannery, who appeared to have stood on his opponent's instep. Flannery played on, kicked it my way. I got in front of my man and took it on my chest.

Goal.

'Reckon they peaked too early,' Flannery said after taking a mark right in front of goal. 'Field's comin back to us.'

He kicked it. Supporters back in full voice.

Ten points behind.

And there we stuck. It began to rain, steady rain. We wrestled with them in the mud, almost everyone ending up in midfield, all mudmen, unrecognisable, exhausted. My thigh was aching, must have opened the wound. The clock ticked on, every second taking Brockley's first Grand Final victory in seventeen years further away.

Out of nowhere, Kingstead kicked another goal. Ball spun free from a collapsing pack, man ran thirty metres and kicked a goal. Supporters in total ecstasy.

Sixteen points behind. Three goals.

As we were picking ourselves up, Billy Garrett said to me, panting, 'Mac, for Christsake, do it. Talk to the little bastard.'

I looked at Lew sitting on the bench, wearing an old overcoat of mine. He didn't look happy. I was his guardian. What would Ned have done? I didn't really have to ask myself the question. I knew what Ned would have done.

I went over to Mick. 'Fuck the golf,' I said. 'Give the boy a run. You only get one chance in life to save a Grand Final for Brockley.'

Mick opened his mouth, looked into my eyes, closed his mouth. He turned towards the bench.

'You're on, fella.'

Lew was up and out of the overcoat, jogging on the spot, big smile.

Minutes to go. Lew on in the centre.

Billy tapped the ball out. It bounced off the shoulder of a Kingstead player, Lew took it out of the air with one hand, slipped between two opponents, perfect balance, ran, one bounce, two bounces, three bounces, sidestepped two Kingstead players, handballed over the head of another one, ran around him, caught his own handball, running, another bounce, kick.

Goal.

Centre bounce. Billy made a superhuman effort, took the ball over his opponent, came down, threw off a tackle, handballed to Lew, who was already running.

Lew ran around three players, stopped, delivered a kick to Gary Weaver, perfectly weighted kick, hit Weaver on the chest.

Weaver kicked the ball to the square, where

Flannery and I and several other Brockley players were in hand-to-hand combat with half the Kingstead side now drafted into defence.

The ball came out of the dark-grey sky. Four of us rose to it, tired men, desperate men, men willing their arms to lengthen.

Lew floated across the front of the pack, fully a metre off the ground, took the ball one-handed, landed like a ballet dancer, perfect pivot, no hesitation, cannon shot through the posts.

Goal.

One goal to victory.

Crowd like Visigoths on a rampage. Grown men would weep in the last light of this day.

Umpire looking at watch. Seconds left.

Centre bounce. No-one was going to take this away from Billy Garrett. He rose like someone called to ascend to a higher place, seemed to grip the ball in a large hand, sent it flying to where Lew was waiting, sent it as if he knew exactly where the boy was, sent it as if they'd arranged it.

Lew went through the Kingstead players with the calm arrogance of someone sent to instruct others on the correct way to play the winter game. No-one put a finger on him. They chased, gave up. Two players collided, heads meeting, fell down senseless.

He came down the field towards me, to where I stood alone, my opponents sure that he was going to goal.

Stopped. Goals in front, thirty metres, no-one within reach of him. Crowd suddenly silent.

Lew kicked, perfect swing of the leg, leg born to kick a football.

Kicked not at goal. Not at exposed, waiting goal. To me.

Like a father kicking to his son in the street. Kick meant to be marked, on the chest, not high, give the boy confidence.

Instead of kicking it himself, could kick it in his sleep, be a hero, he wanted me to kick the winning goal for Brockley. Brockley, seventeen years in the wilderness, object of derision. Lew was handing me the chance to bring the barren years to a close.

I marked the ball under my collarbone. It fell into my hands, stuck there.

The siren went.

Kick to win after the siren. In a Grand Final. People had never recovered from missing one. Moved away. Changed their names. Never played again.

I went back, pulled up my socks.

It looked like a long way, impossible angle.

Flannery walked across behind me.

'Not saying anything,' he said. 'But . . .'

There was not a sound from the crowd. Total silence.

I took a deep breath. No-one should be given this kind of responsibility. No-one.

I ran up and kicked.

Closed my eyes.

Flannery grabbed me from behind, seemed to want to dance with me.

Lew came up, punched my shoulder, put his arm around my waist. I put an arm around his shoulders.

'You little bastard,' I said.

We walked off, shaking hands with opponents, ruffling teammates' hair, listening to the supporters shouting. Mick was kissing players.

In the gloom, I could see Allie, pale head, standing on the bonnet of her truck, fists raised in the air, shouting something. Next to her, Vinnie was doing what looked like the samba.

And then I saw the black Mercedes, person leaning against the grille. Hadn't seen her, spoken to her, since the night I killed two men on her fire escape. Wanted to, scared to, she didn't call.

I cuffed Lew on the back of the head, walked down the line, wet, covered in mud, people patting me on back.

Anne Karsh was in jeans, tartan coat, hair wet, beautiful. Wary eyes, not smiling.

I stopped a metre away. 'Owe you a coffee machine,' I said.

She shrugged. 'Been meaning to throw out that machine for years. Makes really bad coffee.'

We looked at each other.

'Must've read your mind. Threw it out for you. You in the country going back?'

'In the country staying over. Not sure where yet. Leon's divorcing me. Met a neurosurgeon in Switzerland. I get Harkness Park.'

'Nice place,' I said. 'Got the Bobby Hill memorial tennis court. Want to come back to the pub?'

Anne smiled, nodded, touched my muddy arm.

'C'mon, Mac,' Flannery shouted. 'Got to sing the team song. Got to learn it first.'